When an evil spirit comes out of a man, it goes through arid places. Then it says, "I will return to the house I left." When it arrives it finds the house swept clean and put in order. Then it goes and takes seven other spirits more wicked than itself, and they go in and live there. And the final condition of that man is worst than the first.

The Bible

Through Arid Places

Tim Rayner

Matador
5 Weir Road
Kibworth Beauchamp
Leicester LE8 0LQ, UK
Tel: (+44) 116 279 2299
Fax: (+44) 116 279 2277
Email: books@troubador.co.uk
Web: www.troubador.co.uk/matador

ISBN 978 1848763 388

British Library Cataloguing in Publication Data.
A catalogue record for this book is available from the British Library.

Typeset in 12pt Perpetua by Troubador Publishing Ltd, Leicester, UK

Printed in Great Britain by the MPG Books Group, Bodmin and King's Lynn

Matador is an imprint of Troubador Publishing Ltd

To Heather, Stephen, Louise and Alison whose love helps me through my arid places.

To Rob whose experiences in Rwanda provided the genesis of this book and whose editing and advice brought it to completion.

Tim Rayner read modern history at Oxford University. Since university he has worked in business, most recently in two companies which he helped establish. He lives in North London and is married with 3 grown up children. Through Arid Places is his first novel.

The terrible events in Oradour-sur-Glane and Nyarubuye actually happened. However the characters and details in this book are fictional. Through Arid Places should not be seen as an historical account of these events but as a story that seeks to draw truths from them.

CHAPTER ONE

"It was an unspeakable evil." Sister Agathe Deladier spoke quietly and disconsolately as she looked out over Lake Muhazi. Her companion Jennifer Edwards, a twenty four year old British medical student, was silent, sensing the significance of this moment. She looked intently at the old nun but tried not to stare as if this might seem an intrusion into the depths of Sister Agathe's soul. Instead Jennifer contented herself with a visual appraisal of her companion.

Sister Agathe was small and delicate, not in a vulnerable or brittle way, but as if physical development had been an inconsequential element in her growing up. Under her simple blue habit she appeared wiry and straight-backed. Her face was long and thin with furrows ploughing ever deeper across her brow and around her eyes and mouth. However, her chin was resolutely angular and her neck, usually an accurate determinant of age, still relatively tight and firm. The years had been kind to her and even the expansive white hair pushed back from her brow could have belonged to a younger person given its shiny and lustrous appearance.

Jennifer could not guess her age accurately from any of these features but it was Sister Agathe's eyes which indicated that hers had been a long and difficult life. It wasn't so much their pale green colour but the lack of animation as she spoke. It was almost as if her eyes were green marbles – opaque glass hiding the true feelings within. There were aspects of this life which could not be expressed visually.

Yet despite her mysterious eyes, Jennifer sensed that Sister Agathe was a warm, kindly person. Indeed a godly, even saintly woman. The kind of human being who, if you entered a room in which they were sitting alone, created an atmosphere of quiet, holy reflection. One could not be tense or stressed in her presence, but curious about the weariness which appeared to wrap itself around her.

The silence that followed Sister Agathe's opening sentence was out of keeping with the scene over which she looked. The delay in either person responding could have resulted from that moment of wonder which nature inspires. Jennifer knew that feeling from her native Cumbria when, scrambling to the top of the Langdale Pikes, she had surveyed the horseshoe shaped trail to the summit. Nature had chiseled a gigantic granite cupped hand which softly cradled the tranquil Stickle Tarn, blackened by the deep shadow falling over it.

The lake over which they now looked was at the western end of the Gahini mission complex in eastern Rwanda. The community comprised a hospital, rehabilitation centre, school, church and seminary, mostly built by the first Protestant missionaries who had arrived in the 1920s, but developed further by subsequent generations. Dotted around the site were the bungalows that the missionaries had built for themselves and their families. It was from the verandah of one such house that Sister Agathe and Jennifer were surveying the view.

The brown water in the lake looked far more inviting from a distance of 800 metres than it did close up. The occasional snort from a herd of hippos reminded Jennifer that this was Africa, not Cumbria, but in many respects the scene was familiar. The grass was green, not parched white as in many African countries. The lush green banana plantation that fringed the lake emphasized the natural abundance of this place. Rwanda, deep in the heart of this great continent, was rightly known as the Switzerland of Africa.

Hoots of laughter rang out from the nearest section of the lake where Jennifer could see people diving from a small jetty, which protruded about ten metres into the water. Only the bazungu would want to swim in the lake's murky waters. After all, most black people didn't swim and the lake had a much more functional purpose as a source of water for drinking and washing. The white missionaries had built the jetty to avoid having to wade through the slimy, leech infested mud at the side of the lake. Nothing would stop the bazungu from having a dip, thought Jennifer, not even the water snakes or hippos for which Lake Muhazi was their natural home.

As if reading her mind, Sister Agathe resumed, "There was a time when it wasn't so beautiful. No-one was swimming in it. No cows drank from it. No women washed in it. It was partly the stench of rotting flesh which put them off, but it was more the bodies, which got stuck in the mud and branches at the side of the lake. Sometimes the bodies would be dislodged from their resting place by a hippo or a strong gust of wind and the bloated body of a man, woman or child would float silently past like a ghost. That's what disturbed people the most".

Jennifer had wondered since her arrival five days earlier when the genocide would be mentioned. It seemed that most people, expatriates and locals alike, were trying to eradicate those events from their memories in much the same way as the Hutus had tried to eradicate the Tutsis from Rwanda. It was in 1992 that the Hutu Power leader, Leon Mugesara, called on Hutus to send the Tutsis back to Ethiopia along the Nyabarongo River, which flowed through Rwanda on its way to the Nile. This sneering reference to Ethiopia taunted the Tutsis, who had been regarded by the British Victorian explorer, John Hanning Speke, as a superior race emanating from North Africa with the "best blood of Abyssinia" flowing through their veins. He had contrasted them sharply with the inferior negroid Hutus. By 1994, Mugesara's chilling presage had become a reality as rivers and lakes in Rwanda were clogged with the bodies of dead Tutsis.

Jennifer knew enough psychology from her medical studies to know that trying to blank out traumatic events from a person's memory was a necessary coping strategy. They would return to their memories when better able to handle them, almost like accepting a physical scar once the wound has healed.

"Of course, the other factor in the lake being abandoned was that no-one lived near it any more. Everyone had been killed or had fled," continued Agathe in her soft, pleasant French accent. Sensing that the time was right to prolong the conversation, Jennifer asked if the Sister had been at Gahini during the genocide.

"Yes, my dear," she sighed, "when we heard that the Hutu President Habyarimana had been killed we thought there would be a few days of instability and some limited revenge attacks by the Hutus. This had happened many times before but we thought that if we kept our heads down it would soon blow over. But then the shootings started and we knew we had to leave. It was so hard. Many of us had lived here for so long and we had to leave friends behind. We didn't know what would become of them." She paused "…I'm sorry, Jennifer, I can't really talk about it at the moment. The memories are too fresh in my mind, the faces of missing friends too clearly visible. Please excuse me".

With that, the old woman retreated into the house. Jennifer watched as she walked slowly into the mud brick building with its dirty whitewashed walls. She sipped slowly on her hot sweet tea and watched the orange sun slip beneath the horizon at the far end of the lake.

CHAPTER TWO

Sister Agathe slumped onto her bed. "Oh Lord," she prayed, "please help me forgive. Not just sometimes but all the time. The past is such a heavy burden on my heart. Please give me strength to bear that burden through your grace". She had prayed that prayer so many times but each day it was a struggle to see answers, to find hope for mankind. As she lay on her bed Sister Agathe let her mind drift as, once again, she picked up the burden of her past and carried it all by herself.

It was April 1944 and France was under Nazi occupation. The Allies were threatening an invasion that, if successful, would smash Hitler's master plan for European domination. Hitler desperately needed to reinforce his troops in France, to protect both the north and south coasts from Allied attack. He would turn, as he always did in a crisis, to his crack SS divisions. None had a fiercer reputation than the Second SS Panzer Division, known as Das Reich.

Das Reich had been fighting, along with other SS divisions, on the eastern front against Russia. This front had seen the toughest fighting of the war, with the iron determination of two fierce war machines producing battles of epic proportions. Casualties in the east were four times those in the west. Between July and October 1943 alone there were one million of them.

The soldiers of Das Reich would not therefore have been disappointed when they received the call to entrain to France. In truth, despite Hitler's faith in them, Das Reich was now a shadow of its former self. From an all volunteer force its ranks now included conscripts from twelve nationalities including Romanians, Hungarians and Alsatians. Led by General Heinz Bernard Lammerding, himself over promoted, by April 1944 its officers included those from the lower middle or working classes who would never previously have been considered leadership material. Nevertheless, given the fact that fighting units on all sides were depleted after almost five years of war, they were still a formidable force. Spirits were high among Das Reich soldiers as they marched through France from the south. They were at last released from the grinding horror of the eastern front. The prospect of repelling an Allied invasion in France was seen as an opportunity for this elite division to add another glorious chapter to its history. However their hopes of a majestic sweep through France, crushing all opposition with a single blow, were to be cruelly dashed by the guerilla tactics of the French resistance, or maquisards, as they were known locally.

Emboldened by the rumours of invasion and, supplied with arms in increasing quantities by the British Special Operations Executive, the French resistance cells (maquis) undertook sabotage activities along the routes taken by German troops. Das Reich, along with other divisions, suffered losses as roads and railways were blown up in May and early June 1944.

Major Franz Hautmann, the commanding officer of the First Battalion of Der Führer regiment of Das Reich, was horrified by the loss of life suffered by German troops. True, the numbers of casualties were relatively small but Major Hautmann was indignant that his crack fighting machine could be hurt by what he saw as French peasants. Major Hautmann was aged about forty. He was tall with a face which could best be described as pointed. In the same way as the spires of a cathedral point upwards to heaven in unison, so Major Hautmann's features pointed outwards. His nose was sharp and thin while his chin, gathered into an angular promontory, stuck out beyond his slit of a mouth. His jutting forehead, not to be outdone by the other thrusting protruberances, contributed to the impression that his eye sockets had been swallowed by the rest of his face. Hautmann's limp flat black hair could have been greased into place by the Führer himself. None the less, Major Hautmann was not unattractive. His slim taut body was symbiotic with his face and the whole effect was to create an image of purpose – a finely honed and spare warrior, a man for whom Das Reich was a crusade against infidels and cowards. This was his most chilling characteristic – blind obedience to the cause. No small voice of reason or compassion was allowed to intercede.

Hautmann's bearing reflected his upbringing in the south German town of Augsburg. His father, Stefan, was a factory owner, a self made man who instilled into the young Franz the ideals of self sufficiency and determination. His mother had died when he was six and the paternal emphasis in his life, unfettered by maternal compassion, produced a rather bigoted, intolerant child.

Franz's father had turned his factory over to arms production in the First World War. His shells had been used in the Flanders campaigns, rushed to the front just as fast as he could manufacture them. He shared the humiliation felt by most Germans at the Treaty of Versailles. Both father and son were easy fodder for a new idealistic politician who came to be called Adolf Hitler, and they joined his National Socialist Party together. While Stefan's motives for nationalistic fervour were largely due to hurt pride and a sense of injustice, Franz's were more sinister. He bought into the whole idea of Aryan supremacy, the master race whose God given destiny was world domination. Even fellow North Europeans were regarded with disdain. The Poles were inferior and should have seen the invasion by Germany in September 1939 as an opportunity for betterment, a gift from a superior life form bestowing its largesse upon them.

While contemptuous of most foreigners, Franz treated the French with the utmost opprobrium. While he still expected the German forces to defeat all opposition, if they were expelled from France it would be no "victory" for a weak willed people who had caved in at the first sign of an invasion. They had got lucky in having powerful British and American friends. The cleansing of resistance in France could not have been in more dangerous hands than those of Major Franz Hautmann.

* * *

Claude LeClerc had just celebrated his fourteenth birthday on 5th June 1944. He had spent the day, as he had many others, hiding in the maize fields of Farmer Villepreux's farm. He and his friends loved to run along the channels between the maize stalks, which were, by now, about four feet high. It would be even more fun when the stalks reached eight feet in late July. His den in the centre of the field would be truly invisible.

Claude had lived all his life in the village of Oradour-sur-Glane, west of Limoges in central France. There was little to differentiate Oradour from any other small town or village in France in 1944. Residential and municipal buildings had grown up around its main street, Rue Emile Desourteaux, fanning out onto a few side streets off the main highway. The houses were white with red tiled roofs whose only originality appeared to be the varied colours of the shutters which guarded each window. The dwellings were mostly bungalows but some were more of a chalet style with dormer roof windows. Hedges or walls gave most families an element of privacy.

This was a community within which personal space and public spiritedness could happily co-exist. The tramway had allowed the townspeople easy access to the nearest sizeable town of Limoges and provided a conduit for mains electricity. The arrival of a tram was still a source of fascination for Claude and his fellow pupils at the village's boys' school. They craned their necks out of the grubby school windows to see which new arrivals would disembark.

The quiet dignity of Oradour had attracted refugees from more troubled parts – Alsace-Lorraine, Spain, Paris and the usual diaspora of Jews. Its population had doubled to around 650 souls and its boys, girls and refugee schools were 'complet'. Like many of the village's children, Claude enjoyed the company of his schoolmates, whatever their background. While war divided nations, it often brought communities closer together. This could even be true on the battlefield. Crew who had parachuted from a doomed enemy aeroplane would not be fired on and sailors from ships which had sunk would be rescued by those who had fired the shells which had led to the sinking. Claude had not so far regarded the Germans with hatred or resentment. Since occupation four years previously in 1940, the Germans had always been there. Through most of his cognisant years they had been in the locality but their presence had not been particularly invasive. Troop convoys hurtled through the town at infrequent intervals and occasionally German staff cars stopped at the local shops or hotels for refreshment or to ask for directions. Claude was aware that many French people did not welcome the Germans and his father had talked about the maquisard resistance, but he had seen little evidence of their activity. This was unsurprising in that the nearest maquis camp was rumoured to be seven miles to the south west. If it were possible for the greatest conflict in world history to pass by an occupied community then Oradour was that place.

CHAPTER THREE

Major Franz Hautmann was thoroughly annoyed when he arrived in Limoges on 9th June 1944. His journey from the south had been subject to continual delay and frustration. The maquisards had cut down many trees along the route and used them and other detritus to block the roads. Not only did each blockage take hours to clear but each one was a potential ambush and proper protection had to be established before the barriers could be removed. Even so, the battalion came under heavy attack in several places and lost a number of troops. He was not comforted by the killing of several maquisards, together with a few civilians during his passage through the eastern Dordogne. His mood was not improved when he heard that his close friend and fellow officer, Major Heinrick Peters, was missing, assumed abducted by the maquis on the road from Guèret to Limoges.

"These peasants should be exterminated," muttered Hautmann to nobody in particular, "it's demeaning for an elite Panzer division to be cutting up trees and chasing farm labourers across dung heaps. These petty terrorists should be taken care of by local troops, not the SS. How can we possibly be expected to repel the British and Americans when we spend half our time chasing ignorant serfs over turnip patches?"

His frustration was shared by Major Gunther Eberling who had, that same day, entered the town of Tulle, about ninety kilometres south east of Limoges. He was also irritated that the battle for Normandy was being hindered by a bunch of communist snipers, a rag tag outfit of office clerks, teachers, shop keepers, dentists and the like. Eberling was furious that forty German soldiers had been killed by the maquisards and was determined on revenge. A notice was posted on the walls of the town of Tulle stating that, for every soldier who had been murdered, three maquisards were to be hanged. Eberling and his men moved through the town gathering together any men who could possibly be associated with the resistance. However he did not have a shred of evidence against the vast majority of them. Nooses were placed on lampposts together with two ladders, one for the hangman and one for the victim. As each Frenchman was pushed from a ladder with the noose around his neck so the hangman moved on to the next lamppost. Ninety nine men were hanged in this way until the Germans ran out of rope. Eberling then expressed satisfaction that his orders had been carried out and left the bodies hanging in the air for several hours to discourage any further opposition. Residents of the Limoges area now knew that Das Reich had arrived in town.

* * *

Within hours, Sister Agathe Deladier had heard the news of the massacre in Tulle in the village of Corrèze, about 15 kilometres away to the north east. The butcher's boy delivering the meat the next morning was still shaking from the sight of the limp bodies drooping from the lampposts. The Carmelite convent in which she had just commenced her novitiate in 1944 had already experienced the brutal repercussions of Nazi occupation. The convent had been used as a safe house by the French resistance to shelter Jewish refugees. The mother superior, Sister Anne-Marie Devaux, made every effort to help her guests feel at home. Candles and oil from the church were provided to welcome in the Sabbath. Ingredients and utensils from the convent's kitchens were supplied so that the celebration of Holy Days could be observed in the normal culinary way, or at least as normally as possible in these days of rationing and restricted ranges of food products. It was not truly kosher but there was no rabbi within several hundreds of miles to pass judgement.

The nuns took considerable risks in sheltering the Jewish refugees. The Germans were suspicious of religious orders as many maquisards had taken to disguising themselves as nuns in order to carry out guerilla attacks unsuspected. However the Carmelites of all generations since the twelfth century took inspiration from Mary, the Mother of Jesus, and the prophet Elijah. The former was a guarantee of protection and the latter an inspiration towards a burning zeal for God. No Nazi officer would deflect Sister Anne-Marie from her mission.

It was this certainty of purpose and a simple spiritual lifestyle which had attracted the young Sister Agathe. Her vocation was, however, tested to the full by the news that she heard that morning of 9th June 1944. Leaving the delivery boy trembling at the kitchen door, and quite forgetting to receive the parcels of meat that lay in the basket of his tricycle, Sister Agathe ran to tell the news to the Mother Superior. Tearing through the kitchen and down the oak panelled hall she raced up the worn steps leading up to the first floor balcony. Her heart was thumping. If the Germans were butchering innocent Gentile civilians in Tulle how long would it be before they discovered their real enemy sheltering in the convent not twenty minutes' drive away?

Bursting into the Mother Superior's simple room, Sister Agathe realised that she had disturbed her morning contemplations. Reflection and prayer were central tenets of the Carmelite order and Sister Anne-Marie Devaux was punctilious in her observance of these rituals. Aged fifty one Sister Anne-Marie had experienced the horrors of war before. Inspired by the heroic resistance of French forces at Verdun in 1916, she had volunteered to serve as a nurse during the remainder of the conflict. Posted to the Aisne area in northern France she was horrified by the reality of armed conflict. One event had made the most profound impact on her future life.

During the failed French attack on the Germans at Nivelle in April 1917, retreating French troops were pouring into the casualty clearing stations to which Anne-Marie had been assigned. Among those was a young soldier who had been mortally wounded in the stomach. His intestines had flopped out from his torn flesh. The blood was caked and black in the hole where his stomach had been and the stench of his already rotting flesh was overpowering. He was too weak to speak his name and Anne-Marie searched through his haversack to establish his identity. The nurses were taught to find out the names of their patients as quickly as possible as it was immensely reassuring for a wounded soldier to hear his own name pronounced by a friendly voice. It was often the very first stage in their medical treatment. Inside the haversack she found three ordinary objects but the sight of them chilled her to the bone.

One of the objects was a small metal car whose rubber tyres had been worn thin by much racing across wooden floors, no doubt as another race victory was assured. Another was a brown toy bear, one ear hanging by its thread and with its left glass eye missing. Were its injuries the result of a playful scrap with the bear of a sibling, wondered Anne-Marie? Also in the sack was a scruffy blood stained envelope. Anne-Marie opened it and found a card inside. Unfolding the card she read the words "To Jacques on your 14th birthday, with love Mama, Papa, Thèrése and Monique".

Anne-Marie broke down, for once incapable of subordinating her feelings to her professional duty.

"What are we doing?" she cried out loud, "sending children with toys in their pockets to be slaughtered like lambs. How can this be right?"

Suppressing her tears she turned and heard the boy groaning. She gave him a large dose of morphine praying that this would end his suffering. Minutes later he was still and silent. At that moment the glory of war was unmasked as an imposter, not just for its obvious victim but for Anne-Marie Devaux. She was to become Sister Anne-Marie Devaux of the Carmelite order determined that she would do everything in her power to make sure that these horrors would never happen again.

Her dream of building a better world however was just about to be shattered.

"Gracious Mother," shouted Agathe, "have you heard the news?"

CHAPTER FOUR

Samuel Karamira had every reason to feel contented. At the age of thirty six he had just become Head Teacher at Nyarubuye Schol in south east Rwanda. His lovely wife Chantalle had borne him four children, now age four to twelve. His prominent position in local Rwandan society would ensure that they had the best possible start in life. Samuel and Chantalle were from solid Nyarabuye stock. Their families had lived in the area for generations. Tall, light skinned with a narrow nose and thin lips, Samuel had aspirational looks in Rwandan society.

Far from the hustle and bustle of the country's capital, Kigali, the good citizens of Nyarubuye had grown up in peace and stability. Living close to the Tanzanian border they could even claim a modern pan African tolerance, as visitors from across the border were often welcomed into their town. Visitors from western parts of Rwanda may however have been less willing to travel to Nyarubuye. Hills existed there but they were not as green and luscious as in other parts of the country, often rocky and stark in appearance. The land was more arid with tracks of yellow savannah grass punctuated with thornbush and acacia vegetation. But for Samuel there was no finer place on earth. This was his land, his home. Life was good.

On the evening of 7th April 1994, Samuel was returning home from school. He enjoyed the walk from the school along the dirt tracks back to his home. It gave him time to unwind from the pressures of the day. He was continually frustrated by the failures of the Rwandan education system. Primary education was free and compulsory for a period of six years. However many children did not complete even this short period of study. Parental pressure forced children to leave school and start work to support the family. Even though Samuel was now a leader in the Rwandan education system he could see its limitations. The curriculum was narrow and fragmented. Learning was largely 'achieved' by rote and memorising.

Although, technically, education in Rwanda was not organised along tribal lines, in practice most secondary schools discriminated against Tutsis. To Samuel, a Tutsi, education would not be playing its part in creating a multi ethnic society until it treated all children equally. Effective segregation and stilted learning processes were not serving society well. His students were not vacuous but any observer would be hard pressed to conclude otherwise from the products of even his own class. Samuel had tossed these ideas around in his head many times before on his walk home. Before he knew it he was standing at the gate of his house.

He gazed at the small bungalow with its mud walls and corrugated iron roof. He looked with pride at the small glass windows which had been a recent addition and installed at considerable cost. They gave him a certain status in the local community. Glass windows were a sign that you were upwardly mobile much as a conservatory might be in the west. Unlike other days he did not open the front door and shout "I'm home" in Kinyarwanda, before being hugged by Chantalle and his children. Today they were all waiting for him outside the front door. The children's eyes, usually shining and bright, were transfixed on the narrow dirt path leading from the gate.

"Have you heard?" said Chantalle softly, biting her lip as if to suppress the broad grin that usually lit up her face.

Samuel shook his head.

"President Habyarimana has been killed," she continued "and the Hutus are blaming the Tutsis".

Samuel looked puzzled. "How could that be? Why would Tutsis kill a President who was going to give them a share of power after the Arusha Accords were signed. It doesn't make sense."

"I know," said Chantalle "but you had better come in. We have some serious decisions to make".

Samuel was well versed in Rwandan history. He regarded it as a fundamental pre-requisite of a good education for a child to understand his or her origins and the culture within which he or she was growing up. He had introduced such classes at his school. But de-bunking tribal prejudices was like catching soap in a bath. Each time you grabbed it, it slipped out of your grasp. Even his own children slipped into tribal stereotypes on occasions. Last week his six year old daughter, Grace, had asked, "Daddy, why do Hutus have round faces and flat noses? Mireille says it's because they're related to the silver backed gorillas in the mountains. Is it true?"

"Darling, we're all descended from the apes, whatever tribe or country we're from and whatever colour –black, brown, white, yellow. If you laugh at Hutus for being descended from the apes you must laugh at Tutsis, Twa and Belgians too."

"Yes, but why don't Hutus have any cows?"

Samuel just sighed. Ancient Rwandan folklore had assigned the majority Hutu tribe to cultivation of the soil while the minority, Tutsis herded cattle. Cows were more important than crops, went the argument, and therefore Tutsis were more important than Hutus. In reality the distinctions between the tribes were unclear. Hutus and Tutsis spoke the same language, lived in the same areas, followed the same religion and inter-married. Local tribal chiefs could be either Hutus or Tutsis. Many Hutus had cows, the currency for obtaining a wife.

There was, however, some practical outworking of Tutsi hegemony in the nineteenth century as the Tutsi monarchy gained control over much of the country known as Rwanda today. Tutsis were preferred for political and military office and this generated greater financial and economic power. They were destined to lord it over the Hutu "negroes" who originated from the south. The Tutsi's fine aristocratic features appeared to demonstrate their link with northern African stock.

However, Samuel knew that with so much inter breeding it was often imposible to determine someone's ancestry. If he couldn't work it out why should anyone else be able to do so? Yet when the Belgians arrived after the First World War as colonial administrators they sought to bring order to this ethnic chaos. Identity cards were issued labelling every citizen according to their tribe – Hutu, Tutsi or Twa (a minority pygmy tribe). If there was any doubt about a person's ethnic origin, and there often was, then noses could be measured, brain sizes ascertained and bodies weighed. The Belgians saw the need for structure in Rwanda and the Tutsis became the ruling class in this new ordered society. Centuries of largely national identity and peaceful co-existence were swept aside. The European colonial model of control through a ruling elite had thrust the Tutsis into a 'master/servant' relationship with the Hutus.

However by 1959 the Hutus were no longer prepared to be subservient and rose up against the Tutsis. Massacres of Tutsis by Hutus continued throughout the 1960s until half the Tutsi population had fled the country. Meanwhile the Belgians, finding all this too difficult, had granted Rwanda independence and beat a hasty retreat. Hutu majority rule was the predominant ideology.

In 1973 General Juvénal Habyarimana seized power and ensured that Hutus, particularly from his own home area in northern Rwanda, were given key government and military jobs. Tutsis were marginalised and persecuted, resulting in the creation in 1986 of the Rwandan Patriotic Front (RPF) dedicated to reclaiming the rights and status of the Tutsis. Exiled in Uganda, the RPF spent its early years organising itself and accumulating weaponry. Meanwhile, in Rwanda, occasional disappearances of Tutsis continued into the 1990s, many of them carried out by the militias or Interahamwe (translated as 'those who stand together').

In response the RPF occupied a significant part of Byumba prefecture and in February 1993 even had a battalion of soldiers stationed in the parliament building in the capital Kigali. When a peace agreement was signed at Arusha in Tanzania in August 1993 Samuel had looked forward to a new multi ethnic Rwanda, a united government of Hutus and Tutsis and a military dedicated to protecting all citizens. The news that Chantalle had just given him had shattered that dream.

It was with a heavy heart that he walked into the familiar

surroundings of the living room of his home and slumped into the rocking chair reserved for the head of the house. "Yes," he said, his head slumped dejectedly on the sisal back rest as he looked grimly at the family assembled on the floor in front of him, "we have some serious decisions to make".

CHAPTER FIVE

"Henri, the butcher's boy, has just told me that the Germans have hanged ninety nine Frenchmen in Tulle, all to avenge the deaths of a few German soldiers. They would have killed more too but they ran out of rope," blurted out Sister Agathe breathlessly.

"Compose yourself, Sister," said Anne-Marie calmly, "please remember where you are. We must think about this carefully. Please sit down".

"But there's no time. Can't you see that the Germans could be here any minute? If they are butchering innocent Frenchmen for the deaths of German soldiers what will they do when they find the Jews here? The Nazis have warned that they will kill three maquisards or French civilians for every one of their soldiers who die. What would be the ratio of Jews to Germans – a hundred, a thousand? Not that they need any excuse to exterminate the Jews. They've been doing it for ages. You know that this is the first area they will search. The maquis have been active here for years. The Germans think that the maquisards are a bunch of communists, Jews and deserters. Wouldn't they love to drive them out of the hills over there?"

Sister Agathe pointed out through the Mother Superior's window to the thickly wooded countryside into which the maquisards could melt after wrecking a train or setting up a road block. The maquis were now heavily armed with weapons and ammunition from the Allies. Everyone knew for weeks that an invasion was imminent as the weapon drops from the air became a nightly occurrence. Any fighting now between the maquis and Das Reich would be a bloody affair and the convent could be caught in the middle of it.

"Mother Superior, I'm sorry for my haste but I beg you, please let me take the Jews away from here. The Germans have no respect for the house of God. They will turn this place over until they find them. They have always thought we were collaborators and now they have every excuse to prove it. We must contact the resistance further north and try and arrange safe passage."

Sister Anne-Marie got up and started to pace deliberately around her simple room. The floor boards were bare and creaked in protest at every step she took. She stared at the bookshelf opposite which contained all her worldly possessions – a few worn books promoting spiritual truths. Anne-Marie had always said that if she had to put up another bookshelf to contain her possessions she would have succumbed to pride and materialism.

"Sister Agathe, I have never told you of my experience in the Great War, of the child who died in my arms. Some people say that he gave his life in the name of peace…in the name of hope….in the name of the future. But his death was really a victory for hatred, blind obedience, arrogance…How can there be any hope or any future worth its name when children are sent to the battlefield for slaughter. If that is the price for protecting our way of life then the price is too great. That's why I came here. I suppose I was running away, but I could still resist evil, only here it was through prayer and contemplation, through love and good deeds. Now that seems hopeless too."

Despite her impatience at this delay in evacuating the convent, Sister Agathe was unable to speak. Never before had the Mother Superior spoken to her so personally. Not just to her but to any of the nuns as far as Agathe was aware. They had all seen her almost as a living saint, entirely dedicated to serving God and always thinking the best of other people with no doubts in her mind. It was this strength of purpose that had attracted each nun to join the Order. The convent was a place of clear vision and certainty in an ever changing world. Agathe was shocked – how could Sister Anne-Marie now have such doubts? Was evil not to be resisted?

Agathe reflected on her own motives for joining the Order. Yes she had largely been persuaded by Anne-Marie but her journey had started with her disgust at the cosiness of the Vichy government and Catholic church leaders with the Nazis. She hated their triptych of 'Travail, Famille, Patrie' to replace the revolutionary 'Liberté, Égalité, Fraternité'. Above all she was horrified by what she saw as the collaboration of her own brother, Marc, when he joined Les Chantiers de la Jeunesse and went off to work in a German munitions factory. Yes, evil must be resisted, concluded Agathe but she would never support violent means. The convent, the Order, Sister Anne-Marie all seemed to create that ideal of peaceful, God-centred, but resolute, opposition to the forces of evil. Had she been misled?

"Merciful Mother, have you forgotten the text of your sermon last Sunday? It made a great impression on me. 2 Corinthians 4 verses 17-18 – 'For our light and momentary troubles are achieving for us an eternal glory that far outweighs them all. So we fix our eyes not on what is seen but on what is unseen. For what is seen is temporary, but what is unseen is eternal'. How could anything we do for God be hopeless? Yes, for a moment in the vast expanse of time it appears that we are being defeated, but think of the glory that is to come. Think of that smile on the face of God when we finally see what is now unseen. Think of the pleasure that He feels when we do what He commands. Think of the joy in heaven even now if Satan is being resisted. Do you not think the angels are listening to our conversation and imploring us to do what is right? Sister, even if you cannot do this for what is 'seen', do it for what is 'unseen'.

Anne-Marie turned her gaze from the bookshelf, where it had been transfixed, towards Agathe.

"When you came to this convent I was not sure of your vocation. You seemed to be running away from something. Many women hope to escape from society and find a new, better world in this place. Many are disappointed because we are not separate from the world or from other human beings. We are their servants. We are not hiding from the world but shining a light on it. But I now know why you are here. God has sent you to correct me, to remind me that I am a servant of Him and the rest of mankind and to renew my hope in that eternal glory. Please give me the phone and I will call the maquis."

By now the Mother Superior was back to her determined and purposeful self, the veil of doubt and despair lifted from her features. Sister Agathe heard the familiar winding sound as the dial was turned four times. She could hear it ring three times and then Anne-Marie put down the phone. Agathe's heart sank – was she having second thoughts? Had this all been a waste of time? Please don't give up now.

"That's the call sign" said the Mother Superior. "When I ring back he will know what the call is about. We will speak in code in case the exchange is listening."

She dialled again. This time it was answered. Agathe could hear her saying that the chicken had laid eight eggs and that the farmer would be bringing them over. Anne-Marie then listened intently and scribbled on her blotter with her fine fountain pen, the source of the many messages Agathe had already received since joining the convent.

"D'accord. A bientôt." Anne-Marie concluded the conversation brightly as if it had been an everyday discussion about some trivial matter, and replaced the receiver in a deliberate manner.

"He says that the Germans are everywhere, but the network is still operational. It will be risky to leave but if you want to do so you must take our guests to this address. He advises you not to travel on the roads and to keep out of sight. It is now 4p.m. You must leave immediately."

She passed the note to Sister Agathe and both women made their way down to the basement where the refugees were hiding.

Within ten minutes the eight Jewish escapees were ready. They emerged blinking into the daylight of the convent's kitchen. There were two families. Gustav and Reinhild Steinrich had fled from Austria with their three young girls, Miriam, Heloise and Franca. The girls were strikingly pretty with long auburn hair and large, bright green eyes. The family had sheltered with friends in the Mâcon area before being forced to move west as German activity intensified. They had arrived at the convent by chance and at the point of starvation about six weeks earlier.

Paul and Rachel Katz and their thirteen year old son Matthias had lived all their lives in the Corréze area. As the local doctor Paul was a familiar figure in the community. Of German descent, Paul's father and mother raised Paul and his brother David in Corréze in the early years of the century. David had moved away but Paul had trained as a doctor in Paris before returning to Corréze to marry Rachel and establish his medical practice. During 1943, the Germans had been active in rounding up Jews in the Limoges area. By October 1943, Paul Katz, fearing that he would be exposed, given his prominent standing in the locality, approached Sister Anne-Marie for sanctuary. He had been called out many times to the convent to treat the nuns, usually for routine ailments but occasionally for more serious conditions. When Anne-Marie had herself succumbed to pneumonia some months previously, Dr Katz had been a regular and comforting presence. She had no hesitation in providing the sanctuary the family sought. For eight months they had lived in the damp, cold basement, awaiting safe passage or the end of the war. They had begun to doubt if they would ever see either.

The eight refugees looked a pathetic bunch as they gathered in the kitchen. Pale from a prolonged existence in gloomy and damp surroundings and clothed in shabby and musty smelling overcoats they looked resigned to a life of uncertainty and flight. They had accepted the need to evacuate the convent with resignation and little emotion. Their lives had been placed into the hands of others for so long that they had lost the will to speak for themselves and make their own decisions. There were no gradations of danger for a Jew in occupied France. Every knock on the door was a potential arrest and every stranger a potential spy. Even friends could not be trusted. With most people underfed, under clothed, cold and frightened, the prospect of some extra rations for exposing a Jewish family was tempting for some.

"Sister Agathe," said Anne-Marie, "you must leave. I've heard that the Germans are on their way. They are searching the village and will be here soon. May God be with you."

Although Agathe had been pressing the Mother Superior to allow them to leave, she now felt a strange reluctance to go. For the first time she realised the consequences of her actions. Yes, her journey would be dangerous but they would be on the move. They could travel lightly and reconnoitre any potentially dangerous situations. But the convent was a sitting target. The nuns would never abandon the place and the

Germans were thirsting for blood. Suddenly Agathe was gripped by a searing apprehension. Anne-Marie sensed her mood. Hugging her novitiate tightly she spoke earnestly, "Go, Sister, we trust in God. He will protect us."

Tears were beginning to moisten Agathe's eyes as she held onto the woman who had so inspired her. One by one each refugee also embraced Anne-Marie. Silently the group slipped out of the back door. Anne-Marie watched as they walked swiftly up the garden path and through the wooden gate at the end of the vegetable patch. She was trusting in preternatural intervention to save her too.

CHAPTER SIX

Samuel waved to his four children to go and play on the patch of bare earth that masqueraded as a garden at the back of the house.

As ever, Anatolie, the eldest at twelve years of age, led the way. In Rwanda the oldest was often thrust into quasi-parental responsibility at a very young age. AIDS, warfare, disease and displacement had fractured families. Many children were brought up by grandparents or other relatives with the first born treated as the interlocutor with their younger siblings. They could also undertake many of the traditional maternal duties such as cooking, washing and cleaning. Had Anatolie been called upon to meet this challenge she would have passed with flying colours. Her erect posture and flashing brown eyes gave her an aura of authority, largely unquestioned by the others, even her ten year old brother, Jonathan.

Jonathan was small for his age, the consequences of a premature and difficult birth according to Chantalle. He had a fuller face than the rest of the family. His nose was flatter and lips more fleshy than the other children. This had led to taunts of "Hutu" from neighbouring Tutsi children. These jibes and a self consciousness about his height had made Jonathan more withdrawn than others of his age. He preferred to play by himself with his own toys rather than join in the makeshift games of football with bits of plastic bag and strips of inner tube as a ball which were the favoured pastime of other boys in the area. Perhaps his slightly introverted nature made him more sentient than other children of his age. As Samuel watched Jonathan follow Anatolie into the garden the boy turned and caught his father's glance. His look seemed to convey understanding and almost compassion towards his parents and the difficulty of their predicament. Samuel was strangely comforted by this.

The two younger girls, Grace aged six and Marthe aged four, trooped out behind the older children squabbling about who should hold a favourite rag doll, entirely oblivious to the portentous conversation that was about to take place.

Samuel stood up and closed the back door. Chantalle was the first to speak.

"Maybe this will all blow over. These rumours about Hutu reprisals have been heard before. What happens? A few extremists are killed in Kigali, there are skirmishes with the RPF and it all dies down."

"But they have killed the President!" Samuel was animated as he spoke. "Who do you think did this? The Tutsis? No – why should they? For the first time in thirty years the Tutsis have got a sniff of power. Using the RPF army as a threat they could manipulate Habyarimana as they wish. No, this is the work of Hutu Power. They have sacrificed the President to kill the peace process. They never wanted to share power with the Tutsis and Habyarimana was not going to be allowed to bring that about."

Samuel was careful not to use 'we' instead of 'the Tutsis'. He was not a political animal and did not regard the RPF as defending him. Samuel was first and foremost a Rwandan and secondly a Tutsi. None of these things were being done 'in his name'.

Just at that moment there was a loud knock on the door. Samuel and Chantalle froze – the Interahamwe could not be here already, surely. Their friends did not knock, they just came in. They did not need to announce themselves as they were always welcome. Softly Samuel crept towards the front window and looked up diagonally across the glass towards the front door. He could identify the visitor without being seen from this position.

"It's Thomas," he said quizzically but with a measure of relief in his voice.

Samuel opened the door and ushered in his neighbour. He shut the door quickly and checked through the window that no-one was watching. It had already come to this – Thomas was a Hutu and, though one of their oldest friends, might no longer be trustworthy.

"Thomas, why did you knock?" asked Chantalle. "You scared us."

"I did it so that you wouldn't be scared," answered Thomas. "When the militia arrives, do you think they will knock? I assume you have heard the news." Thomas and Chantalle nodded in a resigned manner. "This assassination has been planned for days. The Hutu Power on Radio Rwanda has been hinting all week that something major would be happening. They murdered the President so that they could blame the Tutsis. The reprisals have already started and this time any massacres are going to be big. The militia have been training in this area for months. You must have heard the gunfire. It's not safe for you to stay here, you must leave as quickly as possible".

Samuel replied, "But where would we go, Thomas. This is our home. Surely there will just be some fighting between the Hutu militia and the RPF in Kigali. It won't touch us here. Even if it does, by that time the United Nations will be here to protect us".

"Don't be so naïve, Samuel, the Belgians are already spreading a story that it was the French who shot down the President's plane to stop him handing over the country to the RPF. Remember that the French have propped up Habyarimana's regime for years. For God's sake they even supplied him with the plane that he died in. They have always wanted to protect their little empire in central Africa from their English speaking neighbours like Uganda and Tanzania. What language do the RPF speak? English. Who was Habyarimana's main supporter in Paris? Yes, President Mitterand's own son. Do you really think that the French will let the UN send in thousands of troops to protect you? Without an invitation there is no chance that the UN would move against one of its most powerful members. No, you'll be dead before anyone comes to help you".

Samuel blanched at the word 'you'. Thomas hadn't meant it that way but the conflict was already dividing neighbour from neighbour. Thomas was a Hutu and had an identity card to prove it. He didn't need to go anywhere and was 'we' rather than 'you'. Samuel fingered his card which was in its usual place in his left hand trouser pocket, and which said 'Tutsi' on it. Thomas was right, the card was now a death sentence.

"What are the other Tutsi families doing?" asked Chantalle, "Charles and Mary, Emmanual and Marianne, Evariste, Leon – are they going or staying?"

"They're all going Chantalle. The word is that Bourgmestre Ndagijimana is already compiling lists of Tutsis in the area. You know the power that the Interahamwe have got around here, just wait until they get their hands on that list". He turned imploringly to Samuel. "Old friend, we have known each other since we were children. Do you remember how we used to go up to the church garden and catch butterflies in a bucket, those bright blue ones? You were always the one who put the banana leaves on top of the bucket to stop the butterflies from escaping. We'd then take them home and let them out in the house and watch them fly around until they discovered the way out. We'd find a few the next day spread out on the window ledge, stiff and dry. I don't want to come into this house and find you like those butterflies. There is a way out if you go now before the militia has organised itself. I love you like a brother and sister and despise everything that Hutu Power stand for but we cannot protect you. You must go."

"But where, Thomas, we don't know anywhere else?" cried Chantalle.

"You must go to Tanzania. It's not far and the others will be going with you. If you take enough food and drink for a few days, the Red Cross will be there to help. It already runs refugee camps and you will be safe."

Samuel looked away from Thomas and gazed at the children playing happily in the back garden. He knew that Thomas was right, but how could he leave everything behind that he had spent years building up. Had it all been in vain? What about the school – what would happen to the children? He had spent so long teaching them that education was the only way for them to have a better future. What a fallacy that seemed today. Education had no power over the prejudice and hatred that was now manifesting itself. How had education given the Interahamwe a balanced view of society? He had been wrong all along.

"Chantalle, get our things packed. Only take what we need for a few days and no more than we can carry on our backs. It's only twenty five kilometres to the border. We can be there in a day. Once you and the children are safe I will come back."

Chantalle made for the door to call the children in but then suddenly realised what Samuel had said.

"Samuel, what do you mean, 'come back'? You can't just dump us on the other side of the border and leave. And what do you want to come back for? If it's not safe now, what will it be like next week! How are we going to survive without you?"

"Charles, Emmanuel and Leon will look after you. I cannot just abandon the school and let all the children be slaughtered, the books destroyed and the buildings burnt down. What about the church where we have worshipped all our lives and this home that we have worked so hard to create, the old people who are too frail to walk? I can't just leave them all. I am a head teacher. They will respect me. I promise that I will come back to you."

"But only after you have saved the whole town...single-handedly!" mocked Chantalle. She sighed audibly, knowing that this was not the time to prolong the argument. She had only herself to blame anyway. It was Samuel's strength of character, sense of civic pride and zealous faith which had attracted her to him in the first place. Just like her father, whom she could clearly remember from her pre-pubescent years before his early death. I sound like my mother, she thought, as she started to gather together the children's clothes.

Thomas embraced them and left to spread the word among other Tutsi families.

"Meet at the church in one hour," he said as he rushed out through the front door.

By the time Samuel, Chantalle, Anatolie, Jonathan, Grace and Marthe reached the church, there were about twenty other people gathered there. All were carrying as many possessions as could be crammed into a rag tag collection of bags made out of canvas or banana leaves. One child had a rucsac with 'Italia 90' emblazoned on the back. No doubt some absent minded Belgian tourist had left it behind, only for the bag to become the prized possession of this young boy. Samuel smiled at the incongruity of it – football pervaded life throughout the world, even in the midst of the greatest human tragedy. He recognised the boy as Silas, one of his pupils – a little AIDS orphan who was being looked after by one of the families waiting at the church.

"Where's everyone else?" asked Samuel as he surveyed the small knot of people huddled by the entrance to the church. The Catholic church in Nyarubuye was an imposing building. Built of red sandstone, its frontage would not have disgraced any medium sized town in Europe. From the front it looked a little like a medieval fort. The windows were long slits spread unevenly across the frontage as if to provide vantage points for archers. Each section of wall was of irregular height with parapet slabs at the top from which invaders could be spotted.

On the left hand side of the frontage was the tower, its buttresses reinforcing its forbidding appearance. The tower would have dominated the frontal aspect of the church but for one thing – a white marble statue of Christ above the entrance with his arms outstretched. As Samuel walked up the steps to the door under that statue he felt strangely peaceful. It was as if Christ was welcoming them into His open arms. There they would find protection and peace.

"No-one else is coming, Samuel," said Leon, a local shopkeeper of about the same age. "They do not believe anything bad will happen to them and the Bourgmestre has assured everyone that they will be safe. We have tried to persuade them, but they have heard rumours of massacres before and just do not believe them anymore. We can do no more for them. Quick it's getting dark and we must leave."

As the little group departed, the sound of their steps on the gravel surface in front of the church echoed eerily in the stillness and quietude of an early Rwandan evening. The exodus had begun.

CHAPTER SEVEN

Julius Ndagijimana was in a foul mood on the morning of 9th April 1994, more than thirty six hours after Samuel's small group of refugees had left Nyarubuye. A Bourgmestre in the préfecture of Kibungo province in south east Rwanda, he had received instructions from the new interim government in Kigali which were going to disrupt his day.

"What about my crops?" he muttered grumpily, "I can't leave those idle labourers to look after them. Unless I'm there to get them working they'll be asleep by mid-day".

Ndagijimana's plantations did indeed need his attention. Each morning he would dress and walk out into the courtyard of his luxurious home to survey the plantations of avocado, bananas and beans that stretched for several acres beyond the hedges that fringed his property. If the troubles continue for too long, he thought, my harvest will just rot away. The fax that he held in his hand made that a distinct possibility.

"Patrice!" he barked at the clerk who was cowering in the neighbouring office, "Come here."

The Bourgmestre was indeed a formidable man. Over six feet tall and weighing around one hundred kilos he seemed to dominate his office at the bureau communal rather like an elephant dominates his pen at a zoo. The tribal scars on his cheeks gave his appearance a menacing aspect but his beard was neat and tidy. His green trousers were pressed and his white shirt was starched and clean. This was a man who looked as if he could use force and charm in equal measure as the occasion demanded. Today it was force and not even the smiling photograph of

Pope John Paul II, which hung above Ndagijimana's chair, as if bestowing a papal blessing on the Bourgmestre, could soothe the clerk's nerves as he entered the room.

"Have you updated those index cards yet?" snapped Ndagijimana.

"Yes, Bourgmestre," said Patrice, thankful that he had worked late the previous night to complete the task. "I left them on your table over there."

The Bourgmestre motioned for the clerk to bring the trays of index cards to him. He fingered through the thousands of slim paper cards which contained the name, address, ethnicity and photograph of every resident. Patrice had neatly arranged them in tribal order – Tutsis first, then Hutus, Twas and others.

"Good, Patrice, one of these days you will make a decent clerk worthy of working for such an illustrious leader as myself," Ndagijimana chuckled at his cutting wit. "We have much work to do with these cards today. I want all the Tutsi cards separated into geographical areas, say about fifty in each pile. And get hold of all the Conseillers de Secteur, Responsables de Cellule and the MRND and CDR party chiefs in this commune. Tell them there will be a meeting here today at 1p.m. sharp. I want a list of all those attending within the hour. Understood?"

Patrice nodded and slipped out of the room in as deferential a way as he had entered it. If the Bourgmestre had something to occupy his mind then Patrice hoped he would be left alone. He was, however, filled with foreboding at the task that faced him. There was one Tutsi card that would definitely be 'misplaced' into the Hutu pile – that of his own wife, Odette. And what should he do with the cards of Odette's mother, father, brother, sister, nieces and nephews and his neighbours, the Karamiras, Samuel and Chantalle? Mind you, he hadn't seen them for a day or two, perhaps they were already lying low, he mused.

Patrice had always side-stepped questions about his family. The Bourgmestre once asked him if he was married but in such an off hand way that it was clear he wasn't really interested in the reply. He often did this – asked a question, barely waited for the reply and then launched into a tirade of abuse about something. This was often directed at his "bone idle labourers", "incompetent government officials" or "Tutsi scum". When Patrice nonchalantly replied that he "didn't know why anyone would wish to get married these days", Ndagijimana railed against Tutsis "breeding like rabbits, no, that was an insult to rabbits – like snakes." Patrice hadn't known that snakes bred so prolifically but the Bourgmestre went on without querying his analogy. "All they want to do is infect the Hutus with their poison, to subject them to humiliating subservience as in the past." Patrice nodded compliantly until the rant was over and the Bourgmestre had left the room.

It would not be so easy to protect Odette and her family this time. Patrice opened the top right hand drawer of his desk and stared at a copy of the fax that Julius Ndagijimana had received earlier that morning. The fax had arrived on the only machine in the office. This stood on Patrice's desk. Routinely he read all the faxes that came through, as many of them could be dealt with by him and didn't need the Bourgmestre's attention. Ndagijimana was basically lazy and became very cross if Patrice brought too much work through. By filtering the incoming faxes and letters Patrice could also protect himself from avoidable insults. The fax that had come through that day was brief and stark:

To the Bourgmestre, Kibungo préfecture.

The Republic is in great danger. The forces of the Rwandan Patriotic Front have murdered the democratically elected President of Rwanda, General Juvénal Habyarimana. This invading army is being assisted by Tutsi collaborators in all areas of the country. Their aim is to undermine national unity and displace the legitimate government of this country. You are to identify and eliminate all Tutsi traitors. We will supply you with weapons for the Interahamwe to use to defend local citizens from this subversion. All necessary force must be used to protect our society which is under the greatest possible threat to its existence.

Paul Niyibizi
Minister of Information
Interim Government of the Republic of Rwanda
8th April 1994

Patrice stared blankly at the piece of paper that he held in his hand. He knew exactly what it meant. He had been taking calls the previous day from frightened government officials in Kigali. They were being asked to pay fifty Rwandan francs for every Tutsi head brought into their offices. Urged on by Hutu radio, citizens were commanded to do their patriotic duty and rid Rwanda of Tutsi insurgents. Neighbours were being hacked to death by neighbours, work colleagues by others in their offices. A few doctors killed their patients, while even the odd schoolteacher killed his pupils. All lorries in the capital were being requisitioned to clear the corpses from the roads, so that the military could move around and set up more roadblocks. Any Hutu opposition was also being eliminated. This included Prime Minister, Agathe Uwiligiyimana, who was murdered in the grounds of her own house. The machetes of the Hutu Power Interahamwe were literally dripping with blood.

Patrice shook as he recalled the panicked phone calls of yesterday. He reached for the index cards and deftly moved those for Odette and as many of her family as he could remember, together with the Karamiras and a few other neighbours, from the Tutsi pile to the bottom of the Hutu pile. Just as he was re-tidying the piles of cards the Bourgmestre stormed into the room.

"Give me the Tutsi cards," he blasted. "Come on, I can't wait all day. I will give them to those idle layabouts to sort out. Those officials have got nothing better to do and they know where these vipers live anyway."

Patrice obediently placed the cards into boxes, which he handed over to the Bourgmestre. Each card was now a certain death warrant and Patrice secretly hoped that as many residents as possible had heeded the warnings of local Tutsi leaders that their lives could be in danger. Ndagijimana saw Patrice glance nervously at the piles of Hutu cards scattered across his desk.

"I haven't got time to look through that lot now for any Hutu traitors but put them in boxes and I will do it later. And make sure you get hold of all those officials for this afternoon's meeting." He made a threatening gesture to Patrice which indicated that his life too would be in danger if he didn't follow his leader's instruction.

* * *

By 1p.m. most of the dignitaries in the commune had gathered in the meeting room of the bureau communal. They sat around a large oval table overseen by the green, yellow and red Rwandan flag and a photograph of the Bourgmestre shaking hands with President Habyarimana. Much of the work of the bureau communal had been disrupted by the threat of violence. The health centre was deserted and only the empty boxes of medicine, syringes and bandages scattered all over the floor gave any clue to its identity. No doctors or nurses had reported for duty that day and, even if they had done, there were no patients for them to treat. The administration office was quiet, with the normal chattering of voices and hammering of typewriters replaced by an eery silence.

The officials rose as the Bourgmestre entered the room. Many of them owed their appointment to his patronage and displayed an almost exaggerated sycophancy. However, despite his power in the locality, Ndagijimana was only a middle ranking figure in the government hierarchy.

Rwanda was divided into twelve préfectures or regions. Although the préfectures were the highest level of local government in Rwanda, in reality they had little power. President Habyarimana had consolidated authority into his own hands in Kigali and maintained control through a cabal of his northern Hutu henchmen. Each préfecture was divided into several communes such as Rusumo where Ndagijimana was the Bourgmestre. He felt that the communes were just a convenient tool for Kigali to use to exercise control over the country without giving local people any real power. Nonetheless his distaste for the authoritarian central government did not mellow his attitude to the secteurs (sectors) and cellules (cells – the smallest administrative unit), which reported to him. His control was absolute, his power total. He personally appointed all the main officials in each of the secteurs and cellules. Not only that, but he maintained an informal structure of spies and infiltrators who informed him daily of events in each unit. The Bourgmestre was also a major power broker in the two main political parties in Rwanda, the MRND and CDR.

The MRND had established local militia or Interahamwe to enforce government policy in each locality and the Bourgmestre had been fully involved in the process. As Julius Ndagijimana surveyed the group of about fifty people crammed into the bureau communal's meeting room, he reflected with satisfaction at the thoroughness of his preparation for this moment. Nothing would happen in this commune without his authority and if any group was unwilling to obey his commands he would get it done through someone else, with disasterous consequences to those who had refused to carry out his orders.

"Gentlemen," he opened, "this is a momentous day in the history of the Second Republic. We are in great danger. The Tutsis have murdered our noble President, Juvénal Habyarimana, and are intent on exterminating all Hutus. It is the patriotic duty of all true Rwandans to rise up against the Tutsi invaders and defend our motherland. You will be provided with grenades, machetes and other weapons by the préfecture. These will be delivered to you in the next two days. They can be used by all Hutu comrades to rid this commune of those treacherous inyenzi. No Tutsi can be trusted, even those you have worked with, or lived among, for many years. Even a relative or your next door neighbour is capable of barbarous acts against those who are true patriots. Now that the moment has arrived, they will rise up to drive the Hutus out of our homeland. The Tutsis have been lying low for years waiting for this opportunity to inflict a most terrible revenge on the loyal citizens of Rwanda. Neighbour must defend himself against neighbour and brother against sister. Patrice will give you cards which will identify Tutsis in your area of responsibility. You are to work with the militia to ensure that all such cockroaches are removed from our commune by whatever means are necessary. And I mean permanently removed – do you understand?"

There was a murmur of agreement from his audience, all of whom then besieged Patrice for their cards. In reality they knew that some of the names on the cards were already dead. The Interahamwe had been circling the area for some time blowing whistles and ordering the Tutsi to come out of their homes. They then set fire to their houses and took their cattle. Any who resisted were killed. The militiamen were often drunk and raped any Tutsi girls they managed to catch.

But now it was official. They were obeying government orders. No-one need be spared, no excuses accepted. The real killing could begin.

CHAPTER EIGHT

Sister Agathe secured the gate at the perimeter fence of the convent, not willing to leave any clue as to their hasty departure. She checked in the pocket of her habit for the piece of paper showing the address of the safe house to which they were heading.

"I'm a fool" she muttered, loudly enough for each member of the group to turn around.

"I'm sorry. I just realised that I am still wearing my habit. It's too conspicuous but there's no time to change. We must press on. Maybe I'll be able to change when we get to the safe house. Come, we have a long walk. It's about fifteen kilometres to Madranges and we need to be there before morning."

Agathe had already decided that it would be too dangerous to walk along the country lanes to Madranges. The area was crawling with Germans and a group of nine people, including a nun, walking together would be sure to attract attention. The road to Madranges headed off north-west from the convent passing through the village of St Augustin on the way. Agathe advised the group that they should travel through the fields that were adjacent to the lane. This might involve some clambering over fences and streams but it was the only way to keep out of sight, whilst going in the right direction. It would not be an easy walk particularly with the children. The rolling Limousin hills made for a pleasant afternoon stroll in the summer sun. But a night time walk in April, carrying heavy bags and being uncertain of the route, was another matter.

Madranges was 600 metres above sea level and there would be some steep gradients to be overcome on the way. Agathe was also fearful of the fate which might befall Sister Anne-Marie and the convent when the Germans arrived. She silently mouthed an intercessory prayer.

It was a prescient act, for at that moment Major Gunther Eberling knocked loudly on the sturdy oak door of the Carmelite convent. He spoke good French, albeit with a flat, guttural German accent.

"Open the door," he shouted. "I am a German commandant with orders to search this building."

Sister Anne-Marie and the other nuns were at that same moment praying in the chapel for the safety of the refugees and their own deliverance. One of the younger nuns, hearing Major Eberling's voice, offered to open the door.

"No, Sister," said the Mother Superior firmly, "this is my duty. Please remain here and pray."

With that, she genuflected towards the altar and set off towards the entrance to the convent.

"Open up," shouted Eberling, but more impatiently this time and with further heavy banging on the door.

When it eventually opened Major Eberling surveyed the small, neat, middle aged nun who welcomed him and enquired about his health.

"I am quite well, thank you, Sister," he responded. "May I come in?"

Sister Anne-Marie showed Eberling and two other officers into the visitors' room. The rest of the troops remained with their vehicles on the forecourt of the convent, out of sight of the escaping refugees at the rear.

"Please sit down, gentlemen. May I get you some coffee?"

"No, Sister, I'm afraid we haven't got time to socialise."

Eberling looked around the room and out through the open window, onto the gardens at the side of the convent. Sister Anne-Marie had been careful to show her visitors into a room from which there was no possibility that the Major could see Agathe and her little party. They listened in silence to the effervescent bird song, which joyously filled the room, and smelled the perfumes of early summer, which delicately permeated the convent at this time of year.

"This is a nice and peaceful place you have here. I don't suppose you get many visitors here, do you Sister? Not too many people passing through – very few prying eyes."

Anne-Marie stared at the Major, desperately trying not to betray any flicker of emotion. But it was clear why he had come.

"I don't know what you mean, Major. Our purpose is to spend our time in contemplation and prayer in obedience to our Lord. It isn't a performance for the benefit of other people."

"What I mean, Sister, is that this would be an ideal place for guests to stay for a long period of time…undetected."

Eberling turned on the Mother Superior, his face only twelve inches away from hers, contorted with rage.

"Where are they?" he bellowed, forcing the Mother Superior to press back further into her chair as she emitted a cry of shock.

"Who, who…are you talking about?" blurted out Anne-Marie fearfully.

"You know who I mean," sneered the Major, "the Jewish vermin, the Zionist scum, where are they? Don't make this difficult for me Sister. If you hand them over to me we will leave you in peace."

Anne-Marie was now able to compose herself, praying that Agathe was, by now, well clear of the convent's environs.

"There is no-one here, Major, apart from the other Sisters and myself."

Eberling interrupted, "Sister, I will come straight to the point. Have you, or have you not, been sheltering Jews in this convent? Yes or no?"

Anne-Marie thought for a moment before replying.

"Major, our world is far removed from yours. We don't condemn those who are in need or are different to ourselves. We seek to serve them. In that, we follow the apostle Paul who said that 'there is neither Jew nor Greek, slave nor free, male nor female, for you are all one in Christ Jesus'. Although you are an enemy of our country, if you had come to us in need today we would have helped you."

Eberling was enraged at this ambiguous response, which, in his eyes, was a tacit admission that the convent had given sanctuary to the Jewish enemy. But for the moment he was lost for words. He had been rounding up Jews for months and never before had any Gentile questioned his actions. If they had been collaborating with the Jews they had neither the courage nor the conviction to own up to it. Sister Anne-Marie's honesty had disarmed him momentarily, not just by her unwillingness to lie but by her offer of sanctuary to him. Most French people just spat at him or mouthed obscenities. That was when they weren't trying to blow him to pieces. Here was someone who showed compassion and even Major Eberling could see that she meant it.

However, hardened by years of hatred and butchery, he soon recovered his composure.

"Turn this place over," he barked to his two henchmen. "This is no longer a place of worship. It is a legitimate enemy target. Sister, you have made your choice – your God must save you now."

With that, the three men marched out of the room.

Sister Anne-Marie got up quickly and hastened back to the chapel to join the other nuns. If they were to die it should take place in the house of God while they were on their knees.

Agathe could hear the gunfire emanating from the convent from three or four fields distant. The group stopped and looked back in the weakening evening light towards the building which had been their sanctuary for so long. Wisps of smoke were beginning to appear through the lead roof and the crackle of burning wood could be clearly heard. Male voices exploded from different parts of the house and garden, each episode followed by staccato machine gun fire.

Sister Agathe was transfixed with horror. "I must go back," she said, mesmorised by the terror unfolding in front of her.

"I should never have left. If any harm comes to any of the Sisters I will never be able to forgive myself."

As she set off purposefully back to the convent, Paul Katz ran forward blocking her path and holding her firmly by the shoulders.

"Sister, do you think the Germans are going to stop their destruction just because you are there? If you go back you will become just another victim of this atrocity – another scalp for the Germans. They won't even notice that they are killing another nun. I'm sorry to be so frank but I have seen them at work. They won't stop shooting; they won't put the fire out; not a single life will be saved by your actions. This evil is beyond any human comprehension. It defies all logic. There can be no rational explanations. I am a doctor. I don't know of any biological or medical causes for such actions. They must arise from some deep seated source outside our understanding, but what I do know is, that you cannot defeat this yourself. But if you stay, you can save lives. Please don't go. If not for the adults' sakes, then stay for the children who have their entire future ahead of them. Look at them, please."

Paul Katz gently turned Agathe to face the children – Miriam, Heloise, Franca and Matthias.

"Don't they deserve something better than living like rats in a hole, shaking with fear every time there are footsteps outside? Their voices are so quiet because they have to whisper all the time for fear of being heard. They never have proper conversations, never enough to eat or drink, their teeth fall out through decay and they're taunted by memories that will stay with them for the rest of their lives. We must try and save them so that they can see that life is not always like this, but that there will be a time when they can be happy and safe. But, Sister…if anyone should go back, then it should be me. If they catch one Jew they might be satisfied and go somewhere else. It's the best chance we've got of saving the convent. I beg you, please take the others and go while there's still time."

His voice was breaking up as months of fear and frustration boiled up into a climactic eruption. Tears fell down his face as he turned away from the group so as not to cause them further distress.

Sister Agathe looked despondently from the burning convent to the dishevelled bunch of refugees huddled together like the cattle who had gathered in the far corner of the field.

"It's this way," she said, pointing to a gate about fifty metres away, barely visible now in the gathering gloom, and motioning to Paul Katz to come with them.

No-one said a word as they trudged off into the dark, but the depth of their despair was communicated by the continuous sound of quiet sobbing.

Despite the intensity of their desolation, the little group made good progress as they traversed field after field, climbing steeply in places before dropping down an equal height on the other side. Their boots trampled over fern and heather, grass and wild flowers, as the altitude varied. At times they had to crawl through dense woodland, navigating by the moon and stars on this mercifully clear night.

After about two hours they arrived at the outskirts of the village of St Augustin. Potentially this was the most dangerous part of the journey so far. The fields and woods, which had been their shelter, petered out into a line of houses which bordered the two roads that intersected in the centre of the village.

"Let's rest for a minute," said Agathe as she considered the options for passing safely through the village. "Paul, there is a track just ahead of us beyond that gate over there. As you are a native French speaker and less conspicuous than me," she pointed at the blue habit that stretched from her head to her feet, "would you follow that track and see where it leads?"

Paul nodded, dropped his bag, and headed off down the track. The others slumped gratefully onto the wet grass, the children soon dozing peacefully. He was gone for no more than ten minutes, his presence revealed only by the occasional bark from a dog in a nearby farm. When he returned he had good news.

"Right – the track leads into the centre of the village. There's no sign of anyone at the crossroads and beyond that point we will need to walk on the road for about one hundred metres before we can slip back onto farmland. But it all looks clear, so I suggest we get going. We must be quiet along the track as there are dogs in the farmyard to the right. Most of the houses have shutters bolted tight, so if we are lucky, no-one will see us. Come on, let's wake the children and go."

Each child was gently roused and bags were collected. The group set off down the track towards the centre of St Augustin. It was impossible for nine people to pass noiselessly down the track. Their boots crunched agonisingly on the gravel surface. This set the dogs barking furiously. Within seconds a window on the second floor of the farmhouse was flung open and a gruff voice shouted "Who is it?"

Motioning to the others to continue down the track, Paul Katz replied, "I'm a doctor. I was called to deliver a baby in St Augustin and thought the house was down this track. I am sorry. I must have been mistaken."

"Pity any poor child born in these times," replied the farmer "better not to have been born at all. No sir, you will find no expectant mother around here. Au revoir."

With that the window was closed and Paul hurried on to catch the rest of the group. By then they had reached the crossroads, where they had decided to carry on in family groups until they could pass into fields again. Sister Agathe was to follow at the rear.

With no street lights to betray them, the operation to gain open country again was achieved surprisingly easily. As they reconvened in farmland to the north of St Augustin they exchanged smiles for the first time since they had left the convent earlier that day.

* * *

It was 10p.m. on that same day, 9th June 1944 when Major Franz Hautmann, the commanding officer of 1st Battalion of Der Führer regiment of Das Reich army, arrived at German HQ in Limoges about eighty kilometres north-west of the convent.

"Coffee, Franz?" asked Hermann Schultz, a Gestapo officer whose job it was to gather information about maquis and enemy activity in the area. He ran a group of French informants who were either bribed or intimidated, or both, into revealing the names of resistance members, the location of planned attacks, the timing of Allied weapon drops and the like. Schultz publicly cherished and protected his network of informers but privately he despised them. Fiercely patriotic he would rather have died than betray his own country.

"Thank you," replied Hautmann as he slumped into the heavy dark leather armchair in the modest lounge of the HQ building. "Any news of Peters?"

"Nothing definite but my sources…"

"Your sources!" interrupted Hautmann. "You mean that bunch of

French peasants and beggars. They wouldn't know a German soldier if Hitler himself in full ceremonial uniform goose stepped before them in his jackboots carrying a flag with a swastika on it."

"These French 'peasants' have been remarkably successful in slowing the progress of the mighty Der Führer regiment to a crawl. This has hardly been the most glorious campaign in your regiment's history has it Franz? Perhaps they have a little more 'savoir faire' than you give them credit for."

Hautmann refused to rise to the bait. The frustratingly slow march of Das Reich troops through central France was creating tension and frustration throughout all ranks. It was late and Hautmann really did want to know what had happened to his friend, Heinrich Peters.

"As I was saying, Franz…my sources have told me that Peters is being held by the maquisards in Oradour-sur-Glane, a village about twenty five kilometres away. Rumour has it that he is to be executed tomorrow. But as I only deal with the scum of French society there is no reason for you to believe me," Schultz retorted sarcastically.

"I'm sorry, Hermann, this war is getting to all of us." Hautmann hesitated. "How sure are you about the whereabouts of Peters?"

"To be honest, I don't know. There has been a lot of resistance activity in this area in the last day or two. Sabotage of railway lines, ambushes, abductions…that kind of thing. So there must be a gathering together of maquisards around here to stop us getting further north to repel the Allied invasion. They may well have got Peters and are seeking revenge for what happened at Tulle. The public execution of a high ranking German officer would fit the bill very nicely, don't you think?"

Hautmann nodded grimly. Even if Peters was not being held in this non-descript French village, the locals needed to be taught a lesson. The Germans would look after their own, no matter what the consequences.

"Bauer!" bawled Hautmann to his adjutant who was waiting outside in the lobby, "Come here at once."

Adjutant Otto Bauer marched mechanically into the room and saluted his commanding officer perfunctorily.

"At ease, Otto. I want about 100 men ready for 9a.m. tomorrow morning with two half tracks, eight trucks, a motorcycle and my

Mercedes with a driver. Get hold of Captain Vomecourt. Ask him to report to me at 9.05a.m. tomorrow morning at the latest with all the men correctly assembled and with a map of the route to Oradour-sur-Glane. Also get me a layout of the village showing the location of all public buildings and meeting places. And Otto, when you march into my room, at least look as if you're sincere about it."

"Yes sir!" shouted Bauer, affecting a sergeant major's drill routine as he left the room.

"Sarcastic moron" he breathed as passed through the door and headed off to the barracks where Captain Helmut Vomecourt was billeted for the night.

As he cranked his BMW motorbike into life, Bauer hissed, "I hate this lousy war. I hate Nazism, Aryan supremacy, Mein Kampfe. It's all crap. We're not liberating anyone, not sharing a superior way of life with downtrodden citizens in other countries. No, this war is just bringing untold misery upon millions of innocent people and that includes ordinary German soldiers. All of this just to feed the arrogance and bigotry of a stunted Austrian nobody."

He roared off down the road, venting his frustration on his prized possession which seemed to be wincing under the burden of his erratic riding. He loved his bike which was about the only thing in his life that he was able to control at the moment. The rest of it was just a question of obeying orders.

Helmut Vomecourt was getting ready for bed when the field telephone rang. Already grumpy at the thought of having to bed down on the bare floor of another lousy billet, a phone call was the last thing he wanted.

"Vomecourt," he snapped, barely having lifted the receiver to his mouth. He listened for a few moments and then slammed the receiver back down again. He had heard regional HQ advising him that Adjutant Bauer was on his way and that he had a message of 'the upmost importance'.

"Not that poof," he muttered as he looked around the bleak classroom at the Limoges primary school, "that's all I need."

Vomecourt had no time for anyone who did not share his conviction about the rectitude of the conflict. As the whole campaign reached its climax, with the opportunity to drive the Allied invasion back into the English Channel and deal a final crippling blow to the enemy, there was no place for half–heartedness. Give him a regiment of soldiers from his native Alsace and he could defeat anyone. But all he was ever sent was Saxon nancy boys.

Helmut Vomécourt was born in the Alsatian city of Strasbourg in 1916. His father was a tailor of French origin, his mother a government official of German ancestry. Vomécourt's mixed racial upbringing reflected the historical see-saw of the Alsace-Lorraine region. Originally a part of the German Holy Roman Empire it had been administered by France for much of the seventeenth, eighteenth and nineteenth centuries. The Treaty of Frankfurt in 1871, which ended the Franco-Prussian War, restored the region to German control. However, after World War One, Alsace-Lorraine reverted to France until it was annexed again by Germany in 1940.

Helmut's father was a mild mannered man whose main pleasure in life was fishing in the freshwater rivers and lakes around Strasbourg. He was non-political preferring to call himself an Alsatian rather than French or German. Marietta Vomécourt, Helmut's mother, however, became increasingly partisan following the incorporation of the area into France in 1919. She had been an enthusiastic supporter of autonomy for the region which had been granted by the German government in 1911. When the French were back in control, Marietta found that much of the power formerly exercised by the local government had gone. Her frustration at "French interference" frequently boiled over at the dinner table in the Vomécourt household. Young Vomécourt, being close to his mother, could not help but be suspicious of "Les Francaises" even if he was not entirely sure who they were.

In 1938, however, he found out exactly who they were when he fell madly in love with a French girl from Dijon. They wanted to marry but the girl's parents forbad their daughter from marrying a "Foreigner, and a German at that!" Helmut was devastated. His antagonism towards the French, ignited by his mother, now became a blazing fire, fanned by the bellows of his own rejection. When the opportunity to join the German army presented itself, he grabbed it with both hands. In the SS, Helmut and other young Alsatians were given a status and a cause which brought clarity into the uncertainty of their upbringing. Even conscripts began to embrace the Nazi mission. That wasn't to say that the Alsatians were welcomed into the German army with open arms. They were often treated with suspicion by their German colleagues, sometimes with good reason.

However, many of the more idealistic recruits were able to progress in the German hierarchy and it was a proud day for Helmut when he entered the commissioned ranks of the mighty Das Reich army. He even thought of changing his surname but the habit of the German officials to omit the acute accent on the 'e' and pronounce the final 't' had already given him a name resonant with German authority. The powerful consonant 'V' at the beginning of his name could have originated from anywhere in the Third Reich. So he just quietly dropped the accentuated 'e' and became Captain Helmut Vomecourt, an officer in the SS.

Putting on his overcoat, Vomecourt made for the entrance to the school. He was determined to dispatch Bauer as quickly as possible and so would wait for him outside on the drive. He gazed up at the starry sky, for a moment intrigued by the notion that all combatants in this conflict lived under the same canopy. English soldiers in their trenches could be staring up at the same heavenly lights as Germans in theirs. No matter how much devastation was being caused on the ground, the stars stayed in exactly the same place every night, unmoved by the pounding that was taking place beneath them.

"At least there will be little activity tonight," he muttered. The brightness of the night made weapons' drops and sabotage more dangerous. It was likely that the enemy would wait for cloudier skies. Vomecourt comforted himself with the thought that, once he got rid of Bauer, he would have a restful night's sleep.

Soon Vomecourt could hear the throaty roar of the BMW in the distance and quickly picked out the single headlight piercing the darkness beneath the trees on either side of the school drive. Both men saluted each other in a business like manner. They would never be close but there was no point in making further enemies. The common foe provided enough opportunity for animosity, without internal squabbles.

"Captain," said Bauer, "I have an urgent message from Major Hautmann."

The Adjutant relayed the instructions he had received from the Major less than half an hour previously.

"Otto, answer me one question. How does Hautmann expect me to find another fifty men, another half track and two extra trucks together with a map of a place I have never heard of, let alone been to, in the middle of the night surrounded by French snipers anxious to shoot my head off if I so much as open a window? Is he fighting the same war as I am? Doesn't he know that recruits aren't arriving when they should, equipment isn't being repaired, ammunition is short? And we're just expected to trail off to some half baked French hamlet to look for a needle in a haystack and frighten a few grandmothers? Meanwhile hundreds of thousands of British and American troops have landed on the French beaches without so much as a shot being fired."

"Sorry, old boy, it's called orders. Hautmann shouts at me; I tell you; you say 'Yes, sir'; I tell Hautmann and he goes off happily for another schnapps. Don't you know how the war works? Now, what do you really want me to tell him?" Bauer was at his most gauche.

"Don't tempt me, Bauer. Trouble is, if I did tell you what he could do with his lousy orders you would rather enjoy it. Tell him I'll do my best."

"All right, suit yourself. Good night, Captain," said Bauer as the BMW throbbed back into action.

Vomecourt resigned himself to a miserable night trailing round the other barracks in Limoges trying to beg, steal or borrow men and equipment.

Funnily, the name of the village to which they were going sounded familiar – Oradour-sur-Glane. Vomecourt was sure he had been there recently. All of a sudden he remembered when.

CHAPTER NINE

Father Dominic Lesueuer was sitting in the front room of his presbytery, unaware of the visitors from Limoges who would be arriving the next morning. He was aged about fifty–five, but looked older. Now almost bald the lines on his forehead were deep and prominent. However, as with many bald people the lines came to an abrupt halt at his former hair line. Above that point his skin was smooth and virgin. His small, brown eyes and thin pinched nose gave his face a slightly withdrawn and secretive look. His mouth too was weak and insignificant, hiding the uneven and yellowing teeth of which Father Lesueur was particularly self conscious. Some might have said that he had a rather cynical demeanour, which wasn't diminished by the black priestly cassock he routinely wore. Had this been clean it might have enhanced his facial appearance, but it was usually grubby and stained. The priest wore his cassock as a maid might wear a housecoat – a functional garment that removed any element of choice when getting dressed each morning.

Except, this morning, his routine had been severely disrupted, His head throbbed from the bruising that was vibrantly evident on his forehead, nose and jaw and around his eyes. His face was swollen and an almost completely dark blue colour, apart from a little yellowing around the edges where the bruising was coming out. It was both a vivid and painful reminder of a recent event, which had been the most traumatic of his life.

Father Lesueur cared for the souls of the parish. At least that is what they said at his ordination. In practice it seemed to him that his role was to maintain the rituals of the Roman Catholic Church without questioning whether or not they had any relevance to the care of souls. The masses on saints' days and other special occasions must be held, notwithstanding the fact that most of his flock attended merely out of habit and were likely to rot in hell. Not that Father Lesueur believed in hell. The whole concept of good and evil, heaven and hell, God and Satan was preposterous. Sin was a man made doctrine designed to keep people in check. Why did people steal? Because they didn't have enough to eat. Why did they commit adultery? Because they no longer loved their wives or husbands. Why did they murder? Because they were deranged. Why did they lie? Because the truth hurt either the liar or the person being lied to. Cause and effect. Man had invented God as an excuse for his actions – to avoid taking responsibility for his deeds. Original sin was a cover for behaviour of which human beings were ashamed, but which was really the responsibility of themselves or the society in which they lived.

God was dead, according to Father Lesueur, and nobody really cared much. If he could have found another job at fifty–five he would have done so. But at his age and in wartime this wasn't possible. So he carried on peddling the divine myth, delighting to drop little atheistic hints into his sermons just to see if anyone would notice. They didn't, of course. His sermons were fodder for the masses and they would eat anything.

But now life wasn't quite so easy and simple. At least not since the visit of Captain Helmut Vomecourt a few days previously.

* * *

Father Dominic Leseuer was preparing some of the children in the parish for their First Holy Communion. In the Roman Catholic Church children around seven or eight years of age celebrate this symbol of their faith. The children usually wear white and receive gifts in celebration of their acceptance into the faith. The event has much significance in the Catholic Church. Despite his cynicism, Father Dominic was still much challenged by Napoleon's answer when asked in later years which had been the happiest day of his life. He did not mention any of his military victories or his accession to high office. The happiest day of his life had been his First Holy Communion. If the mighty French Emperor had given it such significance then maybe a humble French priest should at least be respectful.

However, despite his affection for the process of the First Holy Communion there was an altogether darker side to his enthusiasm for the preparation classes. In order to prepare fully each candidate for the celebration and to ensure that they understood the significance of what they were about to do, Father Dominic spent several weeks with each candidate individually in his vestry in the church.

On one such occasion, Father Dominic had been preparing a young eight year old boy called Charles Barthélemy. Towards the end of each class he would sit on the sofa with the child and read them a story. This was a moment he both loved and feared – a moment when he was overcome by both lust and shame in almost equal measure. But the passion that overwhelmed him at this moment he was unable to control. It was a monster so strong and powerful that it would not release him until he had completely succumbed to its crushing grip. He had tried to resist this temptation and after every occurrence he vowed, to whom he was no longer sure, that it would be the last. But it never was.

As he sat on the sofa reading to Charles with his arm around him, his hand slipped down to the boy's leg, bare under his shorts.

"This is our little secret time, Charles, isn't it – when we get really close together, just like Jesus gets close to us. You mustn't tell Mama and Papa because otherwise Jesus won't be your friend anymore. You wouldn't want that would you Charles?"

Charles shook his head as he felt the priest sliding off his shorts. The priest's hands were warm and smooth. Charles desperately wanted Jesus to be his friend and his parents had told him how proud they were that he was taking his First Holy Communion. He didn't want to let them down even though he didn't like what the priest would do next. He had to sit up a little as the priest pulled down his underpants. Charles just shut his eyes and prayed.

At that very moment the door of the vestry flew violently open.

Within a fraction of a second Father Dominic was staring down the barrel of a Parabellum sub machine gun. The finger on the trigger belonged to Captain Helmut Vomecourt who looked in astonishment at the sight in front of him. It took him a few seconds to adjust to the light in the vestry, which the priest had deliberately kept dim, and appreciate what was taking place. But when he did, he could feel the fury erupting inside him. He needed to get the boy out of the church as quickly as possible. He would not want to see what was going to happen to the priest.

"Little boy," he said gently "what is your name?"

"Charles, sir," said the boy quietly, a look of sheer terror in his eyes.

"Well, Charles, I want you to do something for me. Pull up your pants and shorts. Now write down your name and address on this piece of paper."

Vomecourt watched as the boy slowly and studiously printed out his details.

"Charles, I'm going to take you outside to meet some other soldiers. They will take you home in a real German jeep. Would you like that?"

Charles nodded. His friends would be so jealous to see him arrive home in a jeep driven by soldiers, even if they were Germans.

"Wait here," snapped Vomecourt to Father Dominic as he escorted the boy out of the room. "I'll be back."

When Charles was safely on board the jeep, Vomecourt strode swiftly back to the vestry. Father Dominic was seated exactly as Vomecourt had left him, his eyes downcast and his shoulders slumped. If this was an attempt to elicit sympathy from the German army officer it was destined to fail.

"You disgusting pervert!" barked the German in his colloquial French, which Father Dominic recognised as an Alsatian accent. He knew then that his treatment was likely to be harsh. The French deeply resented the complicity of the Alsatians in the German occupation. An Alsatian scalp was highly prized by the maquisards. By now the hatred was mutually intense and Alsatian soldiers took revenge on the French at every opportunity.

"Get up when you are spoken to by a German officer," ordered Vomecourt.

Father Dominic rose slowly to his feet, barely straightening before he felt the crushing blow from the butt of the machine gun on the side of his head. He couldn't tell if it was the warmth of the blood on his face or the stars in his eyes that was the first sensation, but he knew that the second was the vomit in his mouth resulting from the thud of a German boot into his stomach. He writhed on the floor from repeated blows to his head and body, sometimes a kick, sometimes a crack from the leg of a chair, which now lay broken and useless on the floor beside him.

When the German had worn himself out with the repeated beating, he picked up the priest by the scruff of his cassock and stared menacingly at the blood stained face, which was already swollen to such an extent that it was almost unrecognisable.

"Listen to me, you miserable, deviant creep. I could easily kill you now. But I'm not going to, I'm giving you a second chance. You don't deserve it but I'm going to give you the privilege of serving the Fatherland. I shouldn't be associating with scum like you, but I'm feeling generous and you may be useful to me. In a few days time a Gestapo officer will visit you. You are to tell him everything you know about resistance activity in this area. Who are the maquisards? Where are they based? Who are their supporters? What are they planning? I'm sure everyone tells their secrets to the trustworthy local priest!" Vomecourt spat at the Frenchman in derision.

"But even if you don't know now, you'd better find out fast because I'm a pussy cat compared to him. He will visit you on a regular basis and if you don't come up with accurate and regular information, then…" he waved the piece of paper with Charles's address on it, "I think Monsieur and Madame Barthélemy might like to know what you have been up to with their young son. If I don't kill you they certainly would. Do you agree?"

Father Dominic nodded weakly, just as the German landed a valedictory blow on his chest.

Vomecourt was pleased with his day's work. He had entered the church on the off chance that resistance workers, Jews or other enemies of the Third Reich might be sheltering there. He had come away with a cast iron collaborator whose position in the local community would enable him to provide much needed intelligence to save many German lives. It had not been easy to penetrate the maquis in this area. The task had just got a whole lot easier.

Vomecourt also came away with a reinforced conviction about the cause for which he was fighting. The priest epitomised the moral bankruptcy into which France had sunk. Divorce, abortion, homosexuality, paedophilia, immigration had all abounded in the France of the Third Republic. It was time to end this decadence and return France to its traditional values of family life and discipline. He had agreed with Maréchal Petain, who had said, "Ce qu'il faut à la France, à notre cher pays, ce ne sont pas des intelligences, mais des caractères."

Father Dominic had now been readied to play his own part in this process of the character building of the French nation.

CHAPTER TEN

The skies opened as the small group of refugees left Nyarubuye church. The rain came down vertically in sheets, almost as if someone was throwing buckets of water over them. Samuel Karamira cursed the fact that they were undertaking this journey in the rainy season. While it was less wet in the south east than in other parts of Rwanda he expected this rainstorm to be heavy and persistent. Still, he needed to maintain an optimistic outlook for the sake of the others.

"Chantalle," he said brightly, "this rain is good news. Even the Interahamwe won't want to be outside in this and we will be well clear of Nyarubuye before it stops."

"Yes, but the children will be soaked through," replied Chantalle. "They'll not get dry for hours after this. Are you sure this is a good idea? We can always go home and start again tomorrow morning."

"No, it's too dangerous. If the militiamen are rounding up Tutsis now they could be visiting us before tomorrow morning. When we are at home they know exactly where we are. When we are travelling they don't know our whereabouts and, while I know that this rain is unpleasant, it's also the best protection we could ask for. We can be in Tanzania tomorrow and then you and the children will be safe."

The rain and tension dulled the appetite for further conversation and the group silently headed off on the main roadway out of Nyarubuye. They needed to travel south to pick up the main route from Kibungo to the Rusumo Falls in Tanzania. Samuel prayed that no roadblocks had been set up yet. He felt very conspicuous marching along the roadway heavily laden with bags full of possessions. It would be blindingly obvious to any Hutu Power militia that they would be escaping Tutsis. Why else would entire family groups be trudging out of town in the pouring rain? Just in case they were stopped in this way Samuel had raided his secret hiding place before they had left home and had put a pile of US dollars into his pocket. As in many African countries, US dollars were the unofficial currency and available on the black market. Over the years, Samuel had hoarded a supply of notes just for such an eventuality as this. He would try and bribe any militia they encountered, but was concerned they might take the money and kill them anyway. His only hope was that the Hutus would be so busy squabbling about how to divide up the money that they would not notice the group's hasty departure.

By now, the dirt track was a stream. Water filled the tyre tracks on either side of the road and it was increasingly difficult to find firm ground to walk on. The stifled cries as members of the group stumbled in the darkness were more regular now. Despite the rain and gathering darkness Samuel could just make out the coffee plantations on either side of the road. It had always aggrieved him that the flattest and most fertile land was turned over to the production of cash crops for export, while their own families were forced to plant crops clinging to the sides of steep hills. Even now the heavy rain would be washing away their crops, as the water cascaded down the steep inclines, while the crops in the valleys were being nicely irrigated. No doubt the Bourgmestre will enjoy a good harvest, he thought cynically.

His concentration was broken by his ten year old son Jonathan.

"Father, look over there. There are piles of clothes by the side of the road."

Samuel looked across at the bright coloured garments laid out on the grass on the far side of the track. There was something odd about the way they were lying there. Not limp and screwed up but shaped and spread out. Almost as if there was something inside them. He peered through the murk as he crossed the track, shouting to Jonathan and the rest of the group to stay where they were. An increasing sense of foreboding came over him. It couldn't have started yet...surely not.

Samuel retched violently as he saw the first decapitated body lying face down on the verge in front of him, resting at almost ninety degrees to the road. Seven other bodies were lying side by side, each with its head missing. Samuel thought that it was strange he had noticed the symmetry in the layout of the bodies. Surely feelings of revulsion and pity were the natural emotions when faced with such slaughter. Apart from his initial vomiting his reactions had been largely analytical. Where were their heads? Who were these people? What did this mean for him and the rest of the refugees?

As far as he could tell from the headless corpses this looked like a family grouping. Four of them were certainly children and perhaps the other four were parents and grandparents. They had no belongings with them, suggesting that they had fled abruptly or been dragged from a nearby house. He had heard that the Interahamwe would line people up by the side of the road and decapitate them with machetes. This would explain why they had fallen straight down, why their arms were still by their sides, as the nerves and muscles were already inactive by the time they hit the ground. No need to cushion the fall when you are already dead. No chance of clothes riding up over your body when you are motionless on impact. At least it had been quick and, as far as he could see, even the militia baulked at raping dead bodies.

Samuel froze as he heard a rustling sound from the far end of one of the bodies. Surely these murderers weren't still around. At that moment an enormous rat, almost the size of a small dog emerged from the bloodied neck of one of the dead. It had already gorged itself on this unexpected feast and was so bloated that it could only waddle off into the undergrowth to digest its prey. Samuel recollected that the extremist radio station, Radio Mille Collines, incited Hutus to kill children with the phrase, "To kill the big rats you have to kill the little rats". How ironic, thought Samuel that the only rats benefiting from this slaughter were the verminous kind. He retched again at the thought of it.

Samuel was shaken out of his contemplation by the sobs of the women and children behind him. Despite his warning, they had all come over to look at the macabre sight. One of the women had collapsed, others were being sick and everyone looked utterly drained and distraught at this horrific massacre. Samuel called Leon to one side and whispered,

"It's not safe for us to stay on the road. These killers may have just moved further along the track. There could be a roadblock around the corner…or anything."

Leon thought for a moment, his faculties for reasoned decision-making totally subsumed by the horror he now faced. With an effort of will, he was eventually able to concentrate on their predicament and focus on the primary task of survival.

"You're right, Samuel." He looked around. "We must try and make for higher ground. If we can see the road from further up the hill then we can follow it and keep going in the right direction for Tanzania. In any case, this valley should lead to the road for Rusumo."

With that, Leon led the small group off the track and up the hill, initially alongside the same coffee plantation that Samuel had noticed earlier, before the appalling scene of carnage had been revealed. They trudged along the grassy slope, skirting around little clumps of banana trees. Every so often Samuel called for quiet as they approached a smallholding. These were cut into the slope, creating a terrace on which sat a couple of mud built buildings with corrugated iron roofs. The buildings were usually fringed by a wooden fence, often made out of bamboo. Occasionally a dog barked or a chicken clucked but no humans appeared to delay their journey. Samuel thought that no-one, neither Hutu nor Tutsi, would want to reveal their presence tonight. Only the militia would be about. There were no lights shining from the tiny dwellings. The inhabitants were probably cowering inside, more scared of Samuel's little band of refugees than the other way round.

Although this atmosphere of fear and suspicion was heartbreaking for the refugees it was creating a much safer passage than they had dared hope for a few hours earlier. Thus their progress along the valley slopes was surprisingly fast. Samuel could not regard any of this as satisfactory. The regular whimpering of the women and children was testimony to the enormity of this journey, which marked a further stage in the diaspora of the Tutsi people. Life would never be the same again and Samuel feared for the psychological health of his children, particularly

Jonathan, who was already a serious and sensitive child. How would these appalling events haunt him over the coming years?

Samuel also thought about his pupils at Nyarubuye school. How many were already dead? He remembered their shining faces exploding into laughter at some comical behaviour by another child. Would they ever be able to smile again? He recalled the studied concentration on their faces as they grappled with Kinyarwandan grammar. How would they focus on their studies after this? He knew that powers of concentration were often one of the first casualties of trauma. Flashbacks would be a constant enemy of learning for many children for years to come.

But although he had dedicated his life to education these considerations somehow seemed unimportant. There was only one lesson that seemed to matter right now – the lesson of survival. Often those who weren't academic were best at self preservation. After all, they had nothing else to fall back on. They lived or died by their wits. Samuel's doubts and insecurities were surfacing again. How had he prepared his students for this, the biggest exam of their lives? How could he have prepared them? But he would not abandon them – he would return to Nyarubuye soon.

* * *

By 2a.m. the next morning the group had reached the main road to Rusomo Falls, which marked the border between Rwanda and Tanzania. Despite being in desperate need of rest and sleep, Samuel felt that they must press on to try and get as close to the border as possible before sunrise. Leon came up to Samuel. He spoke softly so that the others wouldn't hear.

"Everyone is very tired. We can't walk up any more hills. It'll be safe walking along the road at night. I can't believe that the Interahamwe can have set up roadblocks this far south yet."

"Leon, we can't be sure of that, but I agree that our best hope is to keep going as fast as we can," whispered Samuel. "Alright, we'll stick to the road, but I'll go in front and you lead the others, but only just within earshot and sight of me. If I shout, get off the road as quickly as possible. Put one of the other men at the back of the group, also only just within earshot and he can warn us if there is any trouble coming from the rear."

Thus formed, they resumed their journey. The road was good with few ruts and potholes to impede their progress, the rain had mercifully stopped and spirits had improved. A steady trickle of other refugees were taking the same route. There was strength in numbers and a feeling of solidarity in adversity among those unwittingly caught up in this exodus. For the first time since they had left Nyarubuye, Samuel felt encouraged and that things were finally looking up.

On they walked, kilometre after kilometre. By now the steps they were taking were purely mechanical, walking by instinct. Many of the group were more asleep than awake, wandering off the road when they dozed momentarily. It was impossible to keep the main bunch of refugees together, no matter how hard Leon tried. Cajoling, pushing, pulling, even hitting but nothing worked against the power of total exhaustion and fatigue. As a result, the group was now spread out over several hundred metres and Leon had no idea where Samuel was. He had heard no shout, so he presumed that the road was clear but, even as the sun started to rise and visibility became clearer, there was still no sign of his friend. However there was no alternative but to press on. Leon calculated that there could only be a few kilometres to go and there were still no roadblocks, but the border crossing at Rusomo Falls would be the most dangerous part of the journey. The Interahamwe would surely have sealed off the border. Their only hope was that the presence of Tanzanian border troops would deter the militia from any precipitous action. But the refugees had no passports, no visas, no paperwork allowing them to enter Tanzania. They would be reliant on the goodwill of both sets of border guards. Still there was no alternative but to try and get through.

Samuel Karamira was having similar thoughts five hundred metres ahead. Maybe it hadn't been such a good idea to split up. He daren't go back but was now desperately worried about the rest of the group, especially his own family. He comforted himself with the fact that there had been no roadblocks and no sign of any militia. But as the sun exposed itself above the surrounding hills Samuel was now getting more concerned. He was also greatly fatigued, barely able to flick away the flies that were just starting to become a nuisance. In the distance, above the hill, which he was fairly certain led to the Rusomo bridge, he could see a vast flock of large birds soaring up into the morning sky. Getting closer he could see the bald heads and white plumage of some of the birds swooping down into the valley below. Vultures. Samuel watched transfixed as waves of the birds dropped down below the skyline, only to be replaced by a swarm of their fellows borne upwards by the thermal currents, too heavy to gain altitude by wing power alone.

Samuel too was concerned about the border crossing. What would they face just around the corner at the bridge? There would be two sets of border guards to satisfy: one on the Rwandan side and one on the Tanzanian. Samuel had resolved to arrange safe passage before the main group arrived if at all possible. He fingered the US dollars in his pocket. Money talked – wherever you were in the world, whatever the circumstances. He did not need to depend on goodwill, compassion or charity; all soft currencies at this time of crisis. He had hard currency – the mighty dollar, his passport to safety.

But as Samuel approached the bridge the self confidence generated by the bank notes in his pocket evaporated completely, for he looked down into the swirling Akagera river which marked the boundary between Rwanda and Tanzania and dropped to his knees in disbelief. At first he thought that the river had been used as a mass dumping ground for rubbish, a sort of waste dump, as travellers had been forced to lighten their loads at the border or customs guards had confiscated property and thrown it over the bridge. But then the awful truth dawned on him. This wasn't rubbish, it was corpses, bloated in the fast flowing water. Here a body was caught in the rocks, there in the weeds, some tossed around in the foaming eddies at the edge of the river, unable to escape. Some of the bodies looked white, the skin stretched over the bloated frame. Tall people, short people, children….even babies. A tide of death was being swept towards Lake Victoria, the evidence of slaughter conveniently hidden in a neighbouring land. Samuel remembered the Hutu Power chant of "Send the Tutsis back to

Ethiopia". John Hanning Speke's fallacious claim that the Tutsis originated from "the best blood of Abyssinia" was being thrown in their faces. The Akagera river would not take the bodies as far as Ethiopia but it was in the right direction. An illiterate Hutu peasant drunk on revenge cared nothing for geography. The "Tutsi scum" were being taken out of sight by the swollen river and that was good enough for him to feel that he had done his patriotic duty, by killing a Tutsi and throwing his body out of Rwanda.

Samuel approached the border post, his heart thumping so hard that the reverberations spread throughout his whole body. His temples were thudding and he was sweating profusely. He wanted to take off the clothes on the upper part of his body in order to get cool.

As expected, the border policemen had been joined by five or six Interahamwe militiamen, the most vicious and ideologically motivated section of the Hutu Power movement. It was obvious who was in charge, as the border police looked as scared as Samuel. An enormous militia officer stepped forward to block Samuel's path. His step was unsteady, his breath reeking of African beer from a heavy night of drinking. The officer pulled on the straps of the Kalshnikov AK47 that was slung around his shoulder. Samuel thought that nothing could be more menacing – a drunken, heavily armed Hutu fanatic guarding the Rwandan border. He prayed desperately as the officer struggled to focus on Samuel, momentarily blinded by the rising sun and the effects of his own hangover.

"Identity card," he snapped.

"Sir, I'm sorry but I had to leave in a hurry and I've left it at home. You see there's been fighting down the road and I'm scared for my family. Please may we pass over the bridge?"

"Where's your visa? Or have you left that behind as well?" he sneered, suddenly more lucid and threatening.

"I have no visa. I told you that we had to leave without warning and there was no time…" Samuel could tell that there was no point in elaborating. Any story he fabricated would not be believed. Money talked. He had to trust in the depravity of human nature, that the currency of greed would be stronger than the currency of hate.

However he was inexperienced in bribery and didn't know how to introduce the issue. So he just came straight out with it.

"I can pay you, in US dollars…fifty US dollars."

After a pause the officer approached Samuel. He stood right over him, his foul and alcoholic breath making Samuel nauseous. He spoke softly,

"Are you Tutsi?"

"Sir, this is a business transaction", Samuel was becoming bolder, sensing that the officer was open for negotiation. "I want safe passage for my group to Tanzania. We will make it worth your while to help us. Say 100 US dollars, payable on delivery into Tanzania."

The officer hesitated. He seemed almost as unclear about the procedure as Samuel. In a few days this bargaining would be automatic, a skill honed by dozens of 'transactions'. For the moment, Samuel was one of the first refugees to make an offer in hard currency. The militia had rejected any Rwandan currency – it was already virtually worthless and had no value in any other country. Previous refugees had been sent back at the point of a Kalashnikov or shot and thrown over the bridge.

"Wait here," barked the officer as he walked back towards his colleagues. Samuel hoped this was just a question of agreeing how the spoils would be divided but he knew that it could also be a discussion about whether or not he should be killed.

As this had been going on, Leon and the other refugees had been gathering at the edge of the bridge. Samuel had motioned them back, not wishing to be compromised in the negotiations by the size of the group. The price would be sure to increase if it became clear to the militia that this was several family groupings and that their bargaining power was thus much greater. It was also too dangerous for them to advance further. Besides, they had by now spotted the bodies in the river and were now as statuesque as Samuel had been when first confronted by the horrors of the Akagera. Samuel could see Chantalle and felt reassured that she would have ensured that the children were with her. If only he could get past these guards, who were by now engaged in animated discussion, they would all be safe. He tried not to look too desperate. Even though he actually had no choice, he didn't want to look as if this was his only hope. He smiled weakly at the officer, who was casting repeated glances in his direction.

There was much arm waving by the Interahamwe guards and a lot of pointing at the Tanzanian border post. Samuel could see that this was manned at the moment by just a few Tanzanian policemen. Once the tide of refugees became a flood there would be a much more powerful presence but for the moment the Hutu militia could easily 'persuade' them to let Samuel's group through. He looked back at Chantalle. She was now waving at him agitatedly. Not now, he signalled, tell me when we get over the other side. The officer swayed over to him again.

"200 US dollars and we'll get you into Tanzania."

Samuel nodded and waved the group to come forward. He walked ahead with the officer to ensure that he didn't change his mind. He was gambling that the militia wouldn't double cross them, that they wouldn't want to get the reputation for reneging on a deal – for taking money and not delivering. The flow of funds would then dry up and refugees would seek another, more 'honourable' border crossing. Samuel was sure that the guards would have worked out this angle. He turned to check that the group was still following him. Chantalle was running towards him. He motioned her back determinedly. Any violent movement could provoke a bullet in the back and the end of any chance for any of them to make it to Tanzania. Take it slowly. No histrionics.

At the other side of the bridge, the Rwandan officer went into the border hut. After a brief discussion in Swahili a deal seemed to have been struck. No doubt it would be the first of many that day. The barrier was raised and the group passed through as Samuel carefully counted out 200 US dollars, counting each note laboriously due to his unfamiliarity with their denomination and to allow time for the whole group to get through. The Rwandan officer went into a huddle with the Tanzanian policemen to divide up the spoils while Samuel slipped away. As he walked through the barrier to safety Chantalle grabbed his arm, tears streaming down her face.

"I tried to tell you but you wouldn't let me", she cried "Jonathan's missing. He's not with us."

CHAPTER ELEVEN

Sister Agathe and her little band had an uneventful journey from St Augustin to Madranges where they were to rendezvous with their resistance handler, the man telephoned by Sister Anne-Marie from the convent. Agathe fingered the piece of paper containing the address of their contact. Not much more than twelve hours before, Anne-Marie had written these words on the crumpled paper. Agathe wondered – was it the last thing she ever wrote? How Agathe wished she knew what had happened to the Mother Superior and the other nuns. She didn't know if she should be grieving and praying for the souls of her departed colleagues or whether, by some miracle, their lives had been spared and she could rejoice, praising God for their deliverance. She vowed to return to Corréze to find out their fate as soon as she had safely discharged her guests.

Daylight was dawning as the group reached the final field before Madranges. The village itself was in the heart of the Monédières mountains, about 600 metres above sea level. The fields were lush and green, the cattle already grazing peacefully on the verdant pasture. The grey spire of the village church was prominent, elevated above the surrounding fields. The birds twittered excitedly in their joy at the dawning of a new day. No scene could have been more pastoral or more tranquil, but this would be the most dangerous part of the journey so far. Suppose the network had been infiltrated, the secretive web of agents compromised? They could be walking straight into a trap, right into the lap of the Germans. Not only that, there would be reprisals against the villagers of Madranges. Collaborators would offer information to the Nazis in order to save their own skins. Resistance sympathizers would be identified and shot. However Sister Agathe knew that there was no alternative. She would have to trust the name on her piece of paper. She had no choice.

The group needed to walk along a narrow road to find the white country house that Sister Anne-Marie had identified as their destination. Its slate pitched roof came into view, chimneys stretching into the sky at each gable end. Unusually, the front of the house was not parallel to the road but pointing straight down it, so that their approach could not be hidden from anyone watching from the house or round about it. This feeling of exposure made Agathe especially anxious, although she consoled herself with the fact that the open view also made it easier for them to spot any German activity.

She strode up to the red front door shaded by a giant cherry tree. Sister Anne-Marie had told her to knock four times very slowly. A few minutes later, a thin elderly man opened the door.

"The harvest will be late this year," announced Sister Agathe rather nervously. If they were walking into a trap, this was the moment when it would be sprung. German soldiers would rush out from adjoining rooms and surround them. But all was quiet. The man looked the group up and down before motioning with a delicate upward movement of his head for them to come in.

He led them into a darkened front room, the curtains drawn and the floor bare. There was a heavy clunking sound as they walked across the floorboards to a selection of stark wooden chairs to which they were directed. The group slumped into the chairs, grateful at being able to rest their weary legs at last, oblivious to the hardness of the seats and uncomfortable back rests, which seemed to poke their already emaciated bodies however they tried to arrange themselves.

The elderly man spoke softly.

"I will not ask you for your names or any information about you on condition that you do not ask anything about me." He paused, looking for signs of agreement from each member of the group in turn. Agathe was the first to nod her assent and, while the old man observed the response of the others, she looked around the room. There was no clue as to the occupants of the house. No photographs, no paintings, no letters, no knick-knacks, no ornaments, nothing to reveal the identity, occupation or interests of their host. No clue as to whether anyone else lived in the house or whether the man had any family.

"You must do exactly as I tell you," he went on, when assured of unanimous compliance with his conditions. "Do not question my instructions and do not try and ascertain the whereabouts of any location to which you are taken from now on. Do not try to identify anyone you meet, as to do so might compromise our entire network and lead to lives being put in danger. Do you understand?"

Each member of the group, including the children, who didn't really understand what was going on, nodded bleakly and concentrated on the further instructions.

"In a few minutes you will be taken from this place to another location in the back of a van. The vehicle will be carrying sacks of grain and you will be required to hide under the sacks, out of sight of anyone who might open the back door. You must remain completely silent, do not use a light and do not leave the van until you are instructed to do so. Leave no rubbish behind you when you arrive at your destination – the truck must look as if no-one has ever been in it. If the Germans catch you in the van you are to say that you stowed away unbeknown to the driver. As he was delivering grain at, the name of a place near here known to you, you jumped unseen into the back of the vehicle. I'm afraid you will then be on your own. We cannot help you if the Germans take you prisoner, as to do so could compromise the whole network. We survive by being able to operate totally unseen and unheard and I must insist that, even if you are captured, you say nothing about the resistance network. I realise that this will be difficult as I'm afraid the Germans may torture you but, if you reveal anything about us, there will be no prospect of anyone else escaping in the same way. What's more you will put all our lives at risk."

The old man slowly looked at the faces of each person. He looked straight into the eyes of each man, woman and child, so intently and penetratingly that Agathe felt sure that he was checking for any sign of weakness. Any flicker of doubt that might indicate a potential betrayer.

She wondered how many times he had done this before. Even though every person who passed through this house might be the one who exposed the network, and thus lead to his death, the old man was very matter of fact and business like about the whole operation. She guessed that he could only be so relaxed by having total trust in the network, knowing that each group of refugees had been sent from an impeccable source and that they would be passed on to an equally irreproachable pair of hands. Once that trust was broken and a link in the chain had been removed then the whole pack of cards would come tumbling down. No wonder he was so cautious.

He went on, "You are to destroy any clues as to your identity so that no-one can trace where you have come from or where you are going. Please come into the kitchen."

Here the old man pointed to the wood burning stove and opened the iron door, revealing the blazing yellow and orange flames in the furnace. One by one, the group placed passports, identity cards, correspondence and other personal items into the fire. The symbolism was not lost on Sister Agathe. Long ago in this dreadful war the Jews had lost their self reliance and self respect. Now they had even lost their 'self'. People without names, human beings without their unique identity, not even a number anymore. No tags, no cards, no labels, no history even, as letters, diaries and photographs were consumed by the avaricious flames.

They were by now completely at the mercy of their elderly handler. In leaving the convent they were trusting totally in the network for their safety. Now they had handed over their whole lives to a man they had only known for a few minutes and about whom they knew nothing. They could only trust, not in a 'hoping for the best' way but with complete child-like vulnerability with no prospect of self preservation. Their entire destiny was now in the hands of total strangers.

For the Jews this concept was appalling. Hardened and self reliant through centuries of dispersal and persecution they had made their own way in life. Battling against racism and prejudice and without a homeland, Jews around the world had achieved prominent positions in societies from Australia to Argentina. Dr Paul Katz recognised this in himself. Nothing would have stopped him from becoming a doctor. The child of immigrant German Jews, who arrived in France with nothing, he had been determined to succeed. He was no Zionist, he would not have fought for a Jewish state nor emigrated to Palestine to reclaim holy land. But he felt a burning desire to prove himself, to succeed against all the odds. Perhaps it arose from a desire to right the wrongs of the past. Perhaps it was an innate racial pride and sense of superiority but, whatever his motivation, he had succeeded. He had become a respected citizen, a local grandee, an admired public servant to whom people turned when in trouble. But what was he now? The tears welled up in his eyes as he saw his achievements reduced to ashes in front of him. His prized medical practitioner's certificate was now indistinguishable from the black dust collecting in the removable pan at the foot of the stove. Soon it would be scattered to the four winds – his life's work blown around by the breeze, caught up with the dirt, litter and leaves before finding its final resting place under a hedge or in some ditch. He was no longer Dr Paul Katz, but simply human freight carted from place to place in the back of darkened vans under sacks of grain.

Sister Agathe was conscious of the anguish felt by the other refugees. For her, however, unquestioning trust in another person was an everyday requirement. The convent trusted God for all of their needs. The nuns had no personal possessions, no status, no identity other than as servants of God and their neighbour. Agathe had nothing to throw into the stove as the nuns kept no personal identification other than the minimum required by French law, and even that was left at the convent. Habitually Agathe carried nothing with her – no cards, no money, no keys, no watch, no food – God would provide in whatever situation she found herself. Jesus had said "Do not worry about your life, what you will eat or drink or about your body what you will wear....But seek first His kingdom and His righteousness and all these things will be given to you as well." Never more had she needed to claim this promise than at that very moment. Her faith was going to be tested to the full.

Agathe's prayer was interrupted by the sound of tyres crunching on the gravel driveway of the house.

"Wait here," said the old man as he headed for the front door.
Moments later he returned.

"I'm sorry for the discomfort that this may cause but I must place these scarves over your eyes. I'm afraid you are no longer able to know your location or any details of the vehicle in which you are travelling. I hope you can understand the reasons for this. It is for your own good as much as ours."

Carefully he placed the scarves over the eyes of each person and tightened them before knotting the end. Even daylight was now being denied to them, but the darkness could be their saviour so no-one complained. At least in the dark it was possible to think the best and to have no sensory reason for believing it not to be true. The scarf was like a shield from the worst that Nazi Germany could throw at them and as they got into the van it seemed to provide some comfort and protection.

Each individual was guided silently to a hiding place under the sacks of grain. The air was dusty from the grain and stale from a lack of ventilation. As the van set off so the group bounced around on the sacks, every bump in the road tormenting their already bruised bodies. The journey was passed in complete silence and each time the vehicle stopped, the group barely dared to breathe. The sense of fear was tangible. Indeed, the smell of urine, released by bladders rendered uncontrollable by the tension, penetrated nostrils already sharpened by the deprivation of other senses. The smell was pungent even to the shallowest of breath.

At length the vehicle slowed and took a ninety degree turn. The sound of gravel under the tyres meant that they had either returned to the house from which they had departed or had arrived at a new destination. The refugees waited with bated breath for what seemed an interminable period before one of the double doors at the back of the van opened about a foot or so.

"Allez vite," whispered a voice from the rear of the vehicle. Still with the scarves fastened tightly round their eyes, the group slowly emerged from the sacks of grain and crawled uncertainly towards the sound of the voice and the fresh air that was rapidly chasing out the putrid atmosphere in the van. They were helped down from the vehicle by what seemed like two or three people, who swiftly and silently led them away from the truck a short distance into another building.

Just by the smell of it, the refugees knew that this building wasn't the old man's house, which had no identifiable aroma, thus befitting a residence which was untraceable, unnoticeable and unremarkable. However this house smelt slightly unclean as if neither clothes, curtains nor carpets had been washed for some time. It smelt seedy, unkempt and slightly sinister. While blindfolded they would not have known for sure if, at any time, they had returned to the old man's house, but they would certainly know if they had returned to this place.

Once they were all seated in what they assumed was the lounge of the house, the single resident of the building removed their scarves one by one. Each refugee blinked in the unaccustomed daylight and slowly focused on the bruised and expressionless face of Father Dominic Lesueur.

CHAPTER TWELVE

Later on that same morning, Saturday 10th June 1944, Claude LeClerc was preparing his den in Farmer Villepreux's maize field. That afternoon some of his friends were going to join him for a celebration of his fourteenth birthday, which had occurred a few days earlier, in their den. A quiver of excitement shot through his body at the very thought of it. He had bunked off school that morning in order to get ready. The rest of the children were attending school that day for medical inspections and vaccinations, but nothing was going to stop Claude from preparing properly for his celebrations. He would not be missed and, besides, there would be no lessons that day.

He spared a brief thought for his friends and hoped that their jabs would not affect their enjoyment of the afternoon. He didn't want anyone to be under the weather on his special day. What would Farmer Villepreux say if he knew what was going on? The farmer was public enemy number one among the youth of the village. His farm skirted the northern environs of the village and, with little other amusement around, was a favourite play area for the young people of Oradour. Many had smoked their first cigarette, stolen their first kiss or trapped their first rabbit on his land.

It was almost a rite of passage to have carried out a dare on Farmer Villepreux's estate. Sometimes this might involve creeping up on the farmhouse at night and spraying the front windows with pebbles. This would provoke a furious response from the farmer's four German Shepherd dogs. These beasts were ferocious enough to tackle a fully grown man, let alone a much smaller boy, so the prank was not without risk. The dare was won if the protagonists were able to melt away into the maize fields and woods that surrounded the farmhouse without the animals picking up their scent. Of course the commotion would draw out the grumpy farmer, who would emerge from the house shouting and swearing and firing shots indiscriminately in the general direction of the noise. It was probably this over-reaction to anyone trespassing on his land which made Farmer Villepreux such a hate figure. He had not, as far as anyone was aware, done anything else to justify his status as a bête noire. Indeed, very few of the villagers had ever seen him. However, rumour and exaggeration about his treatment of trespassers, together with his mysterious and reclusive nature and, no doubt, jealousy at his wealth, had created for him an iconic status in the community. He was "that nasty man", "that evil troublemaker" whose very name produced an intake of breath and a shake of the head.

As Claude surveyed his den in the middle of the maize field he was quietly satisfied at having got one over on the wicked farmer. The walls of the den had been made out of maize stalks overlaid with sacking for the roof and sawdust for the floor. All materials had been stolen from Farmer Villepreux, or "borrowed" as Claude liked to put it. For his feast today he had also "borrowed" a flagon of wine and some bread, ham and cheese from his mother. Now he would fish for trout or grayling on the River Glane to complete his menu. This would also involve further trespass on Farmer Villepreux's land which would just add to the pleasure of the feast.

* * *

Dominique Malraux sipped her coffee in the lounge of the Hotel Milord in the centre of Oradour with her friend Denise Renaud. The Hotel Milord was a popular haunt for both locals and visitors alike, although it was hard to know why. The hotel had seen better days and years of heavy smoking had seen its once white walls turn to a rather uneven shade of yellow. The brown leather upholstery seemed to have originated in the nineteenth century and was now worn and stretched. Clumsy stitching indicated numerous attempts to repair splits in the leather where it had given up the fight against continuous wear and tear. The glass light shades which hung from the ceiling were coated with the dust and grime that had accumulated over the years, rendering them ineffective in allowing the dim glow from the light bulbs to penetrate the room. As a result the Hotel Milord was always dark and dingy, but still somehow endearing. Maybe it was the very fact that it had remained untouched by the twentieth century that preserved a sort of comforting charm. The stains were always in the same place, the glasses were always predictably grimy and the tables still sticky with wine that had been spilled several days previously. Dominique found the hotel a reassuring sight after a shopping trip to Limoges.

"Well, of course, I didn't expect to find anything worth buying in Limoges. All that way on the tram and no nylons, chocolates or perfume anywhere," she moaned despairingly.

"You should have gone to the German brothel, darling," replied her companion, Denise Renaud, "you could have got whatever you wanted there."

"Yes, as well as something the doctor might not have been able to treat," laughed Dominique. "Seriously though, if we couldn't afford black market prices I don't know what we'd be eating."

Denise leaned forwards and whispered conspiratorially.

"They say the Allies have invaded. The Germans are deliberately sabotaging crops and food supplies and then blaming the maquisards for the shortages. They are hoping that we will turn on the resistance out of hunger and stop them from preparing the way for the Allies. What they don't realise is that most of us would rather starve to death than help the Germans. Still, with any luck, this wretched war will be over soon."

Instinctively the two women looked round the bar in case anyone was listening. Occasionally German officers would call into the hotel for a drink. But there were none present that lunchtime. It was the normal motley collection of drinkers and diners — a few farm workers quenching their thirsts after a morning tilling the soil, a group of elderly men playing cards at their normal table and a couple of Spaniards, who had sought refuge in Oradour after the Civil War, eating enormous baguettes at a corner table. Nothing or no-one out of the ordinary, but it still added a frisson of excitement to the women's conversation to make vituperative comments against the Germans in public. Yes they reviled them constantly in their own homes but to do so in the Hotel Milord was so much more satisfying.

"Come on, Denise, this war was supposed to be over in December 1939 remember. Haven't you seen all the SS troops the Nazis have brought in from Russia, all the tanks moving north? There's going to be an almighty battle – I just hope we aren't going to be in the middle of it. Sorry, ma chérie, I fear that your nylons won't be available for some time yet!"

* * *

In another part of Oradour, Valérie Brushett and her three year old daughter, Jeanne, were hurrying down the main road from St Junien towards Rue Emile Desourteaux in the centre of the village. They had arranged to meet Valérie's husband, André, at 2p.m. in the Champ de Foire area just off the Rue Emile Desourteaux. The Champ de Foire was a large open area used as the main meeting place for the residents of Oradour. It had seen all manifestations of human life – markets, fun fairs, the rendezvous of secret lovers, fights, family arguments, even death, but for the Brushett family on 10th June 1944 the Champ de Foire was, they hoped, to be a place of reconciliation.

André and Valérie's marriage had been a stormy one. They had married a few months before the outbreak of war in the church at Oradour. For a while their union had been a happy one – a young couple, very much in love, who would not let the deprivation and instability of war upset their marriage. But the stresses and strains of life in Vichy controlled France gradually took their toll.

André was a proud man, patriotic and idealistic. He refused to have anything to do with the National Revolution of Maréchal Philippe Petain. While the Maréchal's emphasis on the countryside, the family and Catholicism might have seemed well suited to a young, by now, father from rural France, André increasingly despised the Vichy regime.

He saw its leaders as cowardly reactionaries who had betrayed the heroes of the 1789 revolution. The Germans were vile oppressors intent on imposing Saxon intolerance on his free spirited countrymen. André also found the day to day struggle for existence an affront to his manhood. There were no jobs, let alone careers, in or around Oradour, so he scratched together a minimum income from casual farming work, labouring and black market wheeling and dealing.

Increasingly he had become drawn into resistance activities, spending days at a time in the Limousin hills, sleeping rough and carrying out raids on German transport movements. Valérie found his nomadic existence a strain on their relationship. They now had a young child who needed her father and even when André returned from an operation he was morose and withdrawn. He wouldn't talk about what he had been doing and spent much of his time sleeping. Unsurprisingly Valérie turned elsewhere for succour and when André found out he stormed out of the house saying that the marriage was over. Valérie had heard nothing from him for almost a year when she suddenly received a letter from André asking if they could meet. He sounded reformed and conciliatory and ready for a fresh start, desperate to be the sort of father Jeanne needed him to be. Valérie didn't know what to think, but she had to give it a go. At least there was no harm in meeting up. But as she turned into the Champ de Foire she had no idea what to expect.

* * *

"Where are you from?" questioned Father Dominic once the blindfolds had been removed from each of the refugees. He stared out of the lounge window to see the van which had brought them to him retreating down the driveway.

Sister Agathe was eerily reminded of the old man's caution not to disclose anything about their background to anyone. Surely the priest knew of this instruction, so why was he asking the question? But it must be all right, she reassured herself. We have been delivered here by the resistance and the Father is part of the network. Perhaps the priest has to keep records of escapees in order that their progress can be tracked.

"Don't you remember?" he asked impatiently. "Which house have you just come from?"

"Father," replied Paul Katz before Agathe had a chance to speak, "we have been blindfolded for days and don't know where we are or where we've come from."

"Liar!" snapped Father Dominic. "Do you want me to help you or not? I must know where you have come from."

"Sir, we are Jewish. You will understand that no-one will reveal anything about their identity or locality to us in case of reprisals. You know the penalty for sheltering Jews and so we don't ask questions as we don't want anyone to suffer on our behalf. That would include you, Father. It's best that you don't know anything about us."

At that moment the door from the kitchen adjoining the lounge burst open. In came three German soldiers, their sub machine guns trained on the small group who instantly huddled together for protection in the face of this latest threat to their survival. Fear showed in their faces but, in truth, the adults at least had long been resigned to their fate. Nevertheless, being betrayed by a priest was a bitter pill to swallow.

Captain Helmut Vomecourt sneered at Father Dominic tempted to make a further mess of his features.

"As with everything in your life that was a pathetic attempt at interrogation. Still you don't deserve anyone's trust do you, you scheming pervert? I suppose you were just too busy lusting after these children to get any proper information about the maquis. However we have heard enough to deal with these stinking Shylocks. Get up. You can come and meet some of the other residents of Oradour-sur-Glane. As for you, Sister," he stabbed his index finger almost into Agathe's face," you will find out what we think of traitors who harbour Jewish filth."

With that Vomecourt and the other soldiers kicked and shoved the refugees out of the presbytery and into the back of an armoured truck. Without delay they sped off in the direction of the Champ de Foire.

CHAPTER THIRTEEN

"When did you last see him?" screamed Samuel to Chantalle.

"I don't know…it's been so dark…I was so tired…I couldn't watch the children all the time," she sobbed.

Turning to the rest of the group Samuel implored them despairingly, "Has anyone seen Jonathan? When did you last notice him? Please, please try and remember."

Silas, the young boy with the Italia 90 rucsac and a pupil at Samuel's school spoke up.

"Sir, he was walking with me until the big fork in the road and then he said he needed to stop as he was so tired. I don't know what happened after that."

Samuel shouted to Leon to look after Chantalle and the children before vaulting over the barrier and rushing back over the bridge. Bullets whistled past his head as first the Tanzanian police and then the Interahamwe took pot shots at him. Luckily, the Tanzanians were not too bothered about people going back into Rwanda, given the massive problems that the refugees were already starting to cause them inside their own country, and made only a desultory attempt to hit him. The Rwandan militiamen were still so hung over that Samuel's biggest danger was from bullets ricocheting off the stanchions of the bridge rather than any direct hit.

He was clear of the bridge in a few seconds and ran frantically back down the road into Rwanda. He did not fear any pursuit – the Interahamwe would not move themselves to stop some madman from going back into Rwanda. There would be plenty of Hutu soldiers on the other side who could deal with him. Still Samuel ran as fast as he could until he could go no further. He stopped by the side of the road, heaving as much from the trauma of losing his son as from the physical exertion. Looking around, all he could see was a stream of refugees going in the opposite direction, a tide of humanity swept towards the border by the fear of genocide. Samuel wanted to tell them that they might end up dead in the Akagera river but he knew it would be pointless. Where else could these people go? Just like him he reflected mournfully, Tanzania was probably their only chance for survival.

Having recovered his breath Samuel carried on, walking as fast as he could and urgently looking from side to side for any sight of his boy. He stopped many times to ask the travellers if they had seen a boy of about ten, small for his age and wearing a blue top and red trousers. Each time he asked he was acutely aware of the impossibility of the task in front of him. There were literally hundreds of small boys trailing along the road and many of them did not seem to have their parents with them. Why would anyone spot just one child sitting by the side of the road, even if he was still there, which was fairly unlikely by now. Most of the refugees were just too exhausted even to look at Samuel and the best response that his question elicited was a weary shake of the head. If only he could find the "big fork in the road", which Silas had said was the last place he saw Jonathan, but there were plenty of those as well. But he had to try – he could not leave his son, his only son.

The adrenalin surging through his body drove Samuel to the edge of human endurance as he continued to race along the road from the border. He cared for nothing other than finding his son. He barely noticed his raging thirst or the blood seeping into his shoes from the cuts to his legs, which resulted from his frequent forays into the undergrowth on either side of the road or from crashing onto the gravel road surface after another collision with a refugee coming the other way. Nothing else mattered, he must find Jonathan but he was becoming increasingly concerned that there was no sign of him. He shouted his name many times until it was echoing around in his head. At times he felt he heard a reply and would shout at the other refugees to keep quiet while he strained to identify the sound. But of course no-one needed to stop talking as they were completely silent anyway. The sheer struggle for survival had made all but the most essential conversation superfluous. Even the occasional sobbing of women and children was barely discernible. In order to cope with the horrors of the situation it was as if each body had shut down all non essential functions and emotions. Talking and even crying contributed nothing to survival and were eliminated. Animal instincts took over – the survival of the fittest. The cries of a manic father were no reason to stop as even the slightest delay could mean the difference between life and death.

Just then the sound of screeching tyres and shotgun fire filled the air. Desperately the refugees threw themselves to the side of the road, burying themselves in the vegetation as much as possible. Samuel jumped behind an acacia tree, its thin trunk bare of branches at a man's height and thus providing little protection. A bullet pinged off the trunk in front of him and he crouched even lower. Three jeeps went past, each with four or five crazy Interahamwe soldiers firing indiscriminately at the refugees. Every so often the jeeps would stop and several soldiers would jump out with gleaming machetes slicing through the air. A group of Tutsis would be mown down in seconds, decapitated in an instant, entire families wiped out with a few heavy blows, having nothing with which to defend themselves apart from a few sticks. Samuel felt that he should intervene, but what could one man do against such force? It would have been a brave gesture to rush at the soldiers but what would it achieve? Another corpse to add to the pile, another head lolling to the side of the torso, not quite severed but utterly useless all the same. He had to find Jonathan so he needed to stay alive, nothing else mattered more than that. The world had gone crazy but he couldn't give up.

As soon as the soldiers were out of range, Samuel regained the road. He felt strangely energised by the delay, even more resolute in the desperate search for his son. Rounding the next corner, he came to a fork in the road. Was this the place where Jonathan had been last seen?

The Interahamwe had clearly stopped at this place. Bodies were littered over the road and in the verges. Some had been shot, others decapitated, and some had been deliberately run over by the jeeps –

several times by the look of things. Samuel was numb, beyond the depths of despair, stuck in a vacuum of emotion yet drained of all hope. Somehow he knew Jonathan was here, call it a sixth sense, call it superstition, call it paternal instinct but he just knew at that moment that his son was a victim of the genocide. Slowly he moved among the corpses. The occasional survivor was wailing loudly over a group of bodies. Samuel wondered if if such wretches were the only ones left alive in their families. What were these poor souls to do, left alone with no other relative to comfort them? The trauma had been bad enough when enduring it with a group of loved ones, but how would anyone cope on their own? Samuel could give no comfort. Compassion had become a victim of the terror too. What was another dead body among so many? Who cared about another grieving relative?

Slowly Samuel turned over each body until its face, if it still had one, was pointing upwards and could be identified. But suddenly there was no need to turn over the next body. Its blue top, red trousers and small frame gave it all the identity that was required. Jonathan was dead. Flat out, face down on a patch of Rwandan dirt, his precious son, a sensitive, intuitive, peace-loving gift from God. Shot through the head in a firing squad.

To Samuel, Jonathan was more than a son. He was a soul mate, a best friend and now a martyr to a cause he neither understood nor cared for. A Tutsi boy who looked like a Hutu and who played with other boys indifferent to their tribal origin. He played with them because they were his friends but now some of their fathers may well have murdered him. Samuel held the boy in his arms, his blood still fresh as it seeped out onto his father's clothes. He wept uncontrollably, his body heaving with spasms of grief. It was over – he had no reason to live anymore. Samuel's life had come to an end just as that of his beloved son's – on a lonely roadside through the gun of a total stranger.

* * *

While Samuel grieved over the death of his son, others in Nyarubuye were grieving too. Not that you would have noticed from a casual glance at the town. It was a beautiful morning. The sun's rays, diffused through the branches of the trees, created random patterns of light on the ground and vegetation had sprung into life, stimulated by the recent heavy rain. The grass sparkled with beads of water that had yet to evaporate in the early morning sun. Birds sang contentedly as if envigorated by the refreshing showers and life seemed good in this peaceful and pleasant land.

But one thing was missing – the noise of human beings; men on their way to work; children chattering excitedly as they made their way to school; women standing in the road, interrupted on their way to market by some juicy gossip. There was a sinister explanation for this. There was only one reason why people would come out of their homes that day and it wasn't of their own choice.

That morning, drunken Interahamwe troops were touring the town blowing their whistles, signalling that all Tutsis should come out of their homes. As each family group emerged their identities were checked against the index cards provided by the Bourgmestre. The soldiers seemed unclear as to the sentence that had been passed by the Bourgmestre on each Tutsi. Was it an execution or just a beating? Should they torch the house or just steal the cattle? As it turned out, the punishment they meted out was totally indiscriminate. Here, a family would be cut down with machetes, their house looted, animals stolen and the building set on fire, there, just a cow would be stolen, some half hearted blows administered to the occupants and then the soldiers would leave. Whatever the outcome the 'justice' was summary and administered without sentence being passed and without any opportunity for the victims to defend themselves. Life hung in the balance depending on the whim of an individual protagonist or whether they were distracted by richer pickings elsewhere. Many a life was saved at the point of a machete when the weapon's owner was called over to an incident in a neighbouring property just as he was about to administer the fatal blow. Resistance was futile and, indeed, it guaranteed certain death. The alcohol-soaked militia were unfailingly roused from their stupor by a fight and the penalty for such inconvenience was clear.

Jeremiah Dusaidi watched proceedings from behind a bush further up the hill from where some of the killings were taking place. Aged twenty, he was a Tutsi native of Nyarubuye, but like most citizens of the town he had thought that tribal murders were something which happened elsewhere – in Kigali or Gitarama perhaps but not in the peaceful outpost of Nyarubuye. Until today that was. When he had seen enough Jeremiah ran back to his parents' house about half a mile away, bursting breathlessly into the front room. His father and mother sat motionless at the table.

His father, Ernest Dusaidi, had been, until recently, a Responsable de Cellule, in charge of an administrative unit of local government. Although this was the lowest level of government, Ernest had amassed considerable power. This was in part due to his reputation as a man "who got things done" in a chaotic municipal infrastructure. In addition, as a prominent Tutsi he was able to act as an intermediary between the Bourgmestre and the local Tutsi population. This worked both ways. If the Tutsis felt that they were being passed over in the allocation of jobs in Nyarubuye then Ernest could represent their concerns to the Bourgmestre. On the other hand, if the Bourgmestre wanted the co-operation of the Tutsis in matters of security or taxation, for instance, then Ernest was the man to deliver it.

Not any longer though, for about five weeks previously Bourgmestre Julius Ndagijimana had summarily dismissed him from his position. No reasons given, no explanations offered but, in reality, Ernest Dusaidi would not have believed them anyway. He had been sacked because he was a Tutsi, pure and simple.

"Father," gasped Jeremiah, "they are hacking us to pieces out there. The Interahamwe pigs are moving from house to house butchering any Tutsis they find, stealing their possessions and then setting fire to their buildings. I have seen it with my own eyes."

"I know, son," Ernest replied solemnly, "Charles has seen it too" as a middle aged man emerged from his hiding place in the bedroom. Charles Rudatigura had been Ernest's trusty assistant in the cellule and was a faithful and close confidante of the family.

Ernest continued.

"We must do something to help our brothers and sisters. I know that we no longer have any official position but the Tutsis are looking to us for leadership. We have to try and stop this killing."

"But what can we do Ernest?" questioned Charles, "We have no weapons and no power. The Hutus have been planning this for weeks. You now know why we were sacked – to clear the way for this genocide."

"Charles, we have known the Bourgmestre for years. Sure, he may have had orders to remove Tutsis from government posts but that doesn't mean he won't listen to us. After all, the RPF are at the border and his keen sense of self preservation will mean that he won't want to be too closely identified with the Interahamwe. You know what a snake he is. Will he want to risk his plantations when the RPF arrive because he did nothing to protect his Tutsi citizens?"

"Rubbish, where *are* the RPF father? In sodding Uganda that's where. How can they help us from there? Tutsi bodies will be piled so high that they will be creating waterfalls on the Akagera before anyone arrives to defend us. Yes the Bourgmestre will say nice comforting words about how he will protect the Tutsis but will he do anything?"

Jeremiah thought about using another swear word for emphasis but considered it unnecessary. There was only one answer to his rhetorical question and his father knew it too.

"I know, but we must try. Remind him of his own self interest. Give him a way out in case it all goes wrong, an opportunity to present himself as someone who did everything he could to stop the killing. There's no harm in that."

Charles and Jeremiah looked at each other. They did not believe the Bourgmestre was open to reason but, as on many other occasions previously, they would not refuse Ernest's request. Paternal and historic authority still counted for something. Maybe they were the only things you could rely on in this crazy country.

CHAPTER FOURTEEN

Vomecourt's armoured truck drove along the Rue Emile Desourteaux towards the Champ de Foire. Sister Agathe could just look out of the ventilation slits in the side of the truck. She had never been to Oradour before but the scene looked very similar to that of any other small French town. There were grey stone built shops and houses lining the main street. A few of the inhabitants were standing on the thick stone steps outside the shops. Rolls of carpet were standing upright outside the furniture store as if standing to attention. Wooden poles carrying the overhead tram power cables were placed at twenty feet intervals on the right hand side of the road. Agathe could see large metal plates attached to the walls of the end buildings on each block advertising brands of cigarettes and drinks.

"Not much chance of anyone buying those at the moment," she said to no-one in particular.

As they were turning right into the Champ de Foire, Agathe heard a drum beating and could just make out a man, whom she assumed was the town crier, accompanied by an SS soldier, shouting instructions to the inhabitants to attend an identity card check on the fairground. The truck came to a halt and the doors soon swung open.

"Get out," barked Vomecourt. "Move it, quickly." He kicked the refugees out of the truck and onto the grassy area of the square, sparing a special blow for Sister Agathe who fell in agony onto the grass. Paul Katz made as if to square up to the German but the nun motioned him back.

"Paul, no. I'm all right, please just do as he says."

Katz turned away only to receive his own crushing blow to the head from the butt of Vomecourt's sub machine gun. He slumped to the ground, momentarily dazed by the power of the blow which, fortunately, had largely just glanced off the top of his head.

Vomecourt was now looking particularly menacing. He knew that the locals, who had already gathered in the Champ de Foire, would know by his accent that he was an Alastian. A number of refugees from Alsace-Lorraine had settled in Oradour, evicted from their homes in that Germanised province. They were known as 'Les Ya Ya's' from their habit of answering questions in French with "Ja, Ja". Their venom would be especially directed at him – an Alsatian who had 'sold out' to the Germans.

"Let that be a lesson to all of you," he bellowed. "Any of you who step out of line will be punished and the next time it will be permanent."

The inhabitants who had already gathered in the square looked at each other apprehensively. At first it seemed a reasonable request from the German soldiers, who had entered houses, bars, schools and shops to gather everyone together for an identity card check. Oradour had seen little German activity and it was perhaps just their turn for a visit. Rumour had it that a German major had been captured in the area and that the SS were seeking the maquisards who may have taken him. Yet the brutality of the soldiers in the Champ de Foire and the sporadic gunfire that could be heard around the town suggested that this might be something more than a routine check.

Sister Agathe surveyed the groups of residents who were gathering in increasing numbers on the grassy area of the square. Two enormous trees at the far end of the fairground provided shelter for some from the early afternoon sun. The road that surrounded the green was gradually filling with German vehicles and troops. Agathe estimated that there were now over one hundred soldiers circling around the grassy rectangle. This seemed to her excessive for a simple identity card check.

"Sister," whispered Paul Katz still a little groggy from Vomecourt's blow to his head. "What do we do when they ask for our identity cards? You know we've destroyed everything and, as the Captain has heard that we are Jewish, we're finished."

"I'm not sure this is really about identity cards. When we had a check in Corréze," replied the Sister, "the Germans just went around the town checking people where they found them. What's the point in making everyone come here? There's more to this than meets the eye."

Agathe was no longer trying to pretend that everything would be all right.

"We must take whatever chance we have to escape."

The two of them looked carefully around the square. It would not be easy as, not only were they flanked by dozens of SS troops, but the square was encircled by buildings. There were no obvious escape routes. The square was now filling with people – babies were being brought by their mothers in pushchairs, elderly people in wheelchairs by their sons and daughters. All humanity from Oradour was now convening on the Champ de Foire.

Dominique Malraux and Denise Renaud were among those at the fairground. They had just finished their coffee at the Hotel Milord when the town crier banged his drum outside and called all the occupants out of the hotel for an identity card check.

"Damn," muttered Dominique annoyed at this imposition on her Saturday routine, "I left my card at home. I remember putting it on the mantelpiece but was running late for the tram and forgot to pick it up."

She explained this in broken German to the soldier who was accompanying the town crier and asked if she could return home to collect it. The soldier perfunctorily refused her request and waved in the direction of the Champ de Foire. Unable to undertake a more prolonged questioning in German she and Denise followed the drift of Oradour residents towards the meeting point.

"What's the point in my attending an identity card check when they know I haven't got mine with me?" she asked Denise.

"Don't know. Maybe they just want to look busy and be able to tell their superiors that they have checked carefully for maquisards in Oradour and found nothing. Bit ridiculous really – would the resistance want to hang out in the centre of town on a Saturday afternoon? They should be searching Farmer Villepreux's woods if they want to find the maquis."

"You're joking – even the maquis wouldn't want to be shot at by that grumpy old crow or mauled by his poxy dogs. They'd choose much safer places."

With that the two women pulled into the fairground, almost colliding with Valérie Brushett and her daughter Jeanne who were anxiously scanning the Rue Emile Desourteaux for any sign of Valérie's husband André. She had heard enough from the others to know that it would be extremely dangerous for André to meet her there. There was no chance of Valérie escaping as half a dozen Das Reich soldiers were guarding the entrance to the Champ de Foire, refusing at gun point any requests to leave. But if she could just attract André's attention she might be able to warn him of the danger. Although he had kept most of his activities secret from her he had always insisted on the same routine being followed when he returned from an operation.

It had become standard SS practice to try and ambush maquisards as they came back home from an assignment. They had singularly failed to catch many resistance fighters in their hiding places in the woods or while carrying out sabotage. The maquis simply knew the area too well and could melt away into the surrounding countryside if disturbed. But they had to return home some time and local informants could be bribed or blackmailed to provide the names and addresses of suspects. Returning home was therefore the trickiest part of the operation for a maquisard. So Valérie and André had a signalling system to warn him of any danger. André would knock on the door three times and when Valérie answered the door she would cross her arms and point her fingers towards her shoulders if it was unsafe to come in. If her arms were by her side then André would know it was safe to enter the house.

Valérie always wondered what would happen if the Waffen SS were waiting in the house for his return and he escaped after she had given him the predetermined signal. Had he ever given any thought to the likely consequences for Jeanne and her? Wouldn't the Germans be likely to vent their frustration on her and their daughter, since it would be quite obvious that one way or another Valérie had tipped him off? But then she had become immune to being second best to the wretched resistance. At this moment though, the secret signal was about the only hope that André had of avoiding capture.

Valérie stood as close to the entrance to the square as possible, arms crossed, fingers pointing to her shoulders. She feigned coldness to make the posture look more natural, but this was scarcely plausible given the warm June sun almost at its apex in the clear blue sky above. Where was he? Come on, André, for once in your life, don't let me down, Valérie pleaded silently. Jeanne was becoming increasingly restless, tugging on her mother's arm to go off and join her friends playing games on the grass, oblivious to the mortal danger facing her father.

Just then André appeared at the far end of the Rue Emile Desourteaux riding on an old black bicycle. Even at a distance he looked tired and red in the face as if he had cycled some distance. He was having to swerve to avoid groups of Oradour residents making their way to the Champ de Foire. He had clearly not yet seen Valérie who was standing on tip toes to make herself as visible as possible, desperate to catch his eye but without drawing attention to herself. Her arms were crossed tightly across her chest with her fingers digging deeply into the soft flesh around her collar bones as if the physical pain would somehow make her signal more obvious to André. Please see me now darling – I do still love you.

He was now within thirty metres of his wife and, as a small clearing emerged in the human traffic, André could clearly see his wife standing close to a group of German soldiers. The 'danger' signal. He had seen it now. Immediately he braked, cursing the screeching sound made by the worn, shiny brake blocks. The bike skidded on the loose road surface and André, losing his balance, tumbled to the ground. Frantically he jumped up, yanking the bike underneath him and pushing the leather seat into his bottom. But his feet never found the pedals. There was no time. The bullets hit his head and back with such ferocity that his whole body was thrown right over the handlebars and onto the steep kerb delineating the pavement from the road. Flesh and clothing were torn from his body and splattered over the neighbouring buildings, his blood already trickling down the gutter. His body lay distended on the gravel as if the sheer force of the bullets had ripped his joints apart. In such a grotesque posture André Brushett breathed his last breath.

The Germans left him where he fell and returned to their duties at the entrance to the Champ de Foire. Just another suspect eliminated. Another traitor left to decompose in the sun. Valérie stood there stupefied with shock – unable to comprehend what had just happened right in front of her, but still retaining enough instinct for self preservation not to rush over and cradle André in her arms even though she longed to do so. The thought that he had died without them being reconciled was an unbearable burden for her to have to carry, but if she showed any emotion, she could well join André in the gutter. She had to control her feelings, if not for her own sake then for Jeanee's. It was because of her that he had come back. It was because of love for her that he had died. No other lives should be lost that day, least of all that of the common bond between them.

The shooting in front of so many villagers led to panic in the square. Groups of residents crowded round the soldiers demanding to know why this man had been killed and what was going to happen to them. The mood was starting to turn ugly and some of the young men were remonstrating angrily with the Germans. The townspeople outnumbered the Germans by about five to one and, even though they weren't armed, a riot by so many people could have been difficult to control, even by the SS.

Just at that moment, a black Mercedes staff car swept into the Champ de Foire. Even before it had stopped, Otto Bauer had jumped from the front passenger side of the car and was opening the rear offside door. Almost immediately, Major Franz Hautmann emerged, seeming to glide out of the car at the same velocity as the vehicle. Thus he was walking at full speed before the car came to a halt. Most of the villagers turned towards the man who had made such an impressive entrance.

The commanding officer of the First Battalion of Der Führer regiment of Das Reich straightened his uniform as he walked over to his officers who were by now gathered together and saluting in front of him. Clearly angered by the commotion that greeted his arrival, he saluted back in an irascible and hasty manner.

"What's going on," he snapped. "Get those people back on the grass and away from our men."

A volley of bullets crackled in the air over the fairground. The SS pushed and shoved the residents back towards the centre of the square. A few scuffles broke out but within a minute or two order had been restored.

"Vomecourt, what do you mean by this?" Hautmann asked curtly. "I gave you a simple order to get all the French peasants from this God forsaken place into the town square. What do I find? Germany's finest soldiers being humiliated by a bunch of ignorant washer women and a few hot-headed youths. We will speak about this again. Get the machine guns set up on tripods to show we mean business and I want the whole group gathered in front of my car, women and children on the right, men on the left. And, Vomecourt, don't mess this up, because if you do, the next group of people you will be facing will be a court martial."

Vomecourt and the other Alsatian soldiers who spoke French well enough to communicate with the villagers moved among the crowd, drawing them together and then separating the men, women and children. Vomecourt knew that Hautmann despised Alsatian soldiers. He would not have spoken to German officers in that way, not even that useless poof Bauer. He had seen the Major's adjutant sniggering as Hautmann vented his anger on the Captain. One day he would get even and show Bauer who was worthy of the Third Reich – a patriotic Alsatian or a traitorous Bavarian. Much as he disliked being treated so harshly by Hautmann, the Major was at least a true zealout, a believer, a patriot and Vomecourt could at least aspire to be like him.

It took several minutes to gather the villagers into groups. Children had to be reunited with adults and farewells said between males and females. There were some arguments about whether an older boy was a child or a man. The assessment of individual soldiers differed and there were old looking children and young looking men in the two groups.

Sister Agathe begged for her little group to be kept together. In vain she argued that they were not residents of Oradour but travellers passing through the town. Couldn't they be allowed to stay together so that they could resume their journey once the identity check was completed? Her request was given short shrift, as she feared it would be. The rest of the group were already identified as Jews and she as a collaborator with them. They would receive no special privileges. Indeed they would probably be singled out for special punishment.

Gustav Steinrich hugged his wife Reinhild and his children, Miriam, Heloise and Franca. Paul Katz embraced Rachel and Matthias. Both men then kissed Sister Agathe thanking her profusely for trying to save them. However they all knew in their hearts that 'trying' was all she had been able to do. If they were to survive from now onwards then they had to save themselves.

Once they were assembled, Hautmann addressed the crowd, his message translated into French by Vomecourt.

"Citizens of Oradour, a few days ago a German officer, Major Heinrich Peters, was abducted by the resistance somewhere between Limoges and Guéret. The Gestapo have advised me that his abductors are based in this area. This is a very serious matter and it is your duty to provide the German authorities with any information you may have about this crime. If you know anything that may help us locate Major Peters and arrest his treacherous captors you must step forward now. The consequences of withholding information will be very serious."

His eyes panned around the assembled crowd. He detected a little nervous movement but most eyes were firmly fixed on the ground. Denise Renaud muttered under her breath to Dominique Malraux, "Duty to provide information, my arse. Even if it was my deadliest enemy holding the Major I wouldn't tell them. I hope he's rotting in a ditch somewhere."

"Hush, Denise, we mustn't attract attention. I need to get back quickly to feed the dog. He'll be starving by now."

"You don't need to go home to find dogs," whispered Denise as she surveyed the small groups of soldiers dotted around the square, "but even dogs' meat is too good for this lot". Both women sniggered.

"Very well," announced Hautmann haughtily when it was clear that no-one would come forward, "there are arms and ammunition hidden in this town and we are going to search for them, house by house. To save us the trouble, if you have any weapons you'd better declare them now."

Farmer Villepreux raised his hand. "I have some 6mm rifles for hunting, Major." There was a titter from a group of young lads gathered near the farmer.

"We know," shouted Etienne Dubois, a friend of Claude LeClerc's, who at that very moment should have been celebrating his friend's birthday in one of the farmer's maize fields, "you've tried to shoot most of us with them".

Etienne looked at the other young men gathered around him. He was desperate to get away as they were, by now, so late for the birthday party that he feared Claude would have given up on them, but he couldn't resist the opportunity to get one over on the old enemy.

"I am talking about offensive weapons intended for use against the German army. This is your last chance to inform us of their whereabouts." Again there was no response.

"I am disappointed that you are not prepared to co-operate so, while we carry out the search, the men are to be divided into six groups and taken to various locations in the village. The women and children are to wait in the church. Your guards will take you to your locations. Do not make this any more difficult than it already is. Anyone resisting our instructions will be dealt with very severely. I'm sure you understand what this means."

Slowly the groups dispersed to their destinations, marshalled by their SS minders. Not a single identity card had been checked that afternoon.

CHAPTER FIFTEEN

Claude LeClerc had been back in his den from his fishing trip for over an hour. He had gutted his little collection of grayling and trout and was cooking them over a few logs which glowed orange on the bare earth. It could not be regarded as smoking the fish, as this might attract Farmer Villepreux's attention, more like grilling. Nevertheless, fish which had been freshly caught by your own hand and cooked in the open air were, to Claude, delicious, their taste enhanced by the condiments of poaching, trespass and danger.

But Claude was growing increasingly impatient. His friends were, by now, an hour late and the fish were overcooked. The cheese was melting in the afternoon heat and the bread was becoming stale. Surely they hadn't forgotten his birthday? They'd never missed this treat before – it was one of the highlights of the year.

Claude decided to try and find them. Leaving the maize field, he circled around the outskirts of the village intending to walk down the Champ de Foire towards the boys' school. Perhaps they had been kept back late for bad behaviour or the inoculations had been delayed. This had happened before, vaccines in France were as scarce as most other products.

On reaching the fairground he noticed a collection of German trucks, half-tracks and cars. He could see the machine guns on their tripods pointing at the grassy area in the centre of the fairground. But there was no-one about. Steathily he slid along the buildings at the edge of the square, expecting to bump into an SS soldier at any moment, but the whole area was completely deserted. Turning right onto the main

Limoges road, he was perplexed by the absence of any kind of human activity. No-one was standing idly on the street corner or tending their gardens and there weren't even any children playing in the street. He couldn't put his finger on it, but there was tension in the air, a feeling that something wasn't quite right, a sinister atmosphere.

On reaching the boys' school, Claude also found it deserted. Pushing on his own classroom door he saw the books laid out on the desks as usual and the blackboard still displaying the chalked equations from Friday's maths lesson. Looking out of the window to the rear of the school, he noticed some torn clothing hanging limply on the wire fence and what looked like a discarded shoe sitting forlornly on the grass nearby. Funny he hadn't noticed those on Friday, he thought.

Returning to the main road, he headed back into the village. He could now see a plume of smoke rising from the road at the far side of the Champ de Foire. He could hear shouting and the sound of shots being fired. Slipping behind the buildings at the eastern side of the fairground Claude could now clearly see in front of him the barn which was, by now, on fire. German soldiers were throwing straw into the building, feeding further the flames which were already leaping up to the roof of the barn.

Every so often Claude could hear a shot being fired. He was puzzled why the soldiers would be firing into a burning building, particularly as they appeared to be aiming at something. It soon became clear to him what that something was as first one man and then some others burst through a door in the rear of an adjoining barn which was also ablaze. He could tell that they were local people and that they had all been injured. One was holding his arm which hung limply by his side, another was literally dragging a useless leg across the courtyard behind the barn. Claude could see blood seeping from multiple bullet wounds in the upper body of the smallest man. A much taller man had hair singed off one side of his head, the bald patch stretched and shiny, glinting in the sunlight. The men dashed into some large rabbit hutches and appeared to burrow into the straw and earth within them.

Claude was horrified by what he had seen, guessing that other men may have been in the barn and been unable to escape. Those who had not been killed by the gunshots would have been suffocated by the choking smoke or burnt to death in the intense heat. He could hear screams as the men pleaded with the Germans to let them out but this just seemed to provoke a further fusillade of bullets from their heartless captors. But there was no sign of his friends. All the men who had escaped were adults and the screams clearly came from males with mature voices. Where were all the children? It was too dangerous to stay where he was and he couldn't help anyone anyway, so Claude crept back onto the Champ de Foire and down the Rue Emile Desourteaux. He retched at the sight of the body of André Brushett still slumped over the pavement, his legs twisted around the bicycle's handlebars.

Another burning building caught his attention, this time a garage. Again a group of German soldiers were hanging around the entrance to the garage, laughing and joking as the building became engulfed in flames. Claude could hear screaming from inside. Squinting through the small gap between the two buildings opposite he could just make out several bodies on the floor of the garage. One or two appeared to be squirming, but with each jerk of an arm or leg the SS troops would unleash a volley of bullets. Soon all movement ceased as putrid, black, belching smoke engulfed the whole building even forcing the soldiers back onto the other side of the road. They were, by now, dangerously close to Claude.

The black smoke was now billowing across the Rue Emile Desourteaux, driven by the flames which were themselves soaring twenty feet into the air. Claude pulled his handkerchief out of his pocket and clasped it over his nose and mouth. The SS soldiers were coughing and moving out of the way of the smoke. They were almost on top of Claude as he crouched in a gap of about eighteen inches between two walls. The smoke was now funnelling down this corridor, driven by the south easterly wind. Claude was choking and could not stop himself from coughing violently as the smoke filled his lungs. He could see the German soldiers turning abruptly in the direction of the noise. Darting back down the narrow gap he could feel the bullets whistling past his body and ricocheting off the stone walls, sharp fragments of rock scratching his face and arms as he fled. Fortunately for Claude, the smoke was so intense that the soldiers could only fire indiscriminately in the direction of the noise. By keeping low he could avoid the most concentrated line of fire and breathe slightly more easily.

At the end of the passage, he turned left, running through adjoining properties into the Champ de Foire. The Germans, anticipating his movements, had run along the Limoges road and turned right into the fairground, emerging just as Claude sped out from the buildings further along the square. He heard the crackle of automatic weapons as he wove between the German vehicles, which provided a welcome screen, as he raced towards the northern end of the Champ de Foire. The bullets pinged off the armour plating of the trucks and skidded into the gravel surface of the road. Claude had no time to plan his escape route. The far end of the square was the most dangerous test so far. It was an open space and he would not have the protection of any vehicles. He would be exposed to fire for a few seconds until he could reach the road leading to the cemetery. Racing past the giant tree under which the villagers had gathered earlier he felt a sharp, stinging sensation in his right arm. I've been hit, he thought in panic, but somehow there was no immediate pain. Energised by the wound, Claude tore down the road to the cemetery. He needed to get out of sight.

The cemetery in Oradour was in an open field situated at the most northerly extreme of the village to the church. Two roads forked around either side and another road headed off to the right just before the fork. Claude calculated that, if the Germans did pursue him this far, this choice of routes would give them a dilemma and they might give up the pursuit. But he had to reach the cemetery first, out of sight of the soldiers. He hurtled over the cemetery wall and crawled in the long grass towards a large upright grave stone that he could see towards the centre of the graveyard. Hiding behind the stone, Claude waited for his pursuers.

He could hear the German soldiers shouting in the general area of the intersections of the three roads. The tramping of boots had ceased, and if Claude's calculations were correct, they were now arguing about which direction they should take and about whether it was sensible to pursue a single child well beyond the boundaries of the main village.

Claude was gambling that they would regard the completion of their killing mission in the centre of the village as more pressing. It seemed to Claude as if an hour had passed but in reality it was probably just a few minutes. He was starting to hyperventilate as the reality of his parlous situation became clearer to him. Please let them leave quickly, he pleaded.

Claude didn't dare look up to see what was happening, as the SS could be anywhere, lying low, just waiting for him to reveal himself. So he just stayed put, shaking with the sheer terror of his situation and the utter horror at what he had witnessed, gasping for breath. Soon he heard shouting again but he could tell from the resigned intonation of the voices that the search was being called off. The sound of boots stomping along the road gradually diminished until he could hear it no more. For the moment at least he had survived.

For the first time, Claude felt that it was safe to inspect his arm. He had been hit in the fleshy part of the upper arm just above the short sleeve of his yellow shirt. He saw with gratitude that the bullet must have glanced off his arm and wasn't embedded in it. But he had lost a fair amount of blood. The top right hand side of his shirt was red, no doubt as the blood had splayed out from the wound as he was running. His lower arm was caked in blood but the crimson fluid was now seeping out of the wound rather than pumping from it. Nature was doing its work as it sought to seal the affected area. By now Claude was breathing more easily but, as he subconsciously relaxed, he was starting to feel faint. Somehow he still had the presence of mind to raise his arm as high as possible to stem the bleeding still further. However he daren't raise it any higher in case he was visible to any solitary soldier who had been asked to stay behind to patrol the area. Claude just waited until his body started to recover and for nightfall to provide some protection for his escape.

He thought of his parents for the first time. Had they been caught up in this atrocity? His father would often go into a bar in Oradour on a Saturday lunchtime for a drink. Had he followed his normal pattern today? His mother would normally have been at home, doing the washing and cleaning, but perhaps she had nipped into the village to buy some provisions. Claude thought it odd that a person's fate could be decided by a split second decision taken without any foreknowledge of what was about to take place. "Oh, come on Pierre, stay for another drink," he could hear his father's friends pleading. One answer meant life, the other death, but which was which? Or maybe both would produce the same result, good or bad. But his father wasn't caught up in the resistance and surely it was only the maquis who had been slaughtered in the barn? Probably it was revenge for some attack on the German army. Surely no innocent civilians could have been involved?

Claude reflected further on his father. Pierre was a natural optimist who saw goodness in everything and everyone. No situation was beyond remedy, no person beyond redemption, as far as Pierre was concerned. But, after what he had seen today, Claude no longer believed what his father had told him. There were people who could not be forgiven and who could never be rehabilitated. There was a place called hell where these people would end up and there was no way out from there. No possible remedy or resolution.

But even Claude's despair couldn't prepare him for what he didn't then know – that things were just about to get even worse than he could ever have imagined.

CHAPTER SIXTEEN

Ernest Dusaidi had been trying to see Bourgmestre Julius Ndagijimana for several days. Each time he was either told that the Bourgmestre was out or that he was busy in a meeting. But today, 15th April 1994, it was going to be different. Enough was enough. The previous day had been the worst so far. It was quite clear that the militia and zealous Hutu civilians were being provided with grenades, machetes and other bladed weapons. The rumour was that these had been distributed by the Bourgmestre for use throughout the prefecture. Rampaging gangs were slaughtering Tutsis with increasing ferocity. Road blockades were preventing refugees from fleeing to Tanzania and anyone attempting to do so was killed. Those seeking to escape across the lakes in the Gisenyi Secteur were being cut down by boatmen with orders to intercept them. Those remaining in their homes were now at serious risk of being killed by a grenade being thrown through a window or cut down by gangs wielding razor sharp machetes.

Initially Ernest, Jeremiah and Silas had been keeping records of such attacks, but now the reports were so frequent that they could not investigate each one or ascertain who had been killed or wounded. The attacks had been particularly vicious the previous night. Burning houses were evident throughout Nyarubuye. Gunshots and exploding mortar bombs could be heard on a regular basis. Hutu gangs seemed to be gathering on almost every street corner and Ernest could see that younger and younger children were now involved with these gangs. So far, his house had been spared. He could only think that this was because of his previous position as a Responsable de Cellule. Maybe the gangs didn't know that he had been sacked or perhaps they simply felt that, if they avoided killing anyone who had been in a position of authority, then somehow their crimes would remain undetected. Whatever the reason, he only had limited time to see the Bourgmestre to try and put an end to this madness.

Ernest, Jeremiah and Silas barged their way into the office of Patrice, the Bourgmestre's assistant.

"Where's the Bourgmestre?" demanded Ernest. Patrice looked up from the piles of identity cards scattered across his desk, which he was trying to sort into some particular order.

"He's given orders not to be disturbed," Patrice replied in a manner which indicated that this was the final word on the matter.

"Stuff his orders!" Ernest snarled as he leant over the clerk's desk, emboldened by the official's offhand response. "At his "orders" hundreds of people are being killed, women are being raped and houses burnt. We insist on seeing him right now."

Patrice shook his head and recommenced shuffling the cards in front of him. Jeremiah grabbed him by the throat.

"Listen, you little sneak, I bet there's an ID card missing from that little pile of Tutsis, isn't there? I wonder who that could be? Perhaps I should go and ask the Bourgmestre if he could find your wife's card. Maybe it got misfiled with the Hutus. Easy mistake to make isn't it? After all, you've so many cards to check through. If you let us in to see the Bourgmestre then that little card can stay in the wrong place. Otherwise your wife's corpse will be piled up with all the rest and yours will be on top of it. You know what they do with Hutu collaborators don't you?" Ernest paused…"Made your mind up yet?"

With that, Jeremiah loosened his grip on the terrified clerk who stammered, "I'll…I'll…see if he…he…can s-spare a few m-minutes to see you." Patrice trotted off dolefully into the Bourgmestre's office.

Clearly Julius Ndagijimana was upset at being disturbed and launched into a screaming rant at his unfortunate flunky. Jeremiah couldn't help but feel a little sympathy for the grovelling sycophant, even though he despised almost everything about him. But more seriously their chance of getting to see the Bourgmestre seemed to be reducing with every expletive that reverberated around the walls of the official's room. How could Patrice manage to calm him down enough even to ask if he would see the Tutsi delegation, let alone produce a positive response to his request? After a while however Ndagijimana seemed to have run out of steam. Voices were hushed, the floor stopped vibrating and the walls shaking. In a few minutes Patrice returned.

"The Bourgmestre will see you now. Come with me."

The three men looked at each other in astonishment and followed the clerk into his superior's office. Jeremiah was impressed. Maybe he had misjudged Patrice. Perhaps there was more to him than met the eye. Calming a beast like Ndagijimana at such a crucial moment was some feat. As he caught the official's eye he nodded in a gesture of both admiration and appreciation. Patrice, unmoved by this small sign of empathy and warmth, left the room without making any response.

The three men surveyed the Bourgmestre's office. There were boxes of machetes and grenades on the floor and a selection of handguns and boxes of bullets on his desk. Ndagijimana fingered one of the guns.

"Just for my own protection, you understand Ernest. These are dangerous times. Since the Tutsis murdered the President no-one is safe, least of all those of us in government. There are many enemies of the state who are seeking to destroy this country."

"It's for that very reason that we want to see you, Julius," replied Ernest refusing to be intimidated by the Bourgmestre's insinuations and his formidable arsenal. "Do you realise what the Hutus are doing to the Tutsis in your prefecture. It's nothing short of genocide. Hundreds have already been killed, thousands have fled. These are your people, Julius, citizens of your government, innocent civilians, entitled to look to you for protection. But what are you doing about it? From the look of things, encouraging and feeding these killers." He kicked over a box of grenades causing Jeremiah and Silas to cower in the corner.

"Don't worry," Ernest continued, "they're not primed but I imagine they soon will be and there's probably one with our names on it. Julius, you have to stop this idiocy."

"Huh!" sneered the Bourgmestre. "You Tutsis have treated us Hutus like dirt for years. Only good enough to dig up a pitiful crop of vegetables on the poxy hills, while your cattle grazed on the lush grass in the valley. Apes, you called us, apes, while sneering down on us over your long Ethiopian noses. Stupid we were, not worth educating, so you took all the school places for your own children. Well it's different now."

He thumped on his desk causing bullets to fall onto the floor, as if emphasizing the fate of the Tutsi population, "Hutu Power will save this country from the traitors within. It's time for us to reclaim our birthright. You Tutsis have trampled on us for too long and now you have even murdered the President to try and subdue us again. Well, it won't be allowed to happen."

Ndagijimana sank back into his chair exhausted by the effort of this vitriol.

"Monsieur Bourgmestre, why not listen to reason?" Silas jumped into the conversation, as he could see that Ernest's antagonistic approach was just going to get them thrown out. "You are a politician, a man who knows how government works. Don't kick them on the way down and they won't kick you on their way up. The RPF are already on their way from Uganda. Sure, it'll take them a little time to get this far but it will happen sooner or later. Even your own commanders fear the RPF. What do you think they've been doing in all these years of exile? Singing patriotic songs and practising their folk dancing? No, Bourgmestre, foreigners have been training them, they've been stockpiling arms, Kagame has been filling their minds with Tutsi ideology. If I may say it, Bourgmestre, your rabble of so-called soldiers won't stand a chance against a proper army."

Julius Ndagijimana narrowed his eyes and, for the first time in the meeting, appeared on the defensive. He knew there was truth in what Silas was saying. Ernest saw it too and could sense that the initiative was moving their way. He tried the personal approach.

"Julius, we have worked together for many years. Yes, we have had our differences, but I always felt that you were a man who listened to reason. When the RPF arrive, wouldn't you like to be known as the one Hutu leader who had tried to moderate the killing – who protected as many Tutsis as possible even at great personal cost? They'll understand that you couldn't stop all the murders. The gangs were out of control. You tried to stop them but they wouldn't listen and threatened to kill you. But you did what you could. We will verify your co-operation with us. In reality we know that if you order the killing to stop most of the militiamen will do as you have instructed because they're frightened of you. That's what we are asking you to do – end the bloodshed and allow us to bury our dead. But we can tell the RPF that you were powerless to prevent the deaths of those who have already died. In the same way as you kept me as the Responsable de Cellule to reassure the Tutsis so we can ask them to retain you as the link with the Hutus. This mad country will only ever work if Hutus and Tutsis co-operate together. The RPF know that. They will be conciliatory. They will want to work with any Hutus who showed compassion to the Tutsis. What will you gain from killing more people when you will no longer be the Bourgmestre in a few weeks? This genocide has played right into the hands of the RPF. They now have the moral, legal, military and even humanitarian excuses to seize power. For your own sake, Julius, even if for no-one else's, you must listen to us – please order them to stop the killing."

For the first time that morning there was silence. The Bourgmestre stood up and gazed at a large map of Rwanda. The northern boundary with Uganda was long enough for any invading force to enter the country quite easily. Hard information was difficult to come by but the Bourgmestre had already heard that RPF troops were in the country. Indeed it was common knowledge that they had never left after the previous invasion before the Arusha Accords were signed. They had a fearsome reputation, not because of their brutality but because they possessed the one characteristic missing from so many African armies – military discipline. While Julius did not intend giving up his cause so easily, there was no harm in keeping an escape route open, a foot in both camps so to speak. His survival instincts had always been strong but they had been sharpened by the tension of the current atrocities.

Eventually Ndagijimana spoke, this time in measured, statesmanlike tones.

"All right, but not because I accept your argument about the RPF but because I am a man of honour. Tell your people to seek refuge in the church. You will be safe there. I will give orders to the troops to treat the church as a place of sanctuary. You have my word that no-one there will be harmed."

The three men stared at each other in disbelief. Jeremiah spoke first.

"Thank you, Bourgmestre. When the others asked me to come here I said that they were wasting their time. You wouldn't listen to any appeal by a Tutsi. But I was wrong. You have listened and have shown yourself to be a friend of all the peoples of Rwanda. Thank you."

With that Ernest, Jeremiah and Silas left the room. Patrice looked up sheepishly as they went past. Jeremiah playfully pushed over a pile of ID cards.

"You won't be needing those now," he said, then whispered in the clerk's ear, "Tell your wife to come to Nyarubuye church straightaway. She'll be safe there."

Mission accomplished, the men walked out purposefully into a bright Rwandan morning.

CHAPTER SEVENTEEN

The Catholic church at Oradour stood proudly on a bend in the Limoges road on the south eastern edge of the village. It was an impressive sight approached from any angle, raised up as it was on a small hill overlooking the low lying environs of the village. It was a sturdy stone built structure with an impressive tower flanked by several turrets. Its steeple was a pyramid shape, topped with a cross. Its nave and side chapels extended out down the hill and were therefore built on two levels, the lowest being nearest to the road to Limoges. The altar was contained in a squat buttress adjacent to a stone built wall that bordered the road. For a village the size of Oradour, the church was indeed an imposing and impressive building.

At about 2p.m. on Saturday 10th June the priest, Father Dominic Lesueur had entered the church through a small sacristy door in the southern transept of the building. On his approach he had seen German troops milling around the eastern entrance to the Champ de Foire and had slipped into the church garden to avoid being seen. From there he was able to pass through a small arch and gain access to the church undetected. Not that it mattered much, his life was no longer worth living. Being caught and executed by the Germans would have been a welcome release. At least then there would have been some dignity in being killed by an evil occupier who was hated by local people. In reality, however, he had been exposed as a paedophile and blackmailed by German troops into betraying his countrymen. Father Dominic felt totally worthless. What's more he hated himself for what he had become.

It was almost as if he were two people in the church building. One, a normal, straight living, rational man of faith, was looking down on the other, a spineless, immoral, child abusing atheist. For the first time in many years he could now see clearly what he was and how he had changed from one person to the other. For all these years he had denied his own sin, had rationalised his disbelief. He had chipped away at his morality and faith, bit by bit. An arm placed around a child trying to read a difficult passage of scripture was harmless, surely? A slight reinterpretation of a few biblical verses was just an aid to understanding, wasn't it? Taking a few coins out of the offering saved the church treasurer from having to write up his expenses, didn't it?

But it never stopped at that. Each little act, largely harmless in itself, was not enough. His desire needed feeding, his appetite grew until he had to consume vast quantities of immorality to be satisfied. He had to climax with every child he taught; not only did he no longer believe in God but he couldn't even understand the concept of goodness; and the church treasurer was constantly berating the congregation for their miserly level of giving. "Well it is wartime," the priest would explain while feeling the weight of the coins in his own pocket.

But for some reason betraying a nun and two families of helpless Jews had given him a lucidity he had not experienced for years. His recidivism was clearly exposed and, more than that, his sin was revealed as a personal injury to God and the priest's victims and, if he felt he had hurt God, then surely God must exist. If God didn't exist then why was he feeling this way. His final act had to be to throw himself at the mercy of that God who could do with him what He wanted. If the God he had wronged so severely could not forgive him, then he would bring his own life to an end. The new upright and rational Father Dominic could not forgive himself without divine intervention and, if there was no forgiveness, there was only one way for society to be rid of such a poisonous and vile pervert.

Father Dominic knelt in front of the altar, staring at the crucifix at its centre. Tears lined his cheeks, his body started to heave with convulsive sobbing. He could not find words to express his feelings – his need for forgiveness was so immense that he felt incapable of expressing his remorse adequately. God could not possibly forgive him. The clear thinking, logical Father Dominic could see that his actions had been so repugnant that God could not even look at him, let alone forgive, and he had no means of redressing the wrong. He couldn't undo the past or repair the damage done to innocent children. The slate could not be wiped clean. He had feelings of the deepest regret but there was nothing he could do to show his repentance, nothing he could even say to express it. The snivelling, repulsive and cheating Father Dominic could do nothing to redeem himself. It was time for his alter ego to take action and put an end to the life of this wretched creature who could not save himself. He drew a knife from under his cassock and stared at the painting of the Virgin Mary,

"Mother of Jesus, have mercy on the soul of this worthless and disobedient servant," he said out loud, the sound reverberating around the empty church.

It was almost as if Father Dominic was carefully positioning the knife over the wrist of another person whom he had just absolved, someone whose life he didn't recognise and about whose existence he was totally ambivalent. It just had to be done. He stared at the blue vein bulging on the surface of his wrist. He would have to cut down deeply to sever the two arteries. Even at this moment of the greatest tension in his life Father Dominic could appreciate the symbolism of bleeding to death before the altar of Christ. He closed his eyes and started to slice through the skin.

Otto Bauer burst through the main entrance door to the church, followed by a procession of women and children who had been sent from the fairground. At the sudden noise Father Dominic rolled over onto the stone floor behind the altar rail, blood dripping from the wound to his wrist. His instinct for self preservation had somehow been stronger than his will to bring his miserable life to an end, or maybe he had just felt that he wanted to die in private. Whatever the reason, he could hear the German guards angrily herding the women and children into the church. Hidden by the first pew, he crawled under the wooden seat towards the side aisle and was just able to slide down the steps into the vestry before anyone could see him. He lay on the floor panting and shaking from the ordeal.

Dominique Malraux and Denise Renaud were among the first to enter the church. The mood of the women had changed from a resigned impatience at having their routine disrupted to a more vulnerable apprehension. If the Germans merely wanted to search all the houses, why did they need to separate the men from the women and herd them off in different directions. Surely they could have stayed in the Champ de Foire until the inspection was over?

"Move down to the front of the church," barked Helmut Vomecourt, sending Valérie and Jeanne sprawling with the butt of his rifle.

"Careful," shouted Dominique, "she's only a child".

Vomecourt stared at Dominique, indignant at this show of defiance at his authority. Grabbing her by the arm he snapped at Otto to get everyone into the church as quickly as possible. Vomecourt had remembered the layout of the building from his previous visit. He pushed Dominique violently down the side aisle and into the vestry. Father Dominic was cowering under the desk, unseen by the two protagonists as they tumbled into the room.

"Get off me, you filthy Alsatian traitor!" screamed Dominique.

She kicked out at the German while picking up the lamp on the table and smashing it across Vomecourt's shoulders. He winced as the pain travelled right down his back.

"You little witch! It should be a privilege for you to be taken by a real man for a change, rather than those French mice who normally infect you with their spineless sperm."

With that, Vomecourt threw Dominique onto the floor of the vestry.

From under the desk, Father Dominic could clearly see Dominique as she hit the floor, one of her shoes flying off under the desk where he sat. He had lain on that same space himself with his own victims. He winced at the thought of it. By now Vomecourt was on top of the girl ripping off her skirt and tearing down her stockings. Dominique was now silent. The priest could not tell whether she had been knocked out in the fall or had calculated that quiet acquiescence was the only chance of saving her life.

He felt the knife in his hand. Gripping the blade strongly he slid out from under the desk unheard above the grotesque grunting of the German. He stood above the writhing attacker, but somehow it wasn't Vomecourt he saw beneath him but himself, his black cassock draped over a small fair haired boy with a bewildered and frightened look on his face. Raising the knife high above his head, he crashed it down on the body beneath. As the knife tore through the flesh he plunged it deeper into the cavities of Vomecourt's chest. He stirred it like a woman straining against a wooden spoon in a big bowl of stew, making sure that the Alsatian major's organs were irreparably damaged. Vomecourt was clearly dead, almost instantaneously.

Father Dominic pushed Vomecourt's body off Dominique. She was conscious, but obviously deeply traumatised. For once in his life the priest had done something to rescue another human being rather than ruin them. He took off his black cloak and laid it on the German. The body looked like Father Dominic. It was meant to, a tangible sign of his repentance.

"Father, forgive me, a worthless sinner," he whispered.

As the bullet from the German officer's gun blew his brains across the room Father Dominic Leseuer entered paradise.

* * *

Dominique felt the priest's body as it slumped heavily on top of her. She was already covered in blood from Vomecourt and now bits of bone and flesh from the priest's skull showered her body. She lay still, silent as the grave, eyes closed shut. The German officer, who had hurried into the vestry in search of the Captain and had shot Father Dominic as the priest was plunging his knife into the German officer, could see that all three people appeared dead. No point wasting any more bullets. He felt for Vomecourt's pulse. There was none. He didn't care. He had hated that monster almost as much as the French had. He turned quickly, shut the vestry door and returned to the main part of the church.

Adjutant Otto Bauer had shepherded the final family into the church, which now contained about 400 people, sitting nervously in family groups in the pews or on the floor. At least they would be safe in here, he thought. He had heard a shot from a direction which appeared to be outside the church. At least it had not been in the nave and no-one had been hurt. Probably it had been some maquisard causing trouble nearby. Bauer was almost wishing the Allies a quick passage to Limoges. He should have deserted months ago but where could he have hidden? Would the French have sheltered a German deserter? Not likely, they would have shot him as an infiltrator. If the Germans had caught him they would have shot him too. He would just have to see it through, but hope that he could get his head down as much as possible and not get shot in the Allied advance. Herding up civilians in quiet French villages, while desultory house to house searches were carried out, was Otto's perfect finale to the war. Not much excitement. Not much danger.

However, as ever, his quiet planning was interrupted by Major Franz Hautmann, who was standing impatiently at the back of the church.

"Otto, where's Vomecourt. Whenever I want him he goes missing. I need him to tell these people what to do."

"I don't know, Major. He was last seen with some French woman – no doubt trying to extend the Fatherland, Sir." Otto winked at his commanding officer.

"Very funny, Otto. Remind me to stop your supply of sarcasm pills. You are becoming increasingly irritating. Bring in that box and put it at the front of the church." Hautmann pointed at a large box wedged between the two entrance doors.

Bauer motioned to another soldier to help him carry the box in. It was large and heavy and the Adjutant noticed a number of strings protruding from its lid and hanging limply over its sides. The box weighed so much that Otto and the other soldier could only drag it across the stone floor and up to the choir stalls. By now the women and children were extremely agitated. The sound of the bullet which killed Father Dominic Lesueur had destabilized the situation and the sight of the box clearly containing explosives was now producing hysteria. Bauer himself was by now deeply disturbed. He reassured the people by smiling and patting some of the children on the head. Had he been able to speak good French he would have reassured them that the box was just a deterrent. If they behaved themselves they would be in no danger. But he was not so sure.

Returning to the rear of the church, Bauer looked at Hautmann. By now he was even more disconcerted. There was a look of revenge in the Major's eyes, a lust for blood was burning bright in his whole demeanour.

"Major," queried the Adjutant, "what is the box for? Surely you don't need to threaten a bunch of harmless women and children with something like that?"

"Who said it was a threat?" sneered Hautmann. "You may be willing to let these peasants kill the flower of German manhood and get away with it but I'm certainly not".

CHAPTER EIGHTEEN

When she could be sure that the guard had gone, Dominique Malraux gently extricated herself from under the priest's body. She rose uncertainly to her feet, checking that she hadn't been injured during the attack. Apart from a little unsteadiness, she had miraculously survived unscathed. Dominique walked slowly and silently to the door, her senses sharpened by the danger that hung in the air like a mist all around her. She leant against the door, her left ear pressed firmly against the wood, listening intently for any sound from the other side.

She could hear muffled crying and shouting, which she guessed emanated from the nave of the church. But she could not be sure that there were no German soldiers guarding the vestry door. Dominique knew that she could not stay in the room as sooner or later she would be discovered. Being in the same place as a murdered German officer would not bode well for her survival. She wondered how Denise was faring, praying that her friend would be safe. She needed to get back into the main part of the church to find out, but she had to be able to defend herself. The priest's knife – where was it? Peeling back the black cloak that covered Captain Vomecourt's body she saw the weapon embedded deeply into his back. Fighting back nausea, she grabbed the handle of the knife with both hands and pulled sharply upwards. The blade made a popping sound, generated by the suction as it emerged from the body. Dominique retched as she was splattered with blood once again. Wiping the bloodied blade clean on the cloak, she slid back to the door. The knife was no match for a gun but at least she had the element of surprise and might be able to strike first. Looking at the prone and lifeless body of the Captain, she could see evidence of the effectiveness of her weapon. Holding her breath, she lifted the latch of the door and swung it open in the same motion.

Hugely relieved, she could see that there was no-one behind the door.

* * *

By now, Sister Agathe had been separated from the Katz and Steinrich families in the nave of the church. Major Hautmann had discovered that the nun spoke both German and French and, in the absence of Captain Vomecourt, was in need of an interpreter.

"Tell the people to sit down and not move around," requested the Major, "we will tell them what to do next in a few minutes."

Obeying his command and speaking as loudly as she could above the general hubbub, Sister Agathe noticed that the Major was motioning to his troops to move towards the main entrance door. The only exception was the soldier who had assisted Adjutant Bauer in carrying the box to the front of the church. He was kneeling down and appeared to be examining the strings that were hanging down the side of the box. As the soldier shuffled further along, Agathe could see with horror that he had been lighting the strings. The fuses were now burning brightly. The heavy box, crammed with its deadly arsenal, would explode in seconds.

The German soldiers were barring any exit from the main door of the church, their rifles now raised and pointing at the women and children. Agathe ducked under the nearest pew as the box exploded and thick black suffocating smoke rapidly filled the church. She could hear people screaming and half choking in the acrid air. They were running to the extremities of the church where the air was fresher. But the Germans were shooting anyone who came into view. From under her pew, Agathe could see bodies starting to pile up at the back of the church.

Many people appeared to be heading for the sacristy, whose door had been broken down by the pressure of those pushing against it. But the soldiers were mowing them down in cold blood. Grenades were now being thrown indiscriminately across the church. Agathe saw one land plumb centre in a baby's pram. It was a vision of hell. Two boys were shot dead as they sheltered in a confessional box. A girl of about three or four was shot six or seven times as she sheltered under a giant pillar.

Agathe crawled under several rows of pews, coughing in the choking smoke but just about able to breathe the few pockets of oxygen trapped under the swirling black cloud. She dragged herself across a side aisle, not knowing where she was heading. Her attention was drawn by the touch of cold fresh air on her face. Looking to her left she could see some steps leading down to an open door. Fresh air was rising up these steps in a futile attempt to drive back the smoke, but it did succeed in lifting the pall slightly so that Agathe could just make out a face and an arm beckoning towards her.

"Over here," shouted the voice.

With an Herculean effort and, despite almost passing out from the effects of inhaled smoke, she pulled herself across the flag stones and tumbled down the steps. Dominique Malraux grabbed her and yanked her into the vestry, where the nun gulped in lungfuls of the relatively fresh air. She saw the bodies lying on the floor but was too intent on survival to worry about how they had come to be there.

"Where do we go now?" she spluttered, black smoke and soot spewing out of her mouth.

Dominique pointed to a small window on the side wall of the vestry, about five feet off the ground. It was slightly ajar and a small draught of fresh air was being drawn into the room. At that moment they could feel the heat of a huge fireball erupting in the church. Agathe had seen the Germans throwing straw, furniture and wood onto the bodies at the back of the church. Obviously this deadly mixture had combusted.

"Quickly, help me up," Dominique cried urgently. The two women pushed the priest's desk under the window and clambered on top. Dominique smashed the glass with a candlestick holder that had been left on the ledge in front of the window.

"Sister, help me through the window."

Agathe grabbed the girl's legs and pushed while Dominque grabbed the window frame and pulled, disregarding the sharp splinters of glass still lodged in the frame. After a few seconds of exhausting effort by both women, Dominique had forced her way through the gap. The glass ripped her clothes and scratched her skin as she pulled herself onto a narrow stone gulley that ran alongside the church. Immediately Dominique turned with her arms and head reaching back into the vestry. Agathe grabbed her hands and was pulled up through the window by a superhuman effort from Dominique.

"I didn't know I was so strong," she whispered as they lay side by side in the shallow gulley. There was a loud cracking sound and a huge billow of smoke emerged from the roof close to where they were sheltering. The fire had obviously caused the roof timbers to collapse dragging down the whole structure. They had only just got out in time. The women could hear sporadic shooting around the church, surmising that escapees were being shot if they attempted to flee the collapsing building.

It was clearly unsafe to move from their hiding place. However, although the gulley was a foot or so below the surface level of the grass in the church grounds, it did not provide adequate protection. Looking around Agathe could see a green tarpaulin propped against a buttress at the side of the church. She motioned to Dominique to crawl towards it. Although the wind direction and intensity of the fire was carrying the smoke upwards and away from the women, hot embers from the burning roof were raining down on them, scorching their hair and any exposed skin. They needed protection but didn't dare run away from the building as German soldiers were shouting and shooting in all directions. The women huddled together under the tarpaulin, leaning back on the stone buttress, ensuring that they were both fully hidden. A window exploded above them, showering hot glass onto their makeshift shelter. The burning glass sizzled on the canvas but the women couldn't risk shaking the cover to remove it. All they could do was sit tight and hope the tarpaulin wouldn't catch fire.

Although secluded in their hiding place, Dominique and Agathe had never felt more vulnerable and exposed. They seemed no more secure than if lined up blindfold in front of a firing squad, never knowing when the fatal bullet would be fired. At any moment a trigger happy German could unload his ammunition into the tarpaulin. The tension was unbearable. Each second that passed could be the last of their lives.

Several SS soldiers passed by and Agathe could tell that they were laughing and cracking anti-French jokes. She could not believe that anyone could regard this overwhelming tragedy, entirely manufactured by human hands, as entertainment. Agathe wasn't naturally lugubrious but she was at this moment almost crushed by a most visceral despair, a despondency of the soul from which no release seemed possible.

Only a physical stimulus could shake the women out of this intense hopelessness. By now the heat that hung in the air and penetrated through the surface of the walls was becoming unbearable. Each felt as if her throat and lungs were being scorched and gasping for clean air only made them inhale more of the burning atmosphere. Dominique whispered to Agathe that they would have to risk running to the far side of the church garden from which they could reach the open countryside. She listened as intently as was possible for the sound of human activity through the thunderous sound of the building being engulfed by the fire. When she was sure that none could be heard, she gingerly lifted the tarpaulin and emerged into the afternoon light. With the most intense relief, Dominique could see no soldiers in the immediate vicinity. Both women got to their feet and slowly crept round the stone buttress.

It was the point of the rifle that Dominique first noticed, but then the unmistakable shape and colour of a German uniform. Adjutant Otto Bauer stood almost on top of her. She instinctively shut her eyes and braced herself against the impact of the bullets, tensing her muscles as if this would somehow provide some protection. But she felt nothing. Opening her eyes again she could see the German officer putting his index finger to his lips and motioning for the women to run to the other side of the garden.

Bauer and the two women ran across the garden towards the wall of the house closest to the church. Just as they approached the wall they were met by a volley of bullets, fired by a German soldier from under the archway that led from the garden to the front of the church. Dominique took the full force of the onslaught and fell only yards from the wall. Otto Bauer lifted his sub machine gun and emptied the contents into the firing soldier, who immediately crumpled to the ground.

"Quick, let's go," gasped Bauer, astonished at what he had just done.

"But we can't leave Dominique," pleaded Agathe, devastated that, after all, her companion had perished only yards from safety.

"Sister, I'm afraid she's dead. We can't stop. Other soldiers will be here any minute."

Bauer helped the nun over the wall and immediately followed close behind. They skirted round the back of a deserted house and along the edge of a field. Keeping close to a hedge that bordered the Limoges road they headed out of the village. Both were shaking and sobbing uncontrollably as the enormity of the horror from which they had escaped began to sink in.

Sister Agathe stole a glance back towards the village. Plumes of smoke were rising from several locations around its centre. The church was now completely engulfed by fire and smoke. Flames were lapping over the tops of the walls above the sacristy. The steeple had partially collapsed and it was obviously only a matter of time before the whole pyramid fell into the tower. Flames and smoke were shooting out almost horizontally from most of the windows. Agathe squirmed agonisingly at the now certain fate of the two Jewish families committed to her care. Regrets were already crowding into her mind. Perhaps they would have been safer in the convent – maybe the Germans wouldn't have found their hideaway, or perhaps they would have been safer making their own way, rather than trusting the Resistance? Should they have headed south, away from the Allied invasion and thus in the opposite direction to German reinforcements making their way north?

But she could never have imagined that the outcome of any of their choices could have been the senseless, stark brutality of this fateful day in Oradour. It now appeared that around 400 women and children had perished in the church and probably hundreds of men in other locations. And all she could do now was pray.

CHAPTER NINETEEN

On finding Jonathan's body, Samuel had wandered aimlessly for several days, merely trying to keep out of sight of the Interahamwe who were marauding in the area. He would have liked to have been able to say that his inertia was due to the difficulty of making the choice between returning to the border to find his family or pressing on to Nyarubuye to try and save his pupils and neighbours. But, in truth, he had no high-minded thoughts at this stage. He was numb, his grief all-encompassing, his sense of desolation total. Nothing mattered any more, not even the fate of the rest of his family. Samuel could never have believed that he could be indifferent to the survival of those he loved. But he had descended to a place where notions of love and compassion for others were absent. He was living in a void, a place set apart from normal existence. He felt nothing except aching loss and hopelessness. He could only just rouse himself to steal a few scraps of food from the many deserted houses round about. There was water in abundance in the many bowsers and tanks attached to houses that had been left abandoned in the vicinity. He could survive physically but there was nothing left of his life beyond that.

Although Samuel had been wandering around without much purpose he had at least had the presence of mind to keep reasonably close to the road to Nyarabuye. Occasionally, when it appeared safe, he would descend to the road and walk towards his home town for a few kilometres before disappearing back into the undergrowth for protection. One day, while tramping along the road to Nyarubuye, a small family group appeared in the distance in front of him. Rwandans are hospitable and friendly people and ordinarily would welcome the opportunity to chat to anyone they met. But times were different now. Every person you met could be your killer. Samuel darted behind a tree at the side of the road, waiting for the group to pass and hoping that he hadn't been seen.

As they got closer however Samuel felt that there was something familiar about the rather bedraggled family walking slowly in his direction. Maybe it was the way they walked or their profiles silhouetted by the sun, which seemed to be tracking their progress. But whatever it was Samuel sensed that he knew them. They were obviously joining the mass exodus out of the country as they were laden down with as many bags of possessions as they could possibly carry. But most people had fled days ago. Why flee now when most of the killings had probably been carried out?

As the figures grew larger Samuel knew the answers to both questions. As the group passed the tree Samuel whispered, "Thomas?"

Thomas Cyiza started at the sound, fearing an ambush, but when he saw the owner of the voice that had startled him, his face broke into a broad grin. The two men embraced and there was much back slapping and hugging. Samuel also embraced Thomas's wife, Amelie and their three children. Thomas had been Samuel's Hutu neighbour who had urged him to flee when the news of Habyarimana's assassination broke.

They sat by the side of the road, genuinely enjoying the knowledge of their mutual survival. Eventually Thomas dared to ask Samuel about the rest of the family,

"Chantalle and the children, Samuel, are they safe?"

There was silence. Samuel knew that he would have to face this question but, now that the moment had come, he didn't know how to respond.

"I left Chantalle, Anatolie, Grace and Marthe on the Tanzanian side of the Rusomo border post. I told them that it would be safe, that the Tanzanians would look after them. But I don't know. They were with Leon and some others. I just hope they made it."

"And Jonathan?"

Samuel looked down. It was the first time anyone had mentioned Jonathan's name since his murder. He had dreaded this moment. It was bad enough dealing with his own grief privately, but now he had to do it publicly as well.

"Jonathan is…dead," he sobbed, cupping his head in his hands and swaying from side to side as if physically trying to displace his sorrow.

Thomas, Amelie and the children were soon sharing his grief, crying with him but yet still trying to comfort the bereaved father. The events of the last few days had strongly polarized relationships between Rwandans. Some had been intent on murdering their friends and neighbours, consumed by a tribal hatred that had been festering for years. They had been able to personalise their feelings of bitterness and injustice onto those with whom, for years, they had lived and worked. One day they were talking to, working with, sharing food among their Hutu or Tutsi neighbours, sharing their joy, weeping at their misfortune, watching their children playing together, joining in festivals and celebrations. The next, they were betraying each other, burning down their houses, raping their women and murdering their kinsmen in a cold-hearted and brutal rage. These were not crimes of passion, committed in the heat of the moment almost before they were aware of their actions. No, these were planned and vindictive assassinations, ethnic cleansing, genocide. No words could adequately explain the motives of those carrying out such crimes.

On the other hand, many Rwandans were brought closer together during the atrocities. Hutus sheltered Tutsis, often at the risk of their own lives. Hutu collaborators were regarded by the Interahamwe as the 'worst of the worst' – traitors for whom any quick death was too lenient. If caught, they faced torture and an excruciating, lingering death. But still they protected their neighbours and colleagues. Some even defended their friends physically, taking up whatever they could find, pieces of wood, hoes, spades, anything with which to beat off the aggressors. The genocide was manufactured to divide Rwandan society on tribal lines but, in some cases, the reverse happened. The bonds between Hutu and Tutsi strengthened. Tribal identities and boundaries disappeared. Suffering was shared, pain and injury borne reciprocally, hearts equally broken. Thomas and Amelie, Hutus, shared such a moment with Samuel, a Tutsi, by the side of that lonely road. They just cried and hugged each other, not speaking until the sorrow could express itself no longer. Spent. Drained. Rock bottom.

Eventually Samuel sighed, as if signifying his return to the physical, tangible world. It had not occurred to him until now that his friends might have been fleeing too.

"Why are you leaving?" he asked.

Thomas replied, "Samuel, it was terrible. I tried to warn them but it was too late. The militiamen with that evil Ndagijimana's little white cards were visiting every Tutsi house in the town. They would call out the family name and when they came out the soldiers would hack them to death with their machetes. They would loot whatever they could from the property and then burn it to the ground. Anyone who survived just ran off into the bush. Many of the bodies were just left where they fell, but every now and then a truck would come by and pick up some of them. I was told that the bodies were dumped in the rivers or lakes.

'Send them back to Ethiopia where they belong', the soldiers chanted. What could we do? Samuel, these were our friends. Earlier on today, Jeremiah Dusaidi, remember him, he's the son of Ernest, who used to be the Responsable de Cellule?"

Samuel nodded.

"Well, he was going round all the houses, at least any that were left, telling all the Tutsis to go to the church, that they would be safe there. Ndagijimana had 'guaranteed' it. I tried to tell him that the Bourgmestre's guarantee was about as useful as a Twa in an orchard. You know, he knows the names of all the fruits but is too small to reach any of them."

They all laughed. Absurd really. The first time Samuel had laughed in days. There was tragedy all around but they laughed and laughed until their sides ached.

Eventually Thomas was able to continue, soberly as he remembered their last few hours in Nyarubuye.

"Anyway, we didn't believe him and tried to tell the other Tutsis not to go. But we knew that we, as Hutus, couldn't stay either. Sooner or later there will be a Tutsi backlash. The RPF will arrive and any Hutus left will be killed. It's the way of our country. Not your way, Samuel, not ours either but it is the way – an eye for an eye, a tooth for a tooth. We wouldn't be safe, so we're going to Tanzania too."

"You are good people, my friends," answered Samuel putting an arm round Thomas and Amelie. "You have nothing to fear."

"You are good too, Samuel, but look what happened to you. There is no fairness in all of this, no logic. We just have to survive."

Amelie had a resigned look on her face and shrugged her shoulders.

"Samuel, we cannot take any risks with the children. Their safety is all that matters to us."

Immediately she had said this, Amelie knew that she was wrong. She hadn't meant it that way – suggesting that Samuel had let Jonathan down in not being able to guarantee his safety.

"I'm sorry, Samuel, I didn't mean it like that. I know you would have done everything you could."

"No, Amelie, that's just the problem. I didn't. I was too busy looking after everyone else to notice that my own son was missing. Can you imagine how that feels? But he still shouldn't have died. They shouldn't have killed him like that. Shot in the back of the head. A little boy. Just a boy…"

Samuel's voice trailed off into silence.

"You know what is so bad," Samuel went on, "I don't feel that I can ever forgive. You know, I have always been a reasonable man – a Christian and a churchgoer. I have always tried to see the other person's point of view. But I'm changing. How can I ever understand people who would do such a terrible thing? And if I can't understand, how can I ever forgive? I could never do to a child what they have done to mine. It's just inhuman. It's as if we are living in another world where the normal rules of behaviour don't apply and where people are driven by a higher authority. I feel as if I'm being drawn into this world. I don't like it but if I came across Jonathan's killers I couldn't be responsible for my actions."

"Samuel, you mustn't talk like this." Thomas was concerned at this change in his friend's attitude. "That's exactly what the killers want to happen. To whip up hatred so that murder leads to murder, to make us all driven by revenge so that the killing goes on. You're playing into their hands. In times of chaos the man with the gun has power. It almost doesn't matter whether it's a Hutu or a Tutsi pulling the trigger. Whatever side he is on, a murderer is still a murderer and he spreads his gospel through a desire for revenge. We have to break this cycle, Samuel, and you won't do it through hatred."

"Yes I know, you're right," answered Samuel. "It's been good to talk to you. You'd better carry on. It's a long walk to the border. Watch out for the militia. I'll be praying that you get there safely."

"But what about you, Samuel?" Amelie interjected. "Aren't you coming with us?"

"No, Amelie. I promised that I would never leave my pupils so I must go back and rescue as many as possible. You say that the Tutsis will be at Nyarubuye church. Well, that's where I must be as well. If Ndagijimana can't guarantee their safety then I must help them escape, now that I know the way and the dangers...."

Samuel's voice trailed away as his thoughts turned once again to Jonathan. Yes, he knew the dangers. And if there was any good that could come out of his death it would be the rescue of the other children. There must be some of his classmates in the church, the sons and daughters of other parents who should not have to endure the pain that Samuel had experienced. This could be Jonathan's legacy.

"Samuel, you can't go back," pleaded Thomas. "What can you do? You are just one man. Do you think the Interahamwe or the Bourgmestre are going to spare you just because you are a bereaved father? They will kill you along with all the others. Come with us. Let's try and find Chantalle and the children. Don't you think they'll be worried about you? Chantalle doesn't want to lose a husband, your children don't want to lose a father. Come."

With that, Thomas held out his hand, but Samuel shook his head. After silently embracing his friends he walked slowly back down the road to Nyarubuye. There was a determined look on his face. Thomas knew it was hopeless to try and persuade him further. But he was apprehensive. He could not be sure that Samuel's determination was due to love and duty or to something altogether more sinister. They watched as he disappeared into the distance, not looking back, not even to wave goodbye. Amelie sighed and motioned to the others to pick up their bags. They must get to Tanzania as soon as possible.

* * *

It took Samuel a couple of hours to reach Nyarubuye church and it was by then about 4p.m. The town was deserted. Even the animals seemed to have fled. Where houses had once stood there were now just piles of blackened ash. Any houses remaining intact showed no sign of human activity. But Samuel couldn't escape the feeling that he was being watched. He felt exposed, even though he was using the back paths and, where these petered out, he was jumping from garden to garden to avoid using the roads as much as possible. The atmosphere was uneasy, threatening. Sporadic gunfire could be heard, sometimes sharp and close at hand, at others more muffled and remote. Mortars were obviously being fired, their presence revealed by plumes of smoke which suddenly appeared on the horizon. Samuel closed his eyes as he imagined the fate of those caught in the path of those bombs. Lives snuffed out in an instant. How quickly the status of people changed in a conflict, from beloved daughter to orphan, from mother to childless widow, from independent father to helpless beggar, from proud homeowner to landless migrant.

Even if Samuel hadn't seen the Catholic church he would have known that he was close from the line of tall trees on either side of the track leading up to it. It was not a particularly impressive vista by western standards but it had an element of grandeur in Rwanda. The tall trees led the eye towards the high tower of the sandstone building. The contiguity of two such large objects, one natural, the other man made, was striking. Samuel could see people everywhere in the church complex. Not just people but animals too. Cattle were grazing on the meagre grass in the church gardens, the proud possessions of the residents of Nyarubuye brought with them to safety.

Some were gathered under the white marble statue of Christ, his hands outstretched in welcome above the entrance. Others were in and around the school classrooms that fringed the main church building. People were standing and talking in the cloisters and the churchyard. Indeed it could almost have been a normal Sunday, with the congregation gathering for worship. As he got closer he recognised several regular worshippers, other near neighbours and even some pupils from his school. There was no sign of any militia or even any government officials. Perhaps he had misjudged the Bourgmestre. Maybe he did respect the sanctuary of the church.

Approaching the entrance, Samuel could see an elegant, upright elderly man talking animatedly with a group of other men. He had typically Tutsi features, a long slim face with a thin straight nose. His short hair was flecked with grey, giving him a distinguished, noble look. He was dressed colonially in a light beige flannel suit, white shirt and brown tie. He could have been attending a cocktail party at the Belgian embassy in the capital Kigali rather than a gathering of displaced, frightened refugees. But Ernest Dusaidi had to keep up appearances for the sake of the citizens who now appeared to be under his care. It was he who had encouraged them to gather at the church for their own safety. He must therefore present the face of normality and security. After all, he had endorsed the Bourgmestre's guarantee of safety. Without his blessing the people would not have gathered at the church. Even though he had not sought leadership of the Tutsi diaspora in Nyarubuye, it appeared to have been thrust upon him.

The discussion between Ernest and the group of men was extremely animated. Samuel listened on the fringe of the gathering, unnoticed in the intensity of the debate.

"Mr Dusaidi," one man ventured, "you cannot expect me and my family to stay in this church indefinitely, without proper food and water. What's more, we are a sitting target. If the Interahamwe want to kill some more Tutsis, well here we are! All nicely collected together in one place, packaged ready for slaughter. What more could they want?"

"He's right," another man agreed, "we must go to the Bourgmestre and insist on safe passage out of Nyarubuye. I'd rather take my chances on the open road than sit around here just waiting day after day. OK, the RPF may be on their way but the Hutus will want to destroy as many witnesses as possible before they arrive."

There was a general murmur of approval from the other men in the group. Ernest thought for a while before answering.

"The Bourgmestre gave me his word that you would be safe. My son, Jeremiah, and Silas Rudatigura heard him too. I have worked under him for many years and I do not believe he would lie to me. However, in view of your concerns I will go and see him and if any of you would like to come with…"

He stopped as a small boy ran into the group, half running, half falling, and planted himself right in front of Ernest.

"Mister, mister," he blurted," the Bourgmestre's here. Look." He pointed to a succession of jeeps and trucks approaching the church.

One of the men cynically exclaimed, "Here we are, Ernest, right on cue. We can all go and ask him how he is going to look after us."

The cavalcade stopped about thirty metres away from Ernest and his men. A cloud of dust was blown up as the each vehicle slid to a halt. Communal police and militia soldiers emerged from each vehicle. Many of the men wore berets and kitenge uniforms bearing MRND and Interahamwe insignia. They were unloading grenades, firearms and machetes and placing them on the ground in front of the church.

The Bourgmestre, Julius Ndagijimana, emerged from one of the jeeps, resplendent in military fatigues. Ernest stepped forwards.

"Julius, what is all this about?" he asked. "Why do you need all these men and all these weapons?" He pointed at the, by now, large arsenal lying on the ground. "We have your guarantee of safety. There is no need for you to come here armed so heavily."

"Ernest, yesterday some of my men were shot at when they approached the church. You are obviously harbouring Tutsi traitors in the place of God and have betrayed my trust in you."

"But Bourgmestre, a few men fired arrows and threw stones at a small group of militia who threatened us. We are not 'Tutsi traitors', we were just defending ourselves against a few soldiers who we assumed must have been renegades. We didn't think that they were anything to do with you as you had promised that we wouldn't be attacked."

"Enough of this," snarled Ndagijimana. "All Tutsis get into the church. Anyone with a Hutu identity card can leave." With that the Bourgmestre started to hand out weapons to the police and soldiers.

A few Hutus started to drift off down the road. As they passed the vehicles one of the soldiers pointed at a man and shouted, "He's a Tutsi." The man reached into his pocket and produced his identity card but before it could be checked he had crumpled to the ground, shot dead by the Bourgmestre's own hand, his Hutu ID card flapping open on the ground beside him.

"No time for any of that," Ndagijimana barked, as he started to fire indiscriminately into the crowd outside the church.

This was the signal for all the other attackers to begin firing. Bodies began dropping to the floor like skittles in a bowling alley – face down on the concrete, slumped over walls, splayed out on the grass, contorted into postures only achievable by the dead. The Tutsis were screaming and rushing around all over the complex. A few brave men and boys were firing arrows into the soldiers or attacking them with homemade spears. But they were shot or struck down by machetes before they could do any serious damage. Once the archers had been cleared from the entrance to the church the soldiers threw grenades into the building, before rushing in and unleashing a fusillade of bullets at the hundreds of Tutsis who were cowering behind the pews. Other militiamen and police began to search all the rooms in the church and school, hacking down anyone they found there. Some fanned out into the bushes and fields surrounding the church, killing any Tutsis who had managed to escape and were hiding there.

Samuel had run into the church when the shooting started, shouting at all those inside to get down. He ran around the church desperately searching for any means of escape. Apart from the entrance there were only two other doors from which anyone could leave the building. By now, bodies had piled up in each exit blocking any means of escape. In any case, militiamen must have been waiting outside ready to kill escapees. Samuel slid under a pew and waited. Soon, he heard the Bourgmestre shouting to his men to finish off those who had been injured, making sure everyone was dead. He could just see the soldiers slashing away violently at bodies in the aisle and under the pews. He felt nothing as the machete crashed down on his own head leading him into a dark and empty void.

CHAPTER TWENTY

Samuel had always been taught at school that hell was a place of 'wailing and gnashing of teeth.' So, can this be hell, he thought? There was no wailing – indeed it was deadly quiet. There was no gnashing of teeth, just a thudding ache that seemed to originate from the centre of his head and spread out to each corner of his skull, before flowing down his spine. And then there was the feeling of heaviness, of an enormous weight bearing down upon him in the darkness. It was cold and damp and there was an unpleasant smell. It was a smell he had not experienced before, but yet he felt he should be able identify it, as it seemed to be human, a bodily odour, something vaguely familiar. So perhaps this was hell. Pain, darkness, heaviness, coldness and an unpleasant odour …but would there be laughter in hell – a kind of drunken, discordant pleasure, punctuated by the noise of smashing glass and raucous cheering?

He tried to move, but the pain in his head became unbearable. Momentarily he passed out, as if each synapse in his brain needed to recover from the surge of pain transmitted through it. His nervous system was overloaded and needed to be reset.

When he came to, he tried once more to move his head and, this time, he could rotate it about forty five degrees to the right. He could now breathe more easily and suddenly realised the source of the smell he had been trying to identify. Blood, human blood. Not just small quantities of it but puddles. It was wet against his face and cold. Maybe he was dead after all or otherwise how could the blood be cold?

He tried to move his left arm but it was wrapped around his head as if protecting his most vital organ. The elbow and upper arm felt wedged into position by a heavy weight bearing down from above. Samuel now turned to his right arm, which was by his side. Concentrating with all his powers he attempted to move it – just an inch at first, then slightly more as he became more confident that it was in working order. Aagh, he felt something cold and sticky and then, moving further along, a piece of fabric, cotton maybe, but caked in a dry substance, making it hard and brittle to the touch. These did not seem to be his own clothes but whose were they?

Now for his legs. His left one, like the rest of the left side of his body, was pinned down but his right leg felt freer. He moved it slightly, then a little more, before striking something hard. This produced a low, muffled moan but Samuel knew that he had made no sound himself. It was dark and he could see nothing, and he was deeply confused both about what had happened to him and his current situation. But there was no other explanation for what he was now feeling and hearing. He was not alone. Other people were lying in the same place with him and, from the silence, some of them must be dead. Overwhelmed, he sank back into the relief of unconsciousness.

When Samuel awoke again it was still dark and completely noiseless. There was no sound of alcoholic merriment. Time seemed immaterial to him, but Samuel guessed it must be early in the morning and he knew that he had to try and leave before it got light to find a safer hiding place. He also had to locate something to drink, as his thirst was now raging. He knew that he must have lost a lot of blood and must now be seriously dehydrated. The noise of the rats rustling around him was disconcerting and the sound of chomping as the vermin started to consume the rotting flesh disgusted Samuel. He wasn't indignant at the rats, as they were just following their natural instincts, but at the humiliation it brought on those around him. Brutally murdered in a church, piled on top of each other in the open air like garbage, and now ripped to pieces in public by predators – there could be no more degrading exit from this life. But somehow his indignation gave him strength as slowly he tried to slide the left side of his trunk out from under the bodies on top of him. He hoped that his left arm and leg would largely extricate themselves, dragged to freedom by the momentum of the rest of his body. But he could not feel his left arm. He could tell that it was resting against his skull from the pressure on his head but, when he tried to move it, there was no response.

Centimetre by centimetre he slid out to his right. Samuel moved slowly, partly from the sheer exhaustion of every movement, and partly to keep as quiet as possible. Even though he could not feel his left arm, it was being dragged free as his head and trunk laboriously edged towards a small open space between Samuel and the next body. Eventually he managed to slip away from under the weight of the bodies, which slumped into the space he had vacated. Samuel just lay there, utterly shattered by the effort of his liberation.

Gradually he began the process of checking the functioning of his limbs. His head ached intolerably but he was able to move it up and down and from side to side. Lucidity was returning to him and he started to appreciate the decisions he must take. A survival plan was taking shape in Samuel's mind and, as it did, he realised that, miraculously, he didn't appear to have suffered any serious brain damage. He could feel his legs and waggle his toes. He tried to lift his right leg and bend it at the knee. Mission accomplished, he then tried the same manoeuvre with his left leg. It was painful, his leg was shaking and it made him feel a little dizzy, but again he was able to achieve a good range of movement.

Samuel had already established that his right arm was in good working order, so he could now use it to feel the front part of his upper body, first the genitals, then the stomach followed by the chest and shoulders. His clothes were ripped and, what was left of them was now brittle with dried blood and other bodily fluids. but so far so good. There did not appear to be any major damage. Samuel knew that he needed to try and sit up to survey the damage to his left arm and ascertain his chances of escape. Every movement was agony but, after several minutes of painstakingly slow progress, he managed to haul himself into a sitting position, his back resting against a pile of bodies behind him. He was breathing heavily partly through the physical exertion of reaching an upright position and partly as a result of the pain that was sweeping through his body. He did not dare cry out and deep breathing was his only way of managing the severe pain as he nudged his body upwards. Samuel would never have believed that such a simple movement could have involved such agony and have taken such an eternity. Never again would he complain at having to fetch a chair for one of his pupils or some wood for the stove for Chantalle.

At this moment his vision of paradise would be taking a few painful steps. It didn't need to be his usual confident swagger, but a shuffle, a stagger, even a crawl. As long as it was carrying him away from this dreadful place, from this fetid grave, anywhere but this hell. Tears started to roll down his cheeks and he began to sob. Every convulsion hurt, but he couldn't help himself. As consciousness and feeling returned to him so did the reality of his situation, the utter horror of recent events but, worst of all, the sheer terror of being completely alone.

After a while his weeping subsided. He was now spent, drained of humanity. Animal instinct was now his only hope of survival. Overwhelmed by sorrow, he hadn't even thought of checking his left arm but now he did so. As he had sat up his arm had flopped down from his head without Samuel feeling it at all. Looking down he could see that it was cut deeply in several places and flesh, muscle and bone protruded in varying proportions from each wound. Blood was still seeping out although it appeared to have a sticky consistency. Samuel could see that he had lost a lot of blood from the wounds. His sleeve was soaked red, but worst of all he could feel nothing beneath his left shoulder. Samuel's guess was that his arm had saved his life. He could only assume, from the position in which he had originally found it, that he had involuntarily raised his arm to protect his head from the machete blows. This had deflected the worst strikes from his head, but his arm had taken a terrible battering. But he had been lucky. The Interahamwe had obviously thrown him on the pile of bodies with his arm still bent over his head in a raised position. This must have acted to stem the blood loss. He knew from his debility that he must have lost a lot of blood, but he was still alive although he urgently needed medical help.

He must make a superhuman effort to stand up. But as he attempted to lever himself up, using his one good arm and both legs, he froze. He could hear something – the sound of a body moving among the dead, a steady panting sound and the noise of clothing being ripped off. Was this one of the guards coming back to finish off any survivors or perhaps a looter looking for any pickings that the guards had missed? He held his breath, not daring to move. His best hope lay in sitting still, putting his head back against the nearest body and feigning death. He hoped that his bloody physical appearance would persuade any potential murderer not to waste any energy on him. The panting and sound of footsteps was getting closer. Whoever it was, they were clearly walking on top of the bodies. Every sinew in Samuel's body was ready to defend himself if he felt an attack was imminent. He had always been a good athlete with a heightened muscle twitch. While it was comforting to know that he was ready for a fight, despite his desperate physical condition, Samuel was concerned that he might be too alert, unable to suppress an involuntary movement as he pretended to be dead.

He was very close now. Samuel could smell his breath – foul and malodorous yet surprisingly alcohol free. Any moment now his opponent would strike. Samuel felt something cold and wet on his face. He could resist no longer and struck out with his right hand, thumping it against his attacker's body. Eyes wide open, rising to his feet, Samuel readied himself for the fight. But the manky, brown wild dog had already departed, looking for easier pickings at the other side of the mound of bodies.

Samuel steadied himself, swaying uneasily as his head spun at a dizzying pace. Must stay on my feet, he thought. It took a supreme act of courage and will to remain upright but, within a minute or two, the swaying stopped. He felt more secure and, for the first time, was able to survey the scene in front of him. He was standing at the edge of a pile of about twenty bodies, at the foot of the steps leading up to the entrance of the church. Some of the bodies were headless, others had no hands or feet. The Hutus were always jealous of our height, he thought. This is their way of cutting us down to size. The bodies looked like sacks thrown haphazardly in a shapeless pile, static and silent.

Moving painfully away from his resting place for the first time,

Samuel could see bodies everywhere. One was spreadeagled grotesquely under the statue of Christ, others were draped over walls and steps. All seemed to have been sliced by machetes and some had clearly had their Achilles tendons cut in two to ensure that they could not run off. Strangely, despite the horror, the bodies looked peaceful, resting almost artistically on the ground, contorted into unique patterns, almost beautiful. Yet these poor souls had died the most brutal and painful deaths. One machete blow could kill but to be sure of death ten, twelve or even fifteen strikes would be necessary, each blow sapping a little more life out of the unfortunate victim. Then they would be left to bleed until the final inevitable outcome.

Rounding the corner of the main frontage of the church Samuel observed a group of about ten or twelve bodies slumped directly under the wall of the building – victims of a firing squad. Samuel wretched as a vivid flashback tortured his mind – another pile of bodies, fallen in line, one of them his son Jonathan. Strangely the bodies appeared to have fallen with their hands outstretched to the front, palms open. One man still had one fist clenched. Samuel stepped forwards, unwilling to violate the dead, but yet intrigued by this unusual sight. Gently he prised open the man's fingers and, immediately he saw what the man was holding, he understood. These were the lucky ones. The man was holding a coin – one Rwandan franc. The guards had missed it. These victims had been able to buy a quick death. One bullet was a merciful end compared to the prolonged hacking by a machete but the soldiers would not waste precious ammunition for no return.

Samuel wondered what the price of an instant death had been – 100? 200? 500 Rwandan francs? At least Jonathan had been spared an excruciating and drawn out passing, despite having had no money with which to bribe his killers. Or maybe one of the other victims had kindly paid Jonathan's share of the cost.

Samuel had not been conscious of any logic to his meanderings around this scene of genocide. However, perhaps subconsciously, his raging thirst had been leading him to the water tank located by the back end of the church. He had passed it many times before but scarcely given it a second look. Now he drank its contents as if it were the river of life. Great gulps of it, choking as he tried to satisfy his unquenchable thirst. Unthinking he immersed his whole head into the tank, pulling up sharply as the coldness of the water hit him and smarting from the sudden pain that tore through his head as the liquid penetrated deep into his wound. Still it felt good – he was alive again.

A little feeling was returning to his left arm, but he knew that he needed medical attention as soon as possible. Samuel circled further round the church, avoiding the piles of bodies that seemed to be lying everywhere. How many had died that day, hundreds, maybe thousands? Suddenly his foot struck a round object, which then rolled noisily away. He picked up the empty bottle of beer and smelt it – banana beer, a local favourite. It had seemed incongruous lying there, as inert as the dead bodies, but a symbol of pleasure rather than pain. Rwandan banana beer had a very high alcohol content and could induce a drunken stupor after only a few bottles. This was fortunate as, lying on the ground a few metres away, were about a dozen soldiers, splayed out on the grass surrounded by piles of broken beer bottles. Samuel now knew the source of the sound of breaking glass he had heard when he first regained consciousness.

No guard had been posted by the soldiers, presumably because they thought they had killed everyone in the vicinity, and the sleeping men looked totally spaced out. Samuel was thus able to skirt around the back of the group with impunity. The embers in the fire were still glowing and the carcass of a calf, which had slipped from the spit on which it was being roasted and had fallen into the fire, was slowly being consumed by the flames. An occasional crackle punctuated the otherwise deathly silence. The men, having slaughtered Tutsi humans, had then slaughtered Tutsi cattle and gorged themselves on the proceeds. It was strange, thought Samuel, that he was almost as outraged at the killing of the cattle as of the humans but, in some respects, it was almost the same thing. Taking what's not yours. Violating another person's property whether it was their life or their cattle was just a question of degree. The root cause was the same and it frightened Samuel that he was starting to identify with that cause. Ethnic cleansing, revenge, jealousy, he could satisfy all three here and now. No doubt he could kill several of the sleepers before anyone woke up.

There were machetes aplenty to hand – gleaming in the moonlight. But with several blows needed to kill each one there was no chance that he could finish the job before being discovered and, in his present state, there was no prospect of escape. Killing one of the soldiers would be signing his own death warrant.

Revenge could wait until he was fitter. But even in his weakened state the rage that was burning within him, after all that he had seen and all that he had been through, would ensure that this slaughter before him and the death of his beloved son would be avenged.

CHAPTER TWENTY ONE

Otto Bauer inched open the barn door and peered inside. It was dark, natural light only penetrating the building through gaps in the corrugated sheeting that comprised the upper part of the barn's walls. Adjusting slowly to the darkness, his eyes searched methodically around the building. It was largely empty although a few sacks of animal feed were piled up against the right hand wall and bales of hay were stored against the left. A few pieces of agricultural equipment were spread over the concrete floor and rolls of rope and flex were hanging haphazardly around its walls.

"Come," whispered Bauer to Sister Agathe in German, pointing towards the bales of hay and silently closing the barn door behind them. Exhausted they slumped onto the hay, throwing their heads back onto the coarse surface. For Agathe, it was the first time she had rested since leaving the convent twenty four hours previously. For the first time the tension that had held her in a tightly coiled spring started to unwind. In place of the adrenaline came a sombre realisation of the enormity and horror of the past twenty four hours. The destruction of the convent, the long walk to Madranges, the betrayal by the priest and the mass murder in Oradour church pressed upon her like a weight, which she could touch and feel, but which there was no prospect of her lifting away.

She could see some of the faces of those who had died starkly vivid in her mind. She had caught a glimpse of thirteen year old Matthias Katz as he had fled across the church towards the sacristy to a certain death. It was a look of terror, pale and wide eyed. No histrionics just an all consuming fear, a headless rush for survival. The image kept flashing across her mind. She was powerless to prevent the flashbacks – the grenade exploding in the baby's pram, the bullets tearing through Dominique Malraux with such force that she was lifted off the ground before she crumpled hideously at Agathe's feet.

She looked at Otto Bauer, still in full military uniform. His cap had fallen over his brow as he had slumped onto the hay. She could clearly see the Death's Head cap badge of Der Führer regiment. It was a grotesque skull and crossbones, the skull of which was distended by slits at the top and the side. The effect of this was to elongate the skull making it look barely human. In shape it was more like a lion's skull with a huge brow and powerful mouth framing broadened eye sockets. Given such an emblem, the brutality of the regiment was hardly surprising.

"You risked your life for me but I don't even know your name," ventured Agathe, desperate for some human contact to try and suppress the horrific images flooding her mind.

"My name is Otto Bauer. I saved your life without knowing your name either. Perhaps it's not so important after all."

"No, maybe not, but I'm Sister Agathe Deladier and I am very grateful. Why did you do it?"

"I've been asking myself that same question too. You know I'm not the heroic type. The Major, I'm his Adjutant you see, used to describe me as a snivelling little weasel. I don't suppose his opinion has changed much but maybe I've been elevated from snivelling to treacherous!"

Otto laughed at the thought of Major Hautmann's reaction to the news of his betrayal.

"I've hated this war from the very beginning. I just didn't have the balls to become a conscientious objector or defect or whatever. Oops, sorry about my language, I had quite forgotten that I was speaking to a lady of your calling."

Agathe smiled. She found Otto's candour refreshing after life in the convent, where she couldn't always be sure exactly what the Mother Superior and the other nuns were thinking behind their holy and demure exteriors.

"Otto, well why didn't you walk out?"

"Because of the pink triangle."

"I don't understand. What do you mean?" questioned Agathe.

"I'm sorry, Sister, of course you aren't German and couldn't be expected to know what it means. If I refused to fight in this meaningless war I would be put in a camp with other objectors. Life would be hard with little to eat or drink, few clothes to wear and only boards to sleep on. The work we would have to do would be punishing and physically draining and the beatings would be regular. I could put up with all of that but they would make me wear a pink triangle, as happened to a friend of mine. They put a pail over his head, stripped him naked and set their ravenous German Shepherds on him. The dogs ripped him to pieces, his screams amplified by the pail over his head. He was eaten alive. If a German wearing a pink triangle went into the sick bay, they didn't come out alive. They would be tortured in the name of medical experimentation."

"But why do people have to wear the pink triangle?"

Agathe was getting exasperated as she didn't understand the point that Otto was trying to make.

"For sexual deviancy…homosexuality by another name. It started at school with a boy in my class. I fancied him like mad. He was tall and slender with a really tight bottom. He had beautiful curly black hair and large, dark brown eyes. I used to sit in class about two rows behind him and just off to the right. I could drool over him the whole time without him ever knowing. Sometimes, early in the morning when the sun was shining it was like a spotlight on him, illuminating every feature. He was like an angel, almost transcendent. For years I kept my infatuation secret, barely saying a word to him. You can't imagine how it consumed me – a love without verbal or physical expression. My obsession was fed by every frustration, every glance unreturned, every smile ignored.

Then one day, my class had the opportunity to go to Berlin to see the Olympics. It was supposed to be a showcase for Nazi supremacy. What nonsense! Anyway I cheered and shouted for Jesse Owens, you know that black American runner. Lots of my friends did too…but not my idol. He just sat there. I was sitting next to him, can you believe it?

I asked him what the problem was. He just shook his head. I put my arm around him…oh heaven…but he still remained silent. But this was my chance. I asked him if he would like to talk about it some time. He nodded and suggested that I came round to his house the next evening. He told me his address, which I must have repeated in my head about 500 times on the way home. I was desperate not to forget it. As I left the bus I touched him again, just on the back of the neck, almost accidentally. Probably no-one else noticed, but I hoped that he felt the warmth of my fingers on the back of his neck and the soft caress of my thumb as I pulled my hand down onto his shoulder. See you tomorrow, I whispered.

I didn't sleep that night and didn't listen to any of the lessons the next day. The teachers shouted at me to concentrate, but I didn't care. I couldn't look at my love during class but right at the end of the day I caught his glance. He was smiling at me. That was all the confirmation I needed.

I must have changed clothes a dozen times to try and find the right look. I didn't have many clothes because times were hard and there were few fashionable garments in the shops but I wanted to make sure that I was wearing the best possible combination of items. I told my parents I was doing my homework. If only they'd known what I was really doing and why! When the time came I picked up my school bag and told my parents that I was going to a friend's house to help him with his homework. I threw the bag into our neighbour's hedge.

I paced around outside his house for some time before I had the courage to knock on the door. I was desperately hoping that he hadn't forgotten but also almost wishing that I didn't have to go through with it. The tension was unbearable. I was a bit disappointed that the door was opened by a large matronly woman whom I supposed to be his mother but she quickly showed me to his bedroom. He was sitting on his bed wearing black shorts and a brown shirt. In his hand he held a small dagger. I knew what it said on it – 'Blood and Honour'. There was a swastika badge on his left arm. He didn't say hello but asked me straight out if I knew what a 175er was. I was rather naïve and had never heard of that term. He explained that it was a name for a homosexual based on paragraph 175 of the German constitution, which made homosexuality a criminal offence. He told me that he was upset at the Olympics because Jesse Owens was a black man. It was an insult to the Hitler Youth for him to be winning gold medals, just as it was for there to be homosexuals living in Germany. He looked me right in the eye. It was a menacing look and I knew exactly what it meant.

I kept quiet after that. When conscription was brought in I had to sign up. I have hated myself ever since. I was too scared to stand up for my identity. I had heard all the horror stories of what the Nazis did to homosexuals and I was a coward – until today. It was as if all the injustices of Nazism were written up on a board in front of me. All I had to do to get rid of them was to shoot at it. I wasn't really killing a Nazi soldier but the whole Nazi edifice. The way it has dehumanised all Germans, forcing us to hide our true feelings and aspirations. Do you know, I didn't even notice which soldier I killed. He could have been a friend of mine. There were one or two decent ones in our regiment. I feel bad about that. It wasn't personal but I just couldn't let another injustice happen. I had seen too many. What happened in the church was beyond evil. No-one will ever be able to explain it. But I just couldn't let you be killed as well. I don't suppose that saving the life of one person will do much good but it was sort of symbolic…"

Otto's voice trailed off into silence as if he didn't really understand what he was saying. Yet somehow he did know that he had been right to do what he did. Perhaps he had just tipped the scales of justice in the right direction. He had maybe brought a little light into the darkness.

Agathe too was silent. There was so much to take in. Less than an hour ago they had been total strangers, even enemies. Now she knew Otto Bauer's intimate secrets – things he probably hadn't told anyone else. Funnily enough, she wasn't shocked. Sister Anne-Marie had always taught the nuns at the convent that homosexuals were sinful. Yet it was just such a sinner who had saved her life, who had committed such an act of self sacrifice that even Christ Himself would have identified with this man.

"Otto", she said gently, "thank you. As you can see I am a Catholic nun who knows very little about your world. If I'm honest, I locked myself away in a convent so that I didn't have to confront difficult issues like this. But everything you have said makes sense. You did the right thing."

"You don't condemn me? A homosexual murderer? Surely your Bible would have a lot to say about people like me?"

"Only in the same way that it has a lot to say about people like me too. Nuns aren't perfect, you know. There are many things about my life that I wouldn't like you to know, but first and foremost the Christian message is about our need for a relationship with God. Anything we do which displeases God is worth getting rid of so that it doesn't weaken that relationship. Anyway the Bible doesn't condemn anyone for being a homosexual, only practising as one. You haven't done that have you, Otto?"

"No, but only because this bloody war got in the way. If I loved someone and he loved me, of course I would want to have sex with him. Is that so shocking?"

Agathe laughed "It doesn't matter if you shock me. Besides, after what I've seen in the last twenty four hours I think I'm incapable of being shocked anymore. What I think about an issue isn't important – it's what God thinks that counts. If the Bible is God's word and it says that some actions or attitudes are sinful then how can I disagree? I can't pick and choose the verses that I like and ignore those I don't like. Right now, sitting with you, the man who saved my life, I wish I could say that your sexuality is your own affair and nothing to do with God. I wish the Bible just said that as long as people love each other then any relationship is all right. But it doesn't say that. I'm not sure why and I don't think I agree with it (may God forgive me for saying that) but I just can't ignore God's truth. God loves you and me but He doesn't love everything we do. I know that it's a hard concept but, Otto, please try and understand how hard it is for me to deal with these issues."

Otto hesitated for a moment. "When we were in the Square, I was talking to one of the Jewish families. The man was a doctor and he spoke German. Hautmann had asked me to question the villagers to try and find out the names of any collaborators or maquisards. For some reason I think he trusted me, or maybe he would have done anything to save the life of the person who had risked everything for him. Either way he asked me to make sure that you were safe. He even had a little money sewn into his coat lining. Here, I have it in my pocket." Otto held out a few francs. "He gave it to me to help you escape. He told me that you had done everything to save his life and the lives of his family. He wouldn't give me any details, for obvious reasons, but he was deeply grateful for what you had done, especially since you hadn't needed to help him. He was Jewish, you were Christian. You were safe in your convent, he and his family were on the run."

Otto was quiet for a moment, sensing for the first time an epiphany as he spoke.

"When someone has taken such risks with their life on behalf of someone else, I know that their faith is sincere and they are perhaps manifesting the behaviour of a higher being. That's not to say that I believe in God, but it does mean that I can't dismiss your beliefs as some intellectual argument that has no basis in reality, that has not been tested in the heat of battle. So if I was in your position, sincere in my beliefs to the point of sacrificing my life, I don't know what I would think. I can understand how difficult it is for you. But I also know that life isn't black and white. I'm not a Christian, but I know that killing is wrong. Yet today I murdered a man. I didn't give him a chance, filled him with bullets. But it was your life or his. Which life was more important and what gave me the right to decide? Someone was going to die and I guess I just decided your life was more valuable than his. Am I condemned for doing that or are there moral decisions that can only be made depending on individual circumstances? If not, how can I live with myself as a murderer?"

The two were silent. Faced with the enormity of the choices before them they could make no further response. It was ironic that they were having the most profound and intimate conversation of their lives in the middle of the most dangerous event of their lives. But perhaps a more trivial conversation would have been out of place. Only questions of life and death really mattered.

The silence was shattered by the big barn door being violently swung open. Otto and Agathe could see two shapes silhouetted against the light background. Each had a rifle nestled into its shoulder, trained directly at the two fugitives.

"Non, non ne tirez pas. Je suis Francaise", shouted Agathe in desperation. Seeing that the two shapes appeared to be pointing their weapons at Otto, who was still wearing full German uniform she pleaded, "Please, wait, I can explain. It's not what it seems."

Otto knew that, had it not been for the nun, he would have been dead and just kept his head down, a forlorn expression on his face, content to place the preservation of his life in the Sister's hands, just as she had done with him in the churchyard.

The two figures marched towards them, rifles still aimed directly and purposefully at their heads. As they got closer, Agathe could make out that the two shapes were both women. One was large and elderly with grey hair tied up in a bun behind her head. She wore a brown cotton smock and black Wellington boots. The other was younger and slimmer with long brown hair draped over her shoulders. She wore green trousers and a black jacket with a fawn coloured scarf wound around her neck.

The older woman motioned with her rifle for them to get up and pointed towards the barn door. Obediently Otto and Agathe stood up and walked slowly towards the light, hands clasped tightly across the back of their heads. Although it was now evening, they blinked rapidly as they came out, unaccustomed to the light.

"À tout droit," ordered the older woman in a rough, deep rural voice.

The party crossed the yard and headed towards a small, narrow farmhouse. Otto felt the point of the rifle pushing him through the low doorway and into a dark room, illuminated only by the embers of a dying wood fire in the stone grate. Agathe stood by his side and surveyed the room as they heard the door being locked and bolted behind them. There was little furniture in the room, just three wicker armchairs and two stools around a solid dark wooden table. The shutters on the front windows of the room were closed, the only daylight coming from two small windows in either side of the door through which they had entered the room. The floor was bare stone, apart from a small rug in front of the fire.

The room gave nothing away as to the identity of their captors. Agathe felt that the surroundings were vaguely familiar, but knew that she had never been there before. The only feature of any note was the red, white and blue flag pinned proudly to the wall above the fireplace. This was just the trigger Agathe needed to remember why she had a feeling of dejà vu – the elderly man's house in Madranges. True he had no flag in his room, but the bare floor, wooden chairs, darkened windows and absence of any personal memorabilia were like a badge of the resistance. If any house was taken by the Nazis there would be no clue as to the identity of its occupants nor, most importantly, that of any other maquisard in the chain.

"Sit down!" barked the older woman pointing towards the wicker chairs as she lowered her rifle. The younger woman still kept hers trained menacingly on the two prisoners.

"Madame, please let me explain." Agathe tried again to put their side of the story. It was a miracle that Otto had not already been shot, but Agathe felt that it was only a matter of time before that oversight was rectified, unless she could persuade them that he was harmless.

The younger woman now spoke, staring cynically straight at the nun,

"You realise that that all sorts of collaborators and traitors masquerade as nuns, priests and even bishops to betray their countrymen. Why should we listen to you?"

"If we were trying to obtain information, is it likely that one of us would turn up wearing a German uniform, especially after what has happened today in your village?" Agathe paused to assess the effect of her argument on the two women. Their silence encouraged her to proceed.

"No, we are not collaborators but we want to tell you how we came to be here and about the awful events that we witnessed only a few hours ago. My name is Sister Agathe Deladier from the Carmelite convent in Corrèze. When the massacre happened in Tulle – you know when so many Frenchmen were hanged from the lampposts – I had to flee the convent with two families of Jews who were sheltering there. It wasn't safe to stay any longer. We knew that the Germans were on the road from Tulle to Corrèze and thought it would only be a matter of time before the convent was raided. So we set off for the old man's house…"

Agathe suddenly hesitated. What if the women weren't part of the resisitance. She had just blurted out details of their escape route. She had promised the old man that she would never to do that.

"His code name is Felix…from Madranges," the younger woman stepped forward. "We have heard about your journey and how you were betrayed by that scum of a priest, Leseuer. What happened to the Jews?"

"I don't know precisely. The women and children were probably killed in the church, but the men were taken somewhere else. They're probably dead too."

"What about him?" she replied, waving the rifle threateningly at Bauer. Not understanding French, Otto had only been able to track the progress of the conversation by the body language of the two women. He sensed that the mood had lightened while Agathe was talking, but suddenly felt threatened again by the aggressive stance of the younger woman.

"I know that it must seem strange to find me in your barn alone with a German officer. I promise you that he means you no harm. Indeed I owe my life to him."

Agathe looked at Otto and explained what had happened at the church in Oradour. She had to stop several times as the sheer horror of what she had experienced overwhelmed her. It was one thing to experience such trauma first hand when all her energies were concentrated on her own survival. It was quite another describing such brutality in the cold light of day. At times she would sob as she recounted a horrific death, at others just stare vacantly out of the window, barely able to comprehend the words that she was saying. Agathe was conscious that the two women probably knew several of those who had been killed. By now they had both put down their rifles and were sitting on the stools listening intently to the traumatic story that was being revealed to them.

As she explained how Dominique had died and how Otto had shot another German soldier to save her life Agathe could sense the ice melting in the women's hearts. It struck her as the only positive aspect of her story, the one truly heroic and selfless act. All those in the church, including herself, had been engaged in a desperate and all consuming bid for survival. Perhaps there had been acts of altruistic bravery, but Agathe hadn't seen any. Those stampeding into the sacristy for safety had been trampling on anyone who had fallen in the crush, even other people's children. Those sheltering under pews or behind pillars had sought to shield themselves from the enemy by hiding behind their countrymen. Only the parents of children seemed to have any instincts other than for their own protection.

When she had finished, there was silence. Even among a group of people grimly accustomed to death after years of war, Agathe's story was harrowing. The older woman, eyes moist as she battled back the tears, hugged Agathe, clinging onto her as if she was the last remnant of a world she had known and which was now gone. The younger woman went over to Otto and embraced him on both cheeks, repeating "Merci" time after time. Eventually she spoke,

"I am sorry. We have not introduced ourselves but you will understand that we must be very careful about our identities. I am Gabrielle and this is my mother, Annette."

Gabrielle pointed to her mother who nodded slightly.

"The people who died today will be remembered as innocent victims of an unjust cause. They died in the defence of the French way of life…our tolerance, our respect for those of other cultures and faiths, our language, our sophistication, our national pride. The Nazis have tried to take these things away from us – to make us hate the Jews, despise our heritage, hate those who aren't like us, turn us into peasants, grateful for any handouts that they deign to give us, people with no intellect or culture. You know they even try to rewrite our history. We women are only good for having babies and cooking. And what does that traitor Petain say, "Ce qu'il faut à la France, à notre cher pays, ce ne sont pas des intelligences, mais des caractères." What does he know about character, my arse."

"Gabrielle, the people who did this are sick, not brainwashed or misguided. Nobody can justify this massacre as trying to improve another nation's culture or purity. You are very idealistic, dear, and that's good in young people, but sometimes you must realise that human beings do evil things because they are psychologically or emotionally ill. Not crazy nationalists or imperialists or any of those other fancy words that you use, but just sick."

Agathe was startled that this country woman who, so far, had only grunted a few terse words was able to articulate her thoughts so succinctly.

"Non, maman, it's more than that," replied Gabrielle. "Sickness cannot explain what happened in the church. You shoot a defenceless boy in a confessional box….because…because your mother didn't love you or you're depressed or you've got low self esteem. No, there will probably be a few soldiers who are psychologically ill, but the sister said there were around fifty in the church. Are they all nutcases? If people do these things because they are ill then why doesn't every loony go round massacring people. These brutes do this because they are obsessed with their cause, brainwashed for years by Hitler and his propaganda into believing they have a right, even a duty, to control the rest of the world, that their race and culture is so superior to the rest that they must impose it on other people. If they can't impose it on a race because they are beyond redemption, like the Jews, they must kill them."

She sighed as if this was not the first time she had made such an oration but had still not converted her mother. Gabrielle continued. "Sister I have been very rude. Can I get you and Otto a coffee?"

Agathe nodded absent mindedly, not even bothering to ask Otto if he wanted a drink. When Gabrielle returned, she asked Agathe, "Why do you think they did it? You are a woman of faith. What does your religion say about this?"

Agathe was quiet for a moment. Still reeling from the events of the day, the last thing she wanted was to be engaged in earnest conversation. But she had been intrigued by the women's discussion. All her recent life she had been surrounded by people who thought in a similar way to her. But the visceral argument of these two women, who were from the same family but had such different interpretations, had challenged her. Sipping her coffee Agathe contemplated the massacre she had just witnessed. So far she had been so bound up in the event that she had not even considered its origins, so personally involved that its causation had seemed an irrelevance. Only the reality burned brightly in her mind. The faces, the screams, the smell and the death but yet she still knew what she must say.

"A few minutes ago you would have shot me, yet now you are asking me the most profound question I have ever been asked. I'm sure that my explanation will be inadequate, but I have never felt that you can explain such terrible events in human terms. If you could explain them then surely we would have done something about it by now, because we would have understood what we needed to do to eliminate the causes. This sort of brutality would no longer be happening, or at least less frequently. But somehow human beings continue to destroy each other. I can understand," she said, looking at the older woman, "why someone who is psychologically disturbed might try and kill another person. Or a wife, who has been beaten by her husband for years might, in an emotional rage, stab him to death. Or maybe," she turned to the younger women, "one nation might invade another to try and impose its 'civilisation' on that country and kill some people in the process. It might try and prohibit its citizens from practising their faith and, perhaps, even use violence to achieve this.

But what I have seen today transcends any such explanation. There was no emotion in the faces of those Nazis as they set fire to the church. They did not look crazy. They weren't shouting fascist propaganda. They weren't performing a patriotic act in order to defend the Fatherland. Whether a group of villagers in an obscure part of France lived or died will make no difference to the outcome of the war. Nazism wasn't threatened by the women and children in the church, or even by the men who were just going about their normal business on a Saturday afternoon. Most of them were more concerned to protect their fishing rods than a maquisard. Others had spent too long in the bar to be any danger to the Germans and the rest were just returning from work. These weren't soldiers or resistance fighters. Anyone could see that. And what can we say about the Jews? Yes I know that Jews have not been popular since the time of Christ, but millions of them have lived in Germany for centuries. Did you know that Yiddish is even descended from the German language? But why are they being rounded up and murdered now? Are the Jews today any worse or unpopular than the Jews of the last century or the one before that?

For me, this is a bigger struggle. It's not about nationalism, politics, mental derangement, anti-semitism, social deprivation or anything like that. It's not even about good and evil. This is a cosmic struggle being played out on earth. It originates from a different dimension to the one that we live in. Spiritual forces are at work here that are greater than anything we can comprehend and that's why with our human minds we can't understand what is going on."

"What do you mean, Sister?" interrupted Gabrielle, "This is all too..... ethereal. It's not a proper explanation that we can relate to."

"But that's my whole point. We can't explain it in human terms. This massacre is just one battle in the war between God and Satan that has been going on since the beginning of the world and will continue until its end. Let me put it another way. It's a bit like a football match. On the pitch, there are eleven players on each side. They are some of the dedicated disciples of either God or Satan. Sometimes there is a prolonged period of attacking play by one side or the other. Maybe even a goal is scored, seeming to give one side the advantage. But the match swings from one side to the other. So this dreadful war has seen Satan thrusting deep into the opposition's half and maybe today, in the massacre at Oradour, his team has scored a goal.

The German Major, I think he is called Hautmann, is so possessed by Satan that he would do anything to give him the advantage. Even if all humanity was screaming at him not to do it, he is so caught up in this cosmic struggle that he has lost all power of rational thought and argument. He is compelled to do it by a higher power that he can't resist. He may well be evil or brainwashed by Hitler or psychologically disturbed but his behaviour today has been pushed beyond anything with which we can identify or attribute to these conditions. Evil spirits travel through arid places trying to find a home, and today they came to rest on Major Hautmann in Oradour."

"But what about us?" queried Annette, the older woman. "We're not on the pitch. And what about Otto here – he's a German but he saved your life. How can he be on the side of the Devil?"

"I didn't say he was, but most of us are in the crowd cheering on one side or the other. Hautmann wasn't acting alone. He gave the order, but others acted on his instructions and, by carrying those out, they were cheering him on. Every now and then one of us may get onto the pitch to do something for the team. Maybe that's what happened to Otto today. I don't know why he did it, and perhaps he doesn't know himself but I do believe he did something for God today."

Agathe could see that the French women were still sceptical but felt that she should let them have a time for reflection. After a while Gabrielle spoke up,

"Sister, so when will this 'match' end?"

"I don't know, but I do know that it will end in judgment for all those on the pitch or in the crowd. God will call those who are on his side to be with Him forever, but those who have supported the other side will be separated from Him forever. I don't really know what that separation will be like but it's obviously not going to be pleasant. I know it may not be much consolation now but that's when Major Hautmann and his like will receive justice."

Annette, who had been looking intently at Agathe as she spoke these words, gave a long sigh. "I used to believe this too, Sister, but it seems so unfair. Most people just aren't like either you on the one side, or the Nazi Major on the other. Most of the time they are good, occasionally bad, but generally they behave morally and shouldn't be punished for the odd mistake. My husband," she crossed herself perfunctorily as she remembered the dead, "was always kind to Gabrielle and myself, always paid his taxes, didn't cheat anyone. Only problem was that he drank too much. But he wasn't a bad man."

"No, I'm sure he wasn't."

Agathe was keen not to appear judgmental of those giving her sanctuary.

"Listen, only God knows people's hearts and understands their destiny, but I do believe they will all be treated fairly. All I am saying is that what I have seen today cannot be explained in any other way. None of us here can identify with the type of people, I use the word loosely, who could set fire to a church full of innocent women and children, lock the doors and shoot anyone who tried to escape. It's inhuman. So why do people behave in this way? If we can't understand this in human terms then the cause must lie outside the world as we know it. If not, I can't make any sense of it."

There was no reply. Not because the women accepted the nun's argument but because there was nothing else to say. The silence was broken by Otto Bauer asking Agathe in German what they were going to do next. She just shook her head. It was the first time that day that she had been given a free choice about anything.

CHAPTER TWENTY TWO

Samuel slipped away down the road from the church. He felt extremely weak. His left arm was now aching constantly and was still sticky with blood. He knew that his open wounds were probably already infected. He didn't know how long he had been lying in the pile of bodies among the rotting flesh, rats and dogs, but it would have been several hours, plenty long enough for his body to have been invaded by all sorts of bacteria, viruses and parasites. But he shuddered when he thought of the major threat posed by the fresh blood that had been dripping on his broken flesh from the dead and dying – AIDS.

The disease was the curse of Africa. Samuel knew enough about AIDS from teaching the children in school to fear the disease above any other. Tens of thousands of people in Africa had already died from it. Samuel always taught the children that they were particularly at risk as the disease had probably originated in the rainforests of Zaire which bordered onto Rwanda. Tribesmen who hunted and killed chimpanzees may have been bitten by the apes allowing the HIV virus to jump the species. As this might have happened as long ago as the 1950s, Samuel knew that the virus was endemic in central Africa and that many of the bodies among whom he had lain would have been HIV positive.

Still he had to press on. He needed medical treatment or he would not live long enough to find out if he had been infected by the virus. It was eerily quiet as he trailed out of Nyarubuye – so normal for the early morning but strange, given the intense human activity that he had witnessed only a few hours earlier. He had read from accounts of previous massacres that one of the strangest sensations for survivors was the return to normality. Markets would re-open within a few hours, schools within a day or two. Buses would start running again, washing would be hung out to dry, people would gather on street corners to gossip. Bodies would be buried and evidence destroyed. Within a few days life appeared to get back to normal. Initially the bereaved were supported by the community, but memories soon faded and goodwill evaporated. Conspiracy theories started to circulate – it wasn't an accident that so and so was killed. He had betrayed his tribesmen in the last uprising or had an affair with his neighbour's wife or had been stealing animals. Samuel had heard them all and suspected that such vituperative comments were already circulating from the massacre at Nyarubuye church.

He was not aware of making a conscious decision to head away from Nyarubuye on the road to Tanzania. But familiarity was a close friend in such circumstances. He knew the route and could anticipate the danger areas. He was also aware that, by now, there would be refugee camps set up in Tanzania where he could get medical treatment. Grimly he braced himself for another long march to the border.

It didn't take Samuel long to realise how much harder it would be this time. His head was throbbing ferociously and every step jarred his injured arm. Whichever way he tried to hold or support it he could get no long term relief. The pain shot through his arm and up to his shoulder. The vibrations through his body were made worse by his heavy step. Samuel could only plod along the hard surface of the road, he had no energy for his normal springy step, where much of the impact was absorbed by his ankles, knees and hips. As he placed each foot heavily onto the ground he felt as if an acute pain was referred right through to the top of his head. This time, however, he could not face walking through the fields and hills where the surface might have been more yielding but where exhaustion would have come upon him more swiftly. He had no alternative but to tramp inexorably along the road out of Nyarubuye.

At least there didn't appear to be any Interahamwe patrols marauding along the road. He had heard rumours that the RPF were now marching on Kigali and taking control of larger areas of the country by the day. He was certain the Interahamwe would not stay and fight. By African standards the RPF was a disciplined and polished army, more than a match for the amorphous hotheads in the Hutu militia. A few burnt out jeeps by the side of the road were evidence that the retreat had begun. This was reinforced by the nature of Samuel's fellow travellers on the road to the border. From the ones he recognised, he conjectured that they were all Hutus trying to escape from any reprisals. By now there was a steady trickle of family groups forlornly marching along the road to Rusomo. Samuel had seen amongst them his neighbours and friends. It was fortuitous that, given his blood stained and bedraggled appearance, none of them appeared to recognise him. For, despite his weariness, hatred burned in his eyes. He felt that, without doubt, if he had been able-bodied he would have taken his revenge there and then. Flashes of the corpses at the church were now tormenting him, nudging him to exact retribution for the suffering they had endured. In time, he thought, but not now. He was strangely unashamed by these odious machinations. He felt possessed – by what or whom he did not know. But it was not pleasant. It gave him a purpose, a reason for making it to the border, a motive even greater than the desire to see his wife and children again. He would make it, he must make it.

* * *

Hours passed and Samuel's progress was slow. By now he had been walking for several hours and was close to delirium. Foolishly he had brought no water from the church with him and was dehydrating severely again. He daren't leave the road in search of water in case he couldn't find his way back again in his debilitated state. Through the mist in his eyes he could dimly make out a white vehicle approaching. Samuel was too tired to attempt an escape. The vehicle seemed to slow down and a man jumped out of the passenger side. Samuel could just make out a red shape on the side of the door as it swung open.

"Let me have a look at you," the man said kindly. Samuel instinctively backed away, even though the man had given him no reason to fear. Indeed his voice was the first gentle sound he had heard in days.

"Don't worry, we're the Red Cross. We just want to help you."

The man spoke perfect Kinyarwanda. Carefully he examined Samuel's injured head and arm and then the rest of his body. Having assured himself that his patient was likely to survive the journey to the border, he helped Samuel into the back of the jeep.

Samuel sat there quietly, barely looking at the three or four other patients slumped in the rear of the vehicle. The stench was appalling but Samuel was so relieved to be off his feet that he barely noticed. The jeep turned round and set off in the direction of the border. The stream of fresh air from the open front window revitalised him somewhat and gave some relief from the appalling smell of the gangrenous wounds. However, his feeling of deliverance was soon replaced by a grim battle against the pain that shot through his body as the vehicle raced along the pitted surface. Every bump was a personal test of survival.

Samuel soon realised that his tongue and lips were bleeding as he bit into them while tensing his teeth against every impact. Every now and then there was a particularly painful jolt as the jeep hit a pile of stones placed at the side of the road by refugee families as supports for their cooking pots. The road had provided a more stable base for their fire than the uneven grass but these obstacles now amounted to torture for Samuel as the jeep scattered them with excruciating regularity. As the vehicle lurched from side to side to try and avoid the worst ruts in the road, it hit anything at the edge of the track. Sometimes the tyres would hit a log or the remains of a hastily removed road block, or a body left where it had fallen. The whole vehicle would judder and both he and his fellow passengers would groan at the unimaginable torment to their bodies. Samuel comforted himself with the fact that their journey should be swift and uneventful, without delays at militia roadblocks. After a while sleep mercifully enveloped him.

He was awakened by the noise and the smell. People were shouting and banging on the jeep. Samuel coughed as the smoke from thousands of wood fires permeated the vehicle. Looking out of the window all he could see were brownish grey dots speckled with blue and white. Peering more closely he could just determine that the grey and blue colours were plastic huts. Thousands and thousands of them stretching as far as the eye could see. The larger white squares appeared to be feeding stations, each with crowds of people queuing patiently in lines which stuck out like tentacles from every side of each marquee. The landscape was largely bare, every tree stripped down to its trunk.

Women and children filed along the road carrying piles of firewood on their heads. Anything combustible was being hurried away to feed the fires which seemed to be burning next to every settlement. The driver of the jeep was constantly sounding his horn to try and clear a path through this sea of humanity. Samuel was surprised at the number of vehicles fighting their way along the main thoroughfare. Large trucks, tankers, Land Rovers and even a sprinkling of motor bikes and bicycles were struggling to make progress along the congested track.

"Where are we?" he moaned, vaguely in the direction of the driver and the kindly man.

The latter looked round. "You are in Tanzania. This is Benaco refugee camp. You will be safe here. We are taking you to the United Nations medical station."

Samuel felt anything but safe. The faces peering into the jeep looked menacing – Hutu menacing. He had seen the same look at Nyarubuye church and tried to shield his face in case anyone recognised him.

"Is this a Hutu or a Tutsi camp?" he queried.

"Both" came the reply, "but more Hutu than Tutsi. They have been arriving incessantly in recent days. They knew the RPF were on the way and were afraid of revenge attacks."

Too right, thought Samuel, his mind wandering back to the images of the bodies floating down the Akagera river under Rusomo bridge.

"I'm looking for my wife and children. How can I find them?" Samuel said after a while, trying to expunge the dark images from his mind.

"Benaco is organised according to the geographical areas of Rwanda," explained the kindly man, "so, if they are here you should be able to find them. But first your wounds must be treated. Here we are."

The jeep ground to a halt inside a makeshift compound protecting two or three large marquees. Several other white Red Cross vehicles were parked around the borders of the compound. The doors of the jeep were flung open and the occupants stiffly emerged, then walked shakily towards the first tent, coughing continuously in the thick smog. However, one traveller did not move out of the jeep and remained with his head leant against the window and his body slumped in the car seat. The driver banged against the side of the jeep. The man did not move. The driver then got into the back of the vehicle and shook the reluctant patient. The man crumpled lifelessly onto the floor. For him the journey had been too much – another genocide victim. One more for the UN statistics but at least this wretch could get a proper burial and his relatives might hear of his fate. Most would not be so lucky. The driver shouted "DOA" (dead on arrival) to a couple of orderlies who were hanging around in the yard and the body was removed to a tent at the rear of the compound.

Samuel gave the unfortunate man no more than a passing glance. He had seen so many dead bodies in recent days that one more did not really register even though he had been sitting close to him for several hours. His own survival required 100 per cent of his concentration. Somehow, genocide dehumanised not only its perpetrators but its victims too.

Samuel dragged his broken body towards the entrance to the medical tent. Every nerve seemed to scream against this unwilling movement. A triage nurse was doing her best to separate the life threatening cases from the less serious. But of course all the patients felt that their injuries were worse than anyone else's. A large middle aged man was arguing passionately with the nurse about his daughter. She appeared to be about ten and was obviously suffering from a fever of some sort. The girl was staring vacantly in Samuel's direction, eyes swollen and sweating profusely.

"Please wait here," implored the nurse, anxious to try and clear the ever lengthening queue in front of her.

"But my daughter is dying," screamed the father, "she must see the doctor now. Please, I beg you, let us go in."

"I will check her temperature and then decide. Please wait with your daughter." She waved him away from the desk. Taking a thermometer from her medical bag the nurse placed it in the girl's mouth and called for the next patient.

No case seemed to be straightforward. Each patient who was told to wait contested the nurse's decision, which prolonged Samuel's wait indeterminately. He had no idea how long he had hung around before it was his turn. It was unpleasant waiting outside the entrance to the medical tent in the fetid air of this densely populated area of the camp. The medical facilities had attracted many refugees to set up their plastic huts nearby in case of emergency. Samuel guessed that they would also feel safer surrounded by Red Cross vehicles and staff. With Hutus and Tutsis huddled together in this confined area there must be trouble from time to time – scores to be settled, tribal boundaries to be reinforced, pecking orders to be re-established.

And then an appalling thought struck him. What if Ndagijimana was in the camp? That monster would have read the writing on the wall before the ink was dry. He wouldn't have risked being captured by the RPF. He could easily be posing as some downtrodden victim of the atrocity, at least until he thought it was safe to re-establish his coterie in new surroundings.

"Hello…..hello….can I help you?" Samuel snapped out of his daydream as the nurse's exasperated voice finally registered.

He pointed at his head and his arm both of which the nurse examined perfunctorily. It was pretty obvious to the nurses which cases were the most serious from a quick visual inspection. They hated triage duty. It didn't challenge them professionally and yet they were in the front line, having to endure the abuse and displeasure of patients from dawn until dusk.

"When did this happen?" she asked, making some brief notes on a white index card.

"Yesterday, in Nyarubuye. I was hiding in a church and the Hutus attacked us with machetes."

The nurse took Samuel into the medical tent, bypassing the man and his daughter whose temperature was obviously not high enough to be life threatening. The man smiled at Samuel, who thought it was funny that the father had calmed down so much merely on account of the reading on a thin piece of glass.

For the first time, Samuel was now worried about his injuries. Having survived the massacre and been able to walk away he had almost become complacent about his wounds. Yes they hurt, but he did not see them as life threatening. He had survived. But he had watched the triage nurse at work. Most people had been told to wait outside, only a few had been ushered into the medical tent and they had all seemed much more seriously injured than he was. Yet the nurse had brought him in to see the doctors without hesitation. Maybe he was more dangerously hurt than he had thought.

Inevitably, however, there was a further delay to be endured. Even the dying have to queue, Samuel thought ironically. He sat on the bare earth floor of the hospital ward. Makeshift beds were lined up along the walls and down the centre of the tent. There appeared to be no bedding, although some patients were covered by a single filthy white sheet. People were also lying on the floor beside and underneath each bed. It was hard to tell who were patients and who were relatives, helpers needed to carry out many of the nursing duties for their loved ones. Some of the patients were hooked up to drips or blood bags. But most just lay there unattended. Surprisingly, there was little sound. Occasionally a low moan or a weak cry for attention emanated from one of the beds. Most of these went unheeded. Samuel thought resignedly that this was probably why nobody bothered to cry out. There was no point. No-one was listening.

There appeared to be only two doctors and a handful of nurses to deal with all the patients in the tent and the dozens waiting outside. Eventually, a white doctor came up to Samuel and asked him in French what had happened. The doctor gently removed Samuel's coat and shirt and examined his left arm. Samuel gazed down at his injured limb, which he had been too tired to check for some time. The wound had become increasingly black around the edges. Pus was oozing out in some areas while, in others, the skin was stretched over what looked like gas bubbles.

"I will need to operate on this as quickly as possible," the doctor spoke in a very business like manner. He quickly checked Samuel's head wound before continuing, "this is not so serious but I will stitch it up at the same time." He pointed over to a line of patients who were lying on the floor outside a tent flap with the words 'Salle D'Opération' on the outside.

"Please join the others and I will see you again shortly."

Samuel sensed that he was not being invited to ask any questions and, besides, he was just too exhausted to do so. He lay on the floor with the other patients and fell asleep.

When he came to he was lying on one of the makeshift beds. He was tired and groggy and his head felt tight, as if encased in a helmet. He was too weak to move and was drifting in and out of consciousness. Despite his condition, he felt comforted by the sensation he felt in both arms. At least they've saved my arm, he thought, before blanking out again.

The bodies pressed down on top of him, squashing his head and trapping his arms and legs. Blood and body fluids dripped down his face before dropping onto his neck. He could taste the blood in his mouth and hear the rats tearing at human flesh. It could have been his own for all he knew. He heard a scream, "Get these bodies off my head. I'm alive, save me!"

He felt a calming hand on his shoulder and heard a soothing voice. "Soyez tranquille. It's just a bad dream." Squinting, Samuel could just see the shape of the white doctor hovering over him.
The dream was still very clear.

"But the bodies are on my head. Get them off, my head feels so tight and stretched."

"Don't worry, it's just the bandages. I had to sew up the cut in your head and bind it tight to help it heal. But I'm sorry, I couldn't save your arm."

Samuel suddenly became lucid.

"What do you mean? I can feel it." He attempted to lift it as if to prove that his arm was still there.

"No, I'm afraid that is just a phantom sensation. It often happens to people who have lost limbs. I had to amputate your arm at the shoulder, but your brain still thinks it's there. It hasn't yet adjusted to the loss of a bodily part. When you came in I could tell that you were developing gas gangrene. That's why there were bubbles on your skin. Toxins were developing underneath which would have killed you very quickly. I had to stop them spreading and I'm afraid that amputation was the only option. I have given you antibiotics to kill off any further infection. With any luck you will make a full recovery. We can fit you with an artificial arm. The Red Cross have promised us a supply, but first you must recover your strength. Please excuse me, as I have to attend to some other patients."

He moved onto the next bed. Samuel just lay there, unable to comprehend that in a few sentences the doctor had just changed his life forever. It felt like bereavement. He was grieving for his lost arm. He hadn't felt that the Hutus could have destroyed any more of him after Jonathan's death, but now they had taken parts of his own body. He felt bereaved all over again. Just as he had needed to locate Jonathan's body in order to grieve properly he now needed to know where his arm was. What had they done with it? It was his — he wanted to see it one final time. He could not bear the thought of it just being tossed into a pit for burning along with all the other detritus of this stinking camp. Yet he knew that this was what had probably happened. The source of infection must be destroyed.

He was now becoming conscious of the throbbing in the stump of his left arm, as the pain killers were wearing off. He shouted out for water but none came. He tried to lift himself up but his whole body screamed at him to lie still. And so the torture went on as it did for thousands of other innocent victims of the genocide that day.

CHAPTER TWENTY THREE

"Samuel, Samuel, my darling, it's me, Chantalle." Samuel was dimly aware of the familiar voice whispering close to his ear. His eyelids felt so heavy he couldn't immediately open them, but Chantalle could detect a weak smile flickering across his face. It was a sound he had been waiting to hear for days. A loving sound, a comforting sound, a peaceful sound, proof that at last there might be some way out of the darkness.

He managed to force one eye open and was just about able to focus on the face of his wife. She was beaming, radiant with joy. She looked like an angel of deliverance. Samuel could barely speak such was the painful weariness pervading his body, but he managed to croak a few words, "Thank God you're safe. What about the children? Where are they?"

"They're fine," replied Chantalle. We have our own hut about ten minutes' walk from here. It's not luxurious but we have enough food, drink, clothing and shelter for our needs. You mustn't worry about us. The best thing that you can do for us is get better."

Samuel was silent for a moment. "Chantalle…Jonathan…" He struggled to say the words. Chantalle rested her hand on his shoulder.

"We know, Samuel. We met Thomas and Amelie. They told us. We have cried and cried over it, but hearing you were safe has helped. The children can't wait to see you."

"How did …?" Samuel was too choked up to complete the question.

"We find you?" Chantalle knew what he was trying to ask. "The Sister here helped us."

The face of Sister Agathe Deladier came into Samuel's view.

"Hello, Samuel, I'm very pleased to have met you." She touched him reassuringly on his right hand.

Chantalle continued.

"Sister Agathe and some of her friends try and reunite families who have been split up. I gave her all the information about you and an old photograph that I had brought with me. Every day she has searched the hospitals, feeding stations and arrival points looking for you. She talked to the drivers of the Red Cross jeeps and one of them said that he had picked up a man of your age and description on the road from Nyarubuye. He told her where he had dropped you off. She came here and identified you from the photograph, although it must have been difficult with that enormous bandage wrapped around your head."

Chantalle laughed, suddenly amused by the thought of Agathe lining up the photograph against only half a head.

"Then she came running back to us. We came straight down...Samuel, the doctor has told us what has happened...about the operation...and everything. I just wanted you to know that I love you as much as ever."

Samuel smiled appreciatively. Maybe he was starting to climb the first few steps out of his pit of despair. The survival of his wife and family and their enduring love for him was the first positive news he had received in days and it felt like the first brick being laid in the wall of his new life.

* * *

Julius Ndagijimana checked the packing list on his clipboard.

"That's fifty bags of twenty kilos each. Have you checked it?"

"Yes, Bourgmestre," answered a small thin man, wearing a blue United Nations helmet, "Fifty sacks of grain."

Ndagijimana ticked the packing list and snapped, "All right, put them away in the tent and don't let any thieving hands touch them. At least not until I've had my supply."

He laughed mockingly. The black market worked everywhere –

even among the lowest of the low in a refugee camp. He surveyed his empire. The grain compound was secured by a stout wooden fence and patrolled by a group of threatening young Hutu thugs. Some of them carried walkie talkies which would occasionally crackle into life. They scowled menacingly at anyone who dared to approach the compound.

The grain was stored in a series of large, white marquees crammed into the compound. The occasional blue markings indicated that the depot was under United Nations control, but it was pretty obvious who was actually in charge. After the massacre at Nyarubuye church, Julius Ndagijimana had received word that the RPF had invaded eastern Rwanda and was making impressive progress. He had also heard that the French, who had supported the Hutu uprising and had justified the murder of Tutsis as self defence, were starting to have second thoughts in the face of international criticism. He feared the RPF as a superior military force. Although less than half the size of the Rwandan national army, and much less than that when all the militias were taken into account, the RPF was a disciplined and efficient outfit. Furthermore the Hutu Power regime had sacrificed the defence of Rwanda's borders and key cities for the completion of the genocide. Their strength had been sapped by such effort and they were in no mood to get killed in the reprisals, which they had felt were inevitable. It was time to play the victim again, and Julius was ready for an Oscar winning performance.

He received an order from the Hutu Power leadership to cease the killing and flee. Julius was swept along in an enormous tide of up to a quarter of a million Hutus streaming over the Rusomo bridge into Tanzania. Except that most were not able to parade to the border in a fleet of jeeps getting progressively drunker as they neared the bridge. However, his image as a down trodden innocent victim of the genocide, a hard working local official who had been desperately trying to stop the violence, would not be supported by such a privileged means of travel. The jeeps were abandoned just out of sight of the border and Ndagijimana and his cronies apparently trailed wearily and uncertainly across the bridge along with thousands of others, making sure, of course, that their images were captured for posterity by the international television crews. In their case their unsteadiness was not a consequence of exhaustion from the long march to the border but the after effects of too much alcohol. Nevertheless the metamorphosis of Hutu Power from oppressor to oppressed was being lapped up by the media and international relief agencies. When Julius arrived at Benaco camp and announced that he was a local government official and could help in keeping order and distributing aid, the UN welcomed him with open arms.

The camp was organised into sectors each of which reflected a different geographical area of Rwanda and refugees were encouraged to congregate in the relevant sector for them. Ndagijimana was put in charge of the Rusomo sector. Nobody seemed interested in his past. Even those Tutsis who had heard about the massacre at Nyarubuye were too scared to expose him. Once a warlord, always a warlord, Ndagijimana had just resurfaced in another location but with his status and power intact. However he was careful to show his humanitarian side whenever foreign officials or film crews came around by making sure that he was personally seen distributing the aid to needy people. After all, he was a compassionate man, there just to serve the community. In this way his power and patronage grew and soon he was largely left alone to run the compound as he wished. Mysterious killings removed any threat to his authority. The mortuaries were full of those who had died from injuries received in Rwanda. A few more bodies sliced by machetes raised no query from the overworked officials. By these means the Bourgmestre of Rusomo resumed his career at Benaco camp. Nothing very much had changed at all.

* * *

It was over a week before Samuel was allowed to leave the field hospital. By now he was starting to adapt to his disability. At first he was constantly trying to use his left arm, the contrary messages from his brain advising him that it was still available for use. Many times he tried to pick up food with it or support himself as he got out of bed. Indeed several times he rolled over onto his stump intending to pull himself up with his left arm, only to find himself screaming with unbelievable pain as his stump rebelled against his request. But a week or so later, the synapses in his brain were ensuring that movement messages were only being passed to his remaining good arm and he was beginning to cope with getting up, eating, dressing, washing and going to the toilet. Chantalle and the children had visited him every day. He was amazed how adaptable the children had become. They told him stories of all the new friends they had made and how some of the school teachers in the camp were now running classes. How they had been playing games with balls made from plastic bags, which the UN and other organisations had abandoned. Their happy chatter brought joy to Samuel's life, but still he grieved deeply for Jonathan. Why couldn't his son be there to share in their games, to sit on his bed and tell him about all the inconsequential things he had done that day and to look forward to a better future when they could return to Rwanda?

Despite his injuries, Samuel became increasingly determined to avenge the death of Jonathan and all those murdered in Nyarubuye church. Somehow he would achieve it, even with one arm. He needed a goal, something to look forward to in this bleakest of situations. That his goal was motivated by hatred and revenge didn't matter. It was his first thought when he woke up in the morning and his last before he fell asleep. The means of his revenge were unclear, the victim as yet unknown but it would be accomplished. Of that he had no doubt. It was now a mission. He didn't care what happened to him. His life was of no account. Even his love for Chantalle and the children was subsumed by his overwhelming desire for retribution. It was now just a question of where, how and when his objective would be met.

* * *

Sister Agathe Deladier sat on a simple camp bed in the UN tent that was now her home. It was a standard issue shelter supplied to those assisting in the humanitarian effort, a modest ridge tent that had seen service in many disasters around the world. Agathe looked tiny perched on the side of her camp bed. Although she had renounced her religious vows after the war she still wore a grey veil as a symbol of her continuing commitment to God's service. A simple light blue skirt and white blouse completed her attire, which was complemented by a grey cardigan for use in colder weather. Seeing the veil everyone was still accustomed to calling her 'Sister' and Agathe was content to be defined in this way. Indeed when particularly burdened with prayer over an important issue, she would don a blue habit and observe the familiar rituals from her days in the convent in France. It seemed to give a structure and purpose to her intercessions.

It was her companion who spoke first.

"How can we have any impact at all in a camp this big?" To emphasize her exasperation Mary Edwardson lifted up the piles of index cards under the weight of which the simple desk in the corner of the tent was groaning. Mary was the antithesis of Agathe. A tall, stocky woman with a jolly round face and long brown hair tied up into a bunch at the back of her head. She was single and aged about forty.

"Talk about needles in a haystack. How can we possibly trace all these missing people and, in the unlikely event that they are alive and just happen to be in Benaco camp, find their families among the hundreds and thousands of Rwandans here. And I don't mean to be racist, but they all look the same to me."

Agathe smiled affectionately.

"When you have been here for a while, Mary, you will realise that Africans look as different to each other as Europeans do. You're just not accustomed to their subtle distinguishing features."

"Agathe, that's hardly surprising. I only came to Gahini for three weeks to cover for Judy in the school after her father's death and here I am stuck in a refugee camp in the middle of Tanzania with no prospect of going back to England in the foreseeable future. So it's not really surprising that I can't tell one Tutsi from another, or from a Hutu for that matter. Now where's that box of cards of missing children?"

Mary rummaged around on the desk while Agathe smiled contentedly. There had been many times when she had not believed that they would escape from Gahini. At first she had thought that the shooting was to frighten away some wild animal that had found its way into the compound. But it grew more intense and there was a lot of shouting and screaming. Soon there was a loud bang on her front door. Someone was shouting, "Where are the Tutsis? Open up or we'll burn your house down."

Shaking with fear Agathe had opened the door.

"There are no Tutsis here, only my friend and myself." She pointed to Mary.

Three militiamen came into the house, one holding a rifle and the other two each brandishing gleaming silver machetes. They searched every room, throwing clothes and bedding over the floor indiscriminately. Helping themselves to any food or valuables that they could find, they headed back to the front door snarling, "If we find that you have been sheltering any Tutsis we'll kill you too."

The one with the rifle fired a couple of times through the door to emphasize the point.

The women looked at each other open mouthed. Could this really be happening? After a few moments Agathe said, "Mary, wait here. I will find out what the other bazungu are going to do."

A few minutes later she returned.

"Quick, we must leave. Collect your belongings together and help me load up the car. The other missionaries are leaving for Tanzania. If we go in convoy we will be safer. We leave in ten minutes."

Agathe looked at her meagre possessions. At least she didn't face any agonising choices about what to take and what to leave behind. Barring furniture and kitchen equipment, all her belongings would easily fit into her yellow Volkswagen Beetle, which was parked outside her house.

"The Hutus are massacring the Tutsis. They blame them for the assassination of the President. Everyone thinks that the killing was engineered by the Hutus so that they could blame the Tutsis and stop the peace process, which was going to hand over some power to the Tutsis. But whatever the reason, it's not safe for us to stay. There is no-one here in Rwanda to protect us apart from a few Belgian troops and they're in Kigali, miles away."

The women loaded up the Beetle and sped off to the church, where Agathe had agreed to rendezvous with the other ex-pats. Agathe desperately wanted to take some of her Tutsi friends with her but their presence in the car would put everyone's lives at risk. It was a heart rending decision and there was no time to say goodbye, but Agathe felt she had no choice. Even if she didn't care for her own safety, she was responsible for Mary and must get her out of Gahini at all costs.

There were three other cars waiting for Agathe and Mary as their Beetle drew up outside the church. The group prayed briefly together before setting off in the direction of Tanzania. It was quite obvious, almost from the start, that the journey was going to be traumatic. It seemed as if every local hothead who wanted to make a name for himself was setting up a roadblock. Sometimes the little fleet of vehicles could travel twenty kilometres without seeing one but, at other times, they were stopped every kilometre or so. Some of the militiamen were extremely menacing, firing rifle shots and waving machetes as a vehicle approached. Others were too drunk to bother with such posturing and seeing the occupants of the vehicles were bazungu, waved them through without any checks. But the missionaries were grateful for their command of the Kinyarwanda language which eased their passage through the trickier obstacles. Agathe pitied any poor Tutsi trying to make the same journey. They wouldn't stand a chance. The militiamen's first question was always, "Have you any Tutsis in your car?" The bodies laid out at the side of the road at regular intervals were a portent of the fate awaiting anyone who answered in the affirmative. Agathe shuddered at the thought of the destruction of this beautiful country – the land of a thousand hills – and its many warm, lovable citizens.

Much of the countryside looked like it always had. There seemed to be dwellings everywhere, not many big towns, but lots of individual houses dotted all along the side of the road and perched on the distant hills. Some were proper cement built residences with a tin roof, others were round mud huts with a thatch. Most were still surrounded by a tall hedge, but in places these had been torn down, the first visible signs of unwelcome visitors.

"I'm so sorry you have had to see this Mary. Rwanda is not like this." Agathe broke the silence which had, until then, been the only natural response to the horror which was unfolding in front of them. She went on, "Normally children would be playing at the side of the road, waving excitedly at every vehicle that went past, desperately hoping that we would toot our horn in recognition. There would be women working out in the fields harvesting bananas or digging up the earth ready for planting. Other women in their brightly coloured clothes would be walking along this road, perhaps with a baby on their back and a sack of vegetables balanced on their heads. Now there is no-one. I used to get cross having to dodge the children or those cows with the big horns if they wandered into the road. Where are they all now?"

"Don't worry about me, Sister," Mary laid a reassuring hand on Agathe's shoulder as she drove, "I can see that this country has gone crazy all of a sudden. The people have all been so friendly and welcoming until now. But this must be terrible for you, this is your home."

"I don't know if I ever told you, Mary, but I came here after the war to escape from all of this. I had seen the most brutal acts carried out by one human being on another in Europe. I thought that perhaps this bestiality was something which affected developed societies. Those who didn't have to worry about having enough to eat but had the luxury of creating ideologies and political systems, even religions, that they wanted to impose on others. Yes, I was even disillusioned with my own church and its shameful collaboration with the Nazis. I thought that if I lived in a simple society where people were just grateful for the rains to germinate their seeds and the sun to ripen their crops there would be no bloodshed. The people here seemed so contented, always smiling and chatting to their friends. Until now. It's as if people have changed sides overnight. Something has turned them into monsters. But whatever happens we mustn't become like them. I have learnt that you can't run away from these problems. They exist wherever you are in the world. Yesterday the Nazis, today the Hutu militia, tomorrow the…oh I don't know." Her voice trailed off as she considered the source of the next act of genocide, but hesitating in case such a presentiment somehow hastened its occurrence.

The women drove on in silence. They, and the others in the little missionary convoy, were already thinking about what they might find in Tanzania and how they might be able to help when they got there.

CHAPTER TWENTY FOUR

There was a tap on the window and then a gentle whisper.

"Gabrielle, Marianne, it's me Eloise. Please let me in."

Gabrielle picked up her rifle and crept towards the door.

"Eloise, are you alone?"

"Yes, Gabrielle, don't worry. There's no-one else here. But I must speak with you."

Gabrielle lifted the latch on the old oak door and opened it a few inches. She peered out, checking that there was no-one with Eloise. She knew the hiding places where anyone wishing to ambush them would lie in wait. Opening the door a little more she expertly surveyed these areas looking for any disturbance in the sand, which the women had placed around each hiding place. The sand was raked flat every day and was visible from most of the windows in the farmhouse. The women would have advance notice of any Germans or collaborators encircling the old farmhouse and could allow any guests to make their escape out through the cellar and along a secret underground passageway into an adjacent paddock. Many lives of those passing through the resistance network had been saved in this way. On this occasion there was no sign of anyone watching the building and Eloise was hustled inside. The door was locked and bolted behind her.

Eloise LeClerc had been the belle of Oradour in her younger days. Even as she approached forty it was still not hard to see why. She had long blonde hair which curled naturally at its ends. Her skin was pale and resembled porcelain that had aged a little, a few cracks evident on its surface. Agathe could easily imagine her blue eyes sparkling at the village ball where she enjoyed the admiration of a worshipping throng of young men. Although she was dressed in a long brown overcoat she still managed to look elegant and, even in her agitated state, contrived to retain her poise and style. Today, however, her once vibrant eyes were sad and downcast.

"What is it Eloise?" asked Marianne.

Eloise looked around at Agathe and Otto. She was not surprised that the women's guests weren't introduced. They never were. Eloise knew that this was not done out of incivility but to protect both her and those passing through the farmhouse. If she didn't know anything then no-one could extract any useful information from her or accuse her of being a collaborator. However, it was the first time she had seen anyone dressed as a Nazi officer and couldn't avoid an alarming stare in Otto's direction. Gabrielle sensed her unease but just smiled to encourage her to answer her mother's question.

"Do you know what's happened in the village?" asked Eloise.

The women nodded.

"I haven't seen Pierre or Claude since this morning and I'm worried sick about them. I wanted to go into the village to try and find them but it's too dangerous to go in by myself. So I was wondering if you would come with me. I thought you might have heard something. You know…through…your contacts."

Eloise hesitated, as if even suggesting that Gabrielle and Marianne might be privy to more advanced information than her might be compromising their position.

"I'm sorry, Eloise we've heard very little apart from what our friends here have told us," pointing to Agathe and Otto. "And, by the way, don't worry about the German uniform – he's one of us now."

Agathe rose and put her arm around the distraught woman. At that moment they could clearly hear the sound of distant gunfire.

"It's not safe to go back into Oradour now. There are more than a hundred German troops in the village. We saw them all in the square. Anyone trying to get back into the village would risk being shot. It's getting dark anyway. I know it will be difficult for you, Eloise, but I think we should wait until daylight."

"My husband and son may be dead by morning. I can't just leave them. They're all I've got in the world."

Eloise slumped onto one of the wicker chairs and started to cry. Deep, agonised sobs emerged from her shaking body.

Gabrielle pulled up her chair close to the weeping woman.

"The Sister is right, Eloise. Please stay with us tonight and we will all go into the village as soon as it's light. There is nothing we can do for them now. We must just wait and pray."

No-one slept much that night. Even with the windows closed the smell of the burning village seemed to pervade the house, the odour trapped in the curtains and soft furnishings. It was a constant reminder of the events of the day, as if any further promptings were necessary. Fear was a close companion for the group that night. Fear of what they might find the next day; fear of a knock at the door as the Germans continued their murderous activities; fear that their community could never recover from the appalling events of a few hours earlier.

It was with relief as well as foreboding that they surfaced the next morning at first light. Marianne found some civilian clothes for Otto. She had kept some of her husband's favourite clothes after he died. She didn't really know why. She knew he wasn't coming back, but it seemed important to keep a hold on the past, provide a reference point. Fortunately, Otto was about the same size although a little slimmer perhaps. Despite the circumstances she couldn't resist a wry smile as she saw the German attired in her husband's Sunday best jacket, shirt and trousers. They hung a little loosely but he would pass as a Frenchman. It brought back memories too of happy times – the village dances on a Saturday night, church services on a Sunday, Bastille night celebrations. But what of the community now, with dancing partners separated on the dance floor, worshippers isolated in the pews, diners eating alone? How would they recover?

No-one felt like eating breakfast. Eloise was desperate to find Pierre and Claude without any further delay but managed to drink a little coffee when pressed by Marianne. It was a Sunday, thought Agathe, the day of rest. Her mind flashed back to the scenes in the church. At least they would now be at rest. She offered up a silent prayer for the souls of the departed.

Close to the farm was a narrow lane which led down onto the road from Limoges to Oradour. Unbeknown to Otto and Agathe, they had followed the line of this lane through the fields from the church the previous day. It was narrow and secluded, which probably explained why the Germans had not paid them a visit the previous night.

The morning was crisp and bright, foretelling a warm and sunny day. It could have been any normal Sunday morning in Oradour except for the wisps of smoke evident in the distance. One of these emanated from the church, which could clearly be seen by the little party. As they approached closer to the church, the sheer intensity of the fire was manifested by the extent of the damage to the building. The main walls of the church, including the tower were built of granite, and were still standing, but they were blackened around every window and door opening. The smoke had created patterns of black and white on the walls. There was a sort of symmetry to these colours as the smoke had consistently sought an upward path from each opening, depositing soot in a fan shape above each aperture, but leaving large areas to the side untouched. Shapes of faces, letters of the alphabet and everyday objects appeared to look out from the ruins like natural graffiti. The spire of the tower had collapsed completely, as had the main roof. The outbuildings were in varying stages of dereliction.

But if there was one thing that capped the image of the blackened building, as the group drew closer, it was the smell. The stench of burnt flesh pervaded the air. It was a pungent, yet vaguely familiar smell – like the roasting of a joint of meat until overdone. Any hope that many other people had escaped from the building was quickly evaporating from Agathe's mind. She spoke softly.

"Do you really want to go in there Eloise? It will be a very distressing sight. Maybe we should wait until they have…you know…removed the bodies."

"It's all right, Sister," she replied, "I need know. Please, let's go inside."

The fire appeared to have burnt itself out in the church. Its sheer ferocity had ensured that anything combustible had burnt very quickly. The smoke they had seen in the distance was being generated by a minor fire in one of the outhouses, which was still smouldering.

The ash was several feet deep in the entrance door, indicating that this may have been a source of the fire. The Germans had lit brushwood, straw and other waste in this area as they left the building, effectively blocking it as a means of escape. The women and Otto waded through the ash and fragments in the entrance door, covering their noses and mouths against the smell and the dust, which blew up from the ash. They were obviously the first people to go into the church. More than twelve hours after the fire had burnt out the ash was still warm but virgin like freshly fallen snow.

The bronze church bells lay melted and misshapen near the entrance door, giving testimony to the intense heat generated by the fire. They had fallen when the steeple had collapsed. As the temperature rose in the church, a flashover would have occurred. Flames carried by the smoke would have destroyed the roof of the church and funneled up through the well ventilated steeple. By now the building would have been like a blast furnace as oxygen drawn in through the increasing number of openings in the church walls and roof fed the flames. The burning bodies provided more fuel for the fire, each adult supplying about eight kilogrammes of body fat. As the fat soaked into the clothing, so it created a sort of wick that kept the fire burning at intense temperatures until even the bones were reduced to ash.

Otto was in tears as he led the women into the main body of the church. He expected to find human remains here but there were few – just piles of ash and occasional fragments of clothing or church furnishings. Just over twelve hours ago he was with the men who did this. He had helped carry the box of explosives into the church. Now there weren't even any dead bodies for most of the relatives to bury, no-one could even know who lay in the remains. How could they have done this? What kind of monsters were they to have killed innocent women and children in such an inhuman and shameless manner?

The party spread out to search different areas of the church. Bizarrely, isolated items appeared to have survived the inferno better than others. The wooden confessional box was severely charred but was still standing, as if protecting the bodies of the two small boys who had hidden inside it. Occasionally a section of pew had survived, sticking up through the ash. Agathe was drawn to the stone altar. It was obvious that a group of children had sought sanctuary here, as some of the bodies were at least partly recognisable.

"Eloise, you must look here." Agathe spoke loudly, but did not wish to shout as any excess noise seemed inappropriate in what was effectively a mass burial chamber.

Eloise looked up from the side aisle about ten metres away, dread filling her mind. She made her way across the church, each step creating an indentation in the carpet of ash, rather like footprints in the sand. On reaching the altar, the woman inspected the bodies gathered around the holy table. Every now and then she let out a muffled scream as she recognised the children of friends…but there was no sign of Claude.

"There is still hope, Eloise," consoled Agathe. "Do you notice something strange about the bodies here?"

Eloise shook her head, not really registering any of the intricate details of the macabre sight. Agathe went on.

"They are all children. No adult sought sanctuary here – in the very place where they might have expected protection. No mother hid here. They gave up this last place of refuge to their children."

After a reflective pause acknowledging this act of maternal sacrifice the two women turned and surveyed the scene of desolation in front of them viewed from the altar steps. The floor of the church was grey with ash, the absence of colour emphasizing the bleakness of the sight facing them. In the main body of the church there were about thirty bodies, partly identifiable but in most cases just a fragment, a hand here, a foot there, a blackened skull poking out from the ash. It was impossible to tell whether or not the body parts were related.

Agathe broke the silence.

"There must have been 400 people in here. The church was packed. Now look at it. Most of the bodies are indistinguishable from the remains of the pews, roof and fittings. Just piles of ash." She stopped, suddenly realising what she had said and surmising Eloise's reaction.

"Eloise, I'm sure Pierre and Claude weren't here." She pointed at the layers of ash in the nave. "Pierre was definitely not here. There were no men in the church. Only women and children, and most of those were accompanied by their mothers or grandmothers. It's unlikely that Claude was here on his own. Please hold onto that hope."

"I am, Sister. It's just…well….nothing can prepare you for something like this. It's as if it's not happening to me. I know it's not a dream because my husband and son are missing, but I could never believe that anyone could do this to other human beings, especially to innocent children."

"Let's go." Agathe placed her arm comfortingly around the younger woman's shoulders.

They made their way back down the side aisle to the entrance door. Agathe had not examined this area before. Here the ash seemed to be less thick and she could even see sections of bare stone floor in the areas closest to the windows. At first she thought sunlight streaming in through the open windows was making patterns on the black and grey ash. Drawing closer, however, she realised with horror what she was looking at – three small heads topped with the remains of long auburn hair. The legs and lower parts of the trunk had been burnt to dust but the upper chest, arms and shoulders were still recognisable. Their arms were linked together as if they had sought safety and comfort in each other's embrace. Perhaps the draught from the window had prevented the fire from burning their faces too badly as, although their appearance was blackened in parts by smoke, their identity was visible.

Fearfully Agathe drew closer, gently clearing away the debris from the faces and upper bodies of the victims. Now there was no doubt. Agathe was looking at the bodies of Miriam, Heloise and Franca Steinrich. She knelt down next to them and hugged the pathetic remains, sobbing audibly but initially with restraint. Soon self control abandoned her and the nun wailed plaintively, rocking from side to side in a desperate attempt to find solace. She had invested so much hope and energy in trying to save these girls and their parents, but it had all come to nothing. It had ended on the stone floor of an alien church in excruciating agony. Why had they ever left the convent? Maybe the

Germans wouldn't have found their hiding place. Or why hadn't they gone south from Corréze rather than north? Why had she survived and these poor children perished? The guilt, sorrow and tension arising from the traumas of the last few days were blended together in great howls of anguish. Doubts came too. If there was a God, where was he now? How could this atrocity have been committed by those He had created? Why hadn't He done something?

Agathe looked up to the heavens and shouted angrily, "Answer me!"

She was unaware how long she had lain cuddling the bodies of the three girls. But she was aware that she was no longer crying. Looking around, Agathe could see that she was alone in the church. Perhaps the others had realised that she needed to be alone with her grief and despair. Or maybe they could just no longer bear to be in that place of horror.

Slowly she rose to her feet, shaking the ash from her clothes and hair. She prayed over the three girls, committing their souls to their Heavenly Father and slowly departed from the building.

Gabrielle, Marianne, Eloise and Otto were waiting in the sunshine outside the church. No-one said anything. The sight that they had witnessed was so beyond human comprehension that communication at any level seemed totally inadequate. They might have hugged, comforting each other through touch. But even that was insufficient. Verbal and physical interaction was impossible – they were inhabiting a landscape in which only the soul could exist and function – the Valley of the Shadow of Death. They could communicate only through the deep grievings of their souls – the companionship of the spirit.

The little group trudged off from the church. There was no methodology in their search, no planning. It just seemed natural to head off in the direction of the Champ de Foire. If the church had not revealed the fate of Pierre and Claude, then maybe the fairground would.

There were still a few German soldiers in the village. Otto and the women instinctively kept out of their sight, but it seemed obvious that the killing was over. It was now about 10.30a.m. on Sunday morning. The few remaining soldiers were loading up their jeeps and preparing to leave. They seemed preoccupied, almost unaware of their surroundings. Otto, however, knew that news of his defection would have spread throughout the regiment and he felt that it was likely that he would be suspected of the German soldier's murder even if no-one had actually seen him do it. The Germans were merciless in taking revenge on deserters and would certainly have taken a break from their preparations for departure to exact retribution. He was concerned that he would be spotted but, in reality, from a distance, no-one would know that he wasn't an unkempt French farmer who hadn't shaved that day. From the look of them, Otto guessed that the soldiers had spent the night in the village. They looked tired and slightly disshevelled. Otto had noticed a pile of empty champagne bottles in the corner of the open space at the side of the church – evidence of a night of celebration. He vomited. He had retained control of his stomach in the church while the others were being sick, but the thought of his former colleagues celebrating while so many young and innocent lives were being destroyed revolted him.

Otto had known the brutality of Hautmann, Vomecourt and the other Nazi leaders but he had retained much of his faith in the humanity of his fellow ground troops. After all they were only obeying orders. Had they disobeyed they would have suffered the same fate as the wretched villagers. But was he the only one to have felt that this unprovoked and barbarous over-reaction could never be justified? The only one whose conscience cried out to him that this could not be allowed to happen, that they had to do something to rescue the women and children from the church? On the evidence of the empty bottles, maybe the answer was yes. How could the other soldiers have been revolted by what had happened and yet content to celebrate as if some major victory had been won?

But what had he achieved by his actions? Dominique Malraux had been killed in cold blood in front of him. Agathe had escaped but she was already out of the church and might have got away in any case. He had shot one of his colleagues. Had the bloodshed been tempered by his actions? He doubted it – hundreds of women and children had still died in that church. But at least he had done something. Call it a protest or a moral statement or whatever you like, but he had switched sides. His mind returned to the discussion about the spiritual football match in the farmhouse of the night before. Agathe had explained it to him in German later on that evening. He had been cheering on his team from the stands, but as the true evil nature of its strategy was revealed he had been compelled to switch sides, get on the pitch and play for the other team. But why? He wasn't a believer. He had no faith. Yet his soul had been stirred, his spirit had rebelled against the evil acts into which he had been drawn. Despite his nausea at that moment Otto vowed to seek the truth behind his actions. Agathe would help him. He knew she would.

* * *

They waited unseen for the last Germans to clear the Champ de Foire and the central section of the Limoges road. They had to hide in an abandoned shop as the troops sped off past the church and in the direction of Nieul. Once they could be sure that the Germans had all left, they came out into the open. By now it was about 11.15a.m.

Walking away from their hideout along the Rue Emile Desourteaux, all Eloise could see was burnt out buildings. Some had no sign of life, or death, within them. No body parts sticking out from the debris, no pieces of clothing clinging tenuously to a block of stone or an iron bar, no personal possessions scattered outside, discarded in a mad scramble for survival. But the garage was a different matter. Its frontage was completely burnt out and the roof had collapsed into the interior. Remains of bodies littered the floor of the workshop. Eloise stepped gingerly and fearfully into the building. From the surviving pieces of clothing and body parts it seemed as if the victims were adult males. The ash was not as thick as in the church, suggesting too that the fire had not been as intense and that fewer bodies had combusted here. But none of the fragments appeared to belong to Pierre and there were no signs of any children having been trapped in the garage.

The other members of the party joined Eloise in surveying the desolation in the once thriving business. Marianne spoke for all of them.

"How many other places are there like this? Our village has been totally destroyed. How could they have done this?"

"It's beyond belief, Mother," replied Gabrielle, wrapping her arm around the distraught Eloise.

"Come, let's go to the school. I know they were inoculating the children yesterday. Hopefully that was over before the killing started, but we need to find out. Will you come with us, Eloise?"

She nodded weakly. By now all hope of finding her husband and child alive had evaporated. It would almost be a relief to find their bodies, such was the mounting trauma that she experienced when entering each building.

They walked along the main street, away from the garage and the church, in the direction of Confolens. A workshop on the other side of the road had been gutted, but apart from a few men's shoes protruding from the ash there was no evidence of those who had perished in the inferno. Without being asked, Eloise shook her head, as she also did in the wine store across the road. The men of the village had obviously been taken to several sites of execution. Bullet holes had created random patterns in any surviving walls. The men had been shot before being consumed by fire.

Agathe broke the silence, speaking in German.

"Otto, I have to ask you this. Did you have any idea that any of this was going to happen?"

"Sister, I swear to you on the Holy Bible, I had no idea. We were told that we were looking for Major Peters who had been abducted in the area. We were ordered to search the houses and bring back any maquis suspects. But we were not ordered to kill. I'm sure that Hautmann has gone way beyond his orders in doing this. And to what effect? He's no closer to finding Peters. It was only hearsay that he was being held here anyway. In fact, even if they had been holding him and he was still alive before the massacre he will certainly be dead now. The French will never be able to forgive the Germans for this. Especially Vomecourt, that Alsatian dog, and his turncoat pups who have butchered their own people. May they rot in hell."

"We will speak later about that, Otto, but first we must check the school."

Even if a visitor that morning had been unaware of the terrible events of the previous day and even if there was no sign of their occurrence, one observation might have had sinister significance. Dogs – they were everywhere, tails between their legs, whining and sniffing around the remains of the buildings seeking out their masters and mistresses. Even the domestic cats, usually so proud and independent, were bowed and forlorn, aware that something was different, maybe wrong, but not sure exactly what. The tragedy had permeated every level of society in Oradour-sur-Glane. Every living being was grieving, but in a sort of incredulous or surreal way.

The boys' school was situated behind the town hall and opposite the tram station and post office. Like most buildings in the village it was a built of local stone. It was a single storey structure comprising several classrooms. Drab and unprepossessing, it must have reinforced the monotony of learning for many students.

Stepping into the building, Eloise was relieved to see that the school had suffered relatively little damage. There had been a desultory attempt to set fire to one or two classrooms and some desks and books had been burnt, but the fire had clearly not taken hold. Perhaps the Germans had lost interest once they had reached the far end of the village. Relieved that her son had not been killed in the school, Eloise could breathe more easily again. But by now her nerves were shattered, the nerve ends raw and exposed by the anguished anticipation on entering each new building and the mixture of relief and anti-climax at each inconclusive discovery. For Eloise the torture continued. Was she ever going to able to establish the fate of her beloved husband and son? If they were alive, how were they going to find each other and how long might it take? Both the agony and the hope lay in not knowing the answers to these questions.

CHAPTER TWENTY FIVE

When Agathe, Mary and the other missionary refugees from Gahini arrived at Benaco, night was falling. Their journey from Rwanda to Tanzania had constantly been interrupted by road blocks and impromptu searches by Hutu militia along the way. But somehow they had made it through each obstruction. Sister Agathe had prayed like she had never prayed before, her faith stretched to the limits as each Hutu thug peered menacingly into the car, searching for Tutsis or Hutu collaborators. Each time they were waved through she shouted, "Thank you, Lord", once out of earshot of the militia. She did not do this in any triumphalist way, as there was likely to be another road block just around the corner, but out of gratitude for their continued survival.

In addition, she was increasingly fearful of the fate of her Rwandan friends at Gahini. They couldn't escape from the country and it now seemed clear that the militia had orders from the highest authority to kill all Tutsis. Not just those who might be a danger to the regime, but all those with a Tutsi ID card or who were suspected of belonging to that tribe. There was no other word to describe this methodology than 'genocide'. Anyone who harboured Tutsis or helped them escape would meet a similar fate, the frequent sight of bodies lying by the side of the road bearing testimony to the scale of the butchery.

The early refugees had established a nascent camp at Benaco. It was a collection of impromptu shelters, constructed from whatever materials the refugees had been able to take with them – wood, plastic sheets, corrugated iron and canvas. They had simply pitched camp where they had dropped in northern Tanzania, unable to go any further, but having reached a safe distance from the border. They had taken with them whatever food and belongings they could carry. The trail of weary people walking from the border had led the missionary convoy to this place. Too tired and tense to make any other arrangements, they parked their vehicles together and slept as best they could in the cars overnight.

Agathe awoke next morning with the certainty that the events of the previous day had just been a bad dream – too appalling to have actually happened. For a few minutes she nursed this happy thought, inhabiting that twilight world between sleeping and waking, where nothing is quite clear and reality is suspended. But gradually the true situation revealed itself to her. It had not been a dream. They were sitting in their cars in the middle of nowhere with vast numbers of humanity trooping past and setting up camp wherever a space could be found.

Looking out of the window, she could see a familiar sight – a white van with a red cross painted on the side. Agathe emerged uncertainly from her Beetle into the morning sun, which was already strong enough for her to have to shade her eyes. She knocked on the window of the van, which had the words 'Tanzanian Red Cross' etched onto the driver's door. The window was wound down and a pleasant young black man spoke in English,

"Can I help you?"

Agathe replied rather nervously, as if unable to focus on a relevant question given the enormity of the tragedy and the unfamiliarity of their predicament.

"Yes, we are Christian missionaries from Rwanda. We left at very short notice yesterday. We have nowhere to go but can offer our services to assist you in your work."

The young man replied.

"Thank you. Stay close by us. We are awaiting further instructions. Other relief agencies have been mobilised and we are awaiting their arrival at any time. Are you able to offer any medical help?" He pointed at a large tent which was being erected about thirty metres away, with the words 'Field Hospital' prominent on the awnings.

"Yes, of course," responded Agathe, "we have a doctor and some nursing staff with us. I will go and get them."

Within a few days the relief operation was in full swing. Huts were being erected for the refugees, food and water points established and field hospitals had started to treat patients. The missionaries from Gahini were put to active use almost immediately, either in the hospitals, feeding stations or, in the case of Agathe and Mary, other family services. For all the frustration of trying to reunite families in the vast camp and the many failures to locate loved ones, the women experienced the most intense satisfaction at each person who found a member of their family or a friend from their village. Sadly, however, for most, their loved ones were dead and it would be many months before their fate was discovered but, in the meantime, they would keep on looking, wandering around the Benaco camp searching for their relatives or anyone they recognised who might know where they were.

A few weeks after Agathe had reunited Samuel and Chantalle, she was sitting quietly in her UN tent having completed another largely unsatisfactory day when she heard a scratching sound on one of the canvas walls of the tent. This was not unusual. Relief workers were pestered day and night by refugees wanting food, drink, clothing, medicines, indeed anything that the displaced Rwandans couldn't be bothered, or were too ill, to queue for. Agathe had learnt not to shout out, "Who is it?", as this would confirm her presence and encourage the enquirer. Many times, receiving no response, the refugee would just go away and join the queue. Agathe was just tall enough to look through the holes into which the brail ropes weaved at the entrance to the tent to see who it was. When she saw her visitor she couldn't get the door open quickly enough. Fumbling with the ropes that held the two pieces of door canvas together she almost fell out of the tent crashing into her visitor.

"Naome, you are safe!" she blurted out, hugging her house-girl so hard that all the breath seemed to be pressed out of their bodies. Despite her joy at seeing her employer again, Naome had to restrain her.

"Sister, you are squashing me. Please let go."

"Naome, I'm sorry but I can't believe you are alive. You're the first person I have seen from Gahini. I've been praying for your safety for so long and now you are here. I've been desperate to know that some people had escaped and, of all my friends, I just can't believe that I've seen you first."

Agathe held open the door of the tent and invited Naome inside.

The two women sat down holding hands, barely able to appreciate the joy of their reunion.

"Let me make tea," said Agathe and she brewed up two cups of the hot, milky, sweet tea favoured by the Rwandans, the provision of which was a special privilege for the aid workers. Agathe looked at her. Naome was about twenty and newly married to Etienne. She had been looking after Agathe since she was about sixteen, after her former house-girl had died of AIDS. She had been diligent and honest, qualities which were not always present in Rwandan domestic staff. At first, having a paid helper was anathema to Agathe. "Why do I need servants waiting on me day and night?" she would often say. "Aren't I able to do things myself? I don't want a slave."

As the years passed, however, she realised that this was the way of things in Rwanda. The locals expected the bazungu to have several servants, perhaps a maid, a gardener and night time security guard. If any European didn't have such employees, the Rwandans would regard them as mean and uncaring. The sum that each was paid was a good wage in Rwanda and an important supplement to the family income. So, over the years, Agathe had employed a series of house-girls and gardeners but assuaged her conscience by treating them as colleagues rather than servants and would help them whenever possible in the event of a family or personal problem. Naome and Agathe had become good friends. When Naome's mother had died Agathe gave her two weeks' paid leave to organise the funeral and observe the period of mourning customary in Rwandan society. She even gave her money to buy food for the many mourners who visited the house. Similarly, Naome would often cheerfully stay late to help Agathe prepare a meal for any visitors that she might have.

Eventually, Agathe asked the question which had been on her lips since they first met.

"Naome, tell me how you managed to escape and what happened to the others."

Naome sighed. She had been expecting this question and indeed, in some ways, had been dreading it as it would compel her to relive the appalling trauma of her escape and the fate of those dear to her. However she needed to confront those memories if she was to move on and, confiding in her dear mistress was perhaps the least painful way to do this.

"Sister, you remember the day you left?"Agathe nodded wincing at the feelings of betrayal that she still experienced. "Well, I was actually in the house when those men arrived. I was just coming in from the garden when you answered the door.You didn't hear me. I had just gone to the market to get some vegetables. I could tell there was trouble and hid in the wood shed. Fortunately, the men didn't see me although they fired a shot at the shed, which made the whole wooden frame shake. I waited until they had left, terrified that they would do a proper search. People had been saying for days that the Hutus would come and kill us but I didn't believe them. I thought we would be safe in Gahini, especially in the mission compound. But, that day, they stayed in Gahini until it was dark. I heard shouting and screaming all day. Some of the voices I thought I recognised.That was the worst part. No, it was worse not knowing whether the voices I recognised were from those being killed or doing the killing. I couldn't bear thinking that some of my friends were killing some of my other friends just because they were from a different tribe. We had lived peacefully together for years. Most times I wasn't even conscious of who was a Hutu and who was a Tutsi. It didn't seem to matter. But on that one day tribalism turned people into killers. I just don't understand why, Sister."

"Naome, it's a question I've asked myself several times in my life. I can't give you a rational explanation. But go on, how did you escape?"

"When it got dark and the noise had died down I opened the door of the wood shed – just an inch or two. I couldn't tell if the militia was staying in your house overnight. I had heard that they had occupied some houses in my sister's village and it was my worst nightmare that they could be in your house for days. I must have listened through the gap for about ten minutes. It was so tense. One mistake and I would have been killed. I couldn't take any risks. I was so stressed, my body was shaking and my head ached unbearingly. And I was dreadfully worried about Etienne. He had gone off early to the market in Rwamagana as usual to sell his vegetables. I kept thinking that the Interahamwe would have gone there first, before they came to Gahini, and he would have been there, right in the middle of the town. He had nowhere to hide and if the Hutus had searched him they would have found his Tutsi ID card. He always carried it with him in case he had to prove his identity to the market officials."

Agathe desperately wanted to know what had happened to Etienne but instinctively felt that she shouldn't ask. Perhaps this was the first time Naome had been able to tell her story. For her it was a cathartic experience, part of the healing process. Agathe should let her continue.

"I kept picturing him in my mind – standing at his stall, selling his stock and happily talking to his customers and the other traders but then I would see the militia coming into the square. They looked and sounded like the men who came to your house, loud and angry, hatred burning in their eyes. And with them were some of the locals. The militia had given them machetes, knives and sticks. They too seemed possessed. I recognised some of them but I don't know why these people had come into my picture. It didn't really matter who they were, it was just enough to know that they were my neighbours and that they shouldn't have been there. But then the picture froze in my mind. Probably I didn't want to know what happened next, or maybe my mind was just not capable of such images."

There was a long pause. Naome wasn't tearful or angry or emotional in any way, just detached, resigned. Agathe had met many people like this in the camp. It was impossible to tell what had happened to them in the genocide or how many of their family members had perished. They just needed space and silence. It was part of nature's coping strategy. It seemed extraordinary that such people weren't pestering her for knowledge of their loved ones. But perhaps their brains had just shut down, switched to survival mode, or maybe they just didn't want to know. "No news is good news" was a saying that

Agathe had heard the British missionaries use. Now she understood its meaning. At the moment she could still imagine that Etienne was alive, as she had heard nothing to the contrary from Naome. There was still hope of good news.

It was a couple of minutes before Naome could resume. She apologised for the delay although she knew she didn't need to. During the silence the women had held hands, but barely exchanged a glance, locked in their own thoughts.

"When I could be sure that everything was quiet I crept out of the shed. I didn't know what to do. I crawled around the side of the house and had a good look inside. There was hardly a sound although I could hear some muffled laughter in the distance. I thought it must be the Hutus getting drunk. But apart from that there was silence. As you know, Sister, normally at this time people would have been having their evening meal, you would hear them chatting and laughing, watching the children running between the houses screaming with delight. There would be lights everywhere. It seemed so strange with everything being dark and still. It made me worry even more that I would be heard and discovered.

I knew it would be dangerous to go back to my house, but I just had to do it. I had to know if Etienne was there or if there was any sign that he had returned home. I would have felt better if I had known that he had escaped from the market. He might then have been able to hide out in the bush or somewhere. I tried to keep out of sight as much as possible, so I crept around the back of the mission buildings, the school, the rehab centre, the hospital, knowing that they would help me to stay hidden. But as I ran from each one I felt really exposed. I thought that it was only a matter of time before someone saw me. There were bodies everywhere. I wanted to check who they were, as I knew their relatives would be worried. At least I could have put them out of their misery. But I just couldn't look. It wasn't that I didn't care, but I had made a conscious decision to stay alive. I couldn't let anything get in the way of that. As it was, every time I stopped, stray dogs would come up to me and start barking. There were only scavenging for food but I was terrified they would alert the militia. If I had stopped to check all the bodies I would have been even more at risk. Was I wrong to be so selfish, Sister Agathe?"

Agathe shook her head. After all, she had left behind all her Rwandan friends when she had fled from Gahini and, again, she had escaped from the church at Oradour when she could have taken others with her. But she had only been concerned with her own survival. Agathe could still vividly picture Dominique Malraux being riddled with bullets and falling at her feet. She had done nothing to help her. She just stepped over the body. As Naome had said, the will to live, the survival decision, overrode all other considerations. Agathe had no right to sit in judgement on Naome.

"But I do feel guilty. People come up to me and ask me if I know what happened to a friend or relative. I always shake my head, but maybe I could have known. Perhaps I stepped over their body. It would only have taken a moment to check their faces, but I didn't do it. Their families have been worrying for weeks and will perhaps never find out the fate of their loved ones. Yet I could have given them an answer – good or bad. But my worst nightmare is that some of those bodies weren't dead. I could have helped them live, but I was too obsessed with myself."

Once again Naome lapsed into a resigned silence. Clearly she was re-living those images of Gahini. They would be with her for the rest of her life, perhaps becoming more vivid and recurrent unless she received psychological help. Agathe determined that she would do everything possible to ensure that Naome was freed from the nightmares.

"When I eventually got home, there was no sign that anyone had been in the house. Everything was just as I had left it. And then I had the numbing thought that Etienne's body might have been one of those at the compound, and I hadn't even looked. With that I broke down completely. I sat on the floor in the dark with my back against the wall and just cried for hours. There seemed to be no hope. I felt completely alone. In a way I hoped that the Interahamwe would find me and kill me too. Life was not much worth living without Etienne, you and the rest of my family. I didn't know what had happened to any of them. I stayed in the house for several days, eating up what little food was left in the store and drinking from the rain water tank in the garden. During the day I hid under some bushes outside. The militiamen were still searching the houses and it was too dangerous to stay inside during the day. At least I could escape from the garden. I had worked out a route which would at least give me a chance of survival if I was discovered. So I just lay there, hidden under the leaves and branches until nightfall when I crept back into the house to eat, drink and sleep.

One day the militia searched the house. I could hear them smashing down the front door and throwing the furniture around. Luckily they didn't come into the garden. They must have assumed we had fled. I was worried that Etienne would come back and see the house deserted and leave again. But as far as I am aware he never did. When the food had nearly run out, I knew that I must leave. So I took what was left, together with some containers of rain water, some clothes and bedding and set off. I didn't really know where to go, but I went in the general direction of the border.

Lots of other people were walking too. There were road blocks everywhere, sometimes every few hundred metres. I didn't dare go through one. Even though I didn't have my Tutsi ID card they would suspect that I was one. Even people with a Hutu ID card were being stopped if they looked like a Tutsi. And I couldn't really pass for a Hutu, could I Sister?"

Both women laughed. Naome had often claimed with pride that she was descended from Mwami Kigeri Rwabugiri, a Tutsi king in the mid nineteenth century, who was credited with creating the Rwandan state. However, in his expanded empire he also perpetuated the dominance of the Tutsis, promoting many to the top military and political posts. Thus the stereotypes of Tutsi as master and Hutu as slave were reinforced, creating the resentment which fuelled the genocide. The Mwami was regarded as divine and infallible. Although Agathe would never be able to verify Naome's claims to be one of Mwami's descendants she did sometimes notice a slightly aristocratic air to her. She was generally helpful and obliging but some things were beneath her. Even though Etienne, her husband, grew vegetables for sale in the market, she would never work in Agathe's garden. When asked, she merely asserted that other classes were cultivators, not hers. To Agathe, this meant that Hutus grew crops while Tutsis kept herds of animals. She often wondered whether Etienne felt inferior, given his wife's traditional views. But, while some attitudes in Rwanda died slowly, it was a generally fluid society and lines of demarcation were blurred. Etienne and Naome seemed to love and support each other and that was enough. If Naome was truly descended from monarchy then maybe it wasn't unreasonable that her attitudes were deep rooted and would take longer to reform.

But the women's laughter was not solely linked to Naome's alleged aristocratic connections with the Tutsis. She also looked the part. No-one would ever mistake her for a Hutu. She was the archetypal 'Ethiopian', tall at five feet nine inches, with a long face that appeared to have been stretched still further by a vice, given its exaggerated proportions. She was light skinned with thin lips and a narrow nose. This latter feature was subdivided into a prominent bridge and pointed tip, which added to the superior aspect of her appearance. The lower part of her face was drawn together into a narrow chin. Her's was a landscape altogether different to the stockier stature and rounder features of the traditional Hutu.

Naome continued.

"So I had to leave the road well before each road block and skirt around it through the countryside. This wasn't always easy. Often the land was laid bare, with few places to hide and I would have to go a long way off line in order to stay hidden. Sometimes I got lost and couldn't find the road again. If I stayed too close to the road the soldiers would fire at me. One time they even hit me, but luckily the bullet passed through the mattress I was carrying on my back. Still, I threw myself to the ground so that they would think that they had killed me. I didn't move until nightfall.

Every night I had to sleep out in the open. There were plenty of deserted homes, but I was terrified that the owners would return or soldiers would use them as billets. So I thought it was safer to stay outside in the countryside. But I didn't sleep much. I was so tense –

every little noise seemed to wake me. You don't realise how many small animals are ferreting around in the undergrowth until you get in their way.

Eventually I got to the border at Rusomo. By then I had eaten all my food and had drunk all the water. This didn't worry me too much as I was sure that I could get some more supplies when I got to Tanzania. I still had some money left and a few valuables, which I could trade. But when I got to the border it was closed. Soldiers were everywhere, firing at anyone who tried to get close to the bridge. There were thousands of us milling around. After the first day, I was getting very thirsty and quite hungry. There was absolutely nothing to eat or drink. All the fruit had been stripped off the trees and the berries from the bushes.

Next to me was a Hutu family, a mother, father and two young children. They could see that I was suffering and shared what little water and food they had with me. I tried not to take too much as I didn't want to deprive the children, who already looked quite distressed. They were from Kibungo and had heard that the RPF had invaded Rwanda and were scared that there would be reprisals from the Tutsis. So they fled. Yet here they were, sharing their final morsels of food and precious drops of water with a Tutsi and a stranger at that. Our country is not so bad, you see!

A rumour was sweeping around the refugees that the RPF weren't far away from Rusomo. One brave person went up to one of the soldiers and told them. He got beaten for his trouble, but you could see the soldiers telling each other and starting to look worried. They were cowards really. They weren't going to stay for a fight and risk getting killed. Within an hour or two they had all deserted, and we could just walk across the bridge into Tanzania. There were so many of us that it took several hours to get across the border. I tried not to look down from the bridge as there were decomposing bodies on the banks of the river. You could smell them even from the bridge. Every time I saw dead bodies I thought that Etienne could be one of them, but I would probably never find out. Someone would probably tip all these bodies into the river, or they would just rot where they had fallen. I was despairing of ever seeing Etienne again – dead or alive.

When we got into Tanzania the Red Cross told us to come to Benaco. As we got closer to the camp there were little stalls by the side of the road selling meat, vegetables, firewood, pots and pans. So I bought some food and water and gave as much as I could spare to my Hutu friends. They were even selling homemade beer so we bought a couple of bottles and celebrated our deliverance in style. I don't know what happened to the Hutu family. They were sent off to the Kibungo zone and I never saw them again. I owe my life to them, but other Hutus may have killed Etienne. I just don't understand it.

When I arrived here I was directed to the zone where all the Gahini people were gathered and they soon told me that you were here. I just had to come and see that you were all right and show you that I had escaped. They also told me that you might be able to find Etienne, if he was still alive and had made his way to Benaco."

"I'm so pleased to see you, Naome," the two women hugged again, "and I will do everything possible to find dear Etienne. Look, I will prepare a record card for him right now."

With that, Agathe started writing on one of the small white index cards, which formed the database of all missing persons reported at the camp.

CHAPTER TWENTY SIX

The boys' school was at the western end of the village, opposite the tram station and post office. While Otto and the women could see that a few other properties further away from the centre of the village than the school had been burnt, it seemed that the Nazis had largely run out of steam at this point. Perhaps they had lost interest, or maybe they were just plain exhausted. It was a chilling thought to Agathe that even cold bloodied murderers needed rest and refreshment. Whatever the motivation, Dupic House, which was a few buildings away from the boys' school, seemed to have been the last structure to have been burnt. A quick search revealed no sign of any bodies or parts of bodies at this location.

The group trudged forlornly back to the centre of the village. They had checked most of the buildings on either side of the road, but realised that they hadn't visited the Champ de Foire, the square at the centre of the village, which had, in pre-war days, hosted fairgrounds and other attractions. It was a place where the villagers had, in the past, met together to celebrate the joy of living – to have fun, to be exhilarated by the latest fairground ride, to laugh and drink together. As they walked into the square, Eloise couldn't help but envisage it filled with happy and excited people. She imagined Pierre grabbing her by the hand and both getting drenched as they bobbed for apples. When he was younger, Claude had been thrilled by the marionettes with their brightly coloured outfits and extravagant movements. Eloise had clung onto him tightly as they sat on a white horse on the merry go round, Claude gurgling contentedly at the thrill of the ride. How she wished she could hold him now – she would never let go again.

As it was, all that Eloise could see were the Mayor's burnt out car near to the entrance to the Champ de Foire and a few personal possessions scattered around the square. She searched eagerly among the latter for any sign that Pierre or Claude had been there. But once again she found nothing. By now Otto and Marianne were peering down the well at the far end of the Champ de Foire. There was no obvious evidence that any bodies had been tipped into the well, but they could only see a few metres down before visibility faded.

"Let's go down this road at the side of the square," directed Gabrielle, pointing to a narrow route back onto the Rue Emile Desourteaux, "there are a few buildings down there that we can search."

As they walked down the road their hearts sank. They could smell death again. Not just the bitter smell of burnt timber, but the sweeter tang of roasted flesh. The barn on the right of the street appeared to mark the seat of the fire. It was a substantial structure with stone walls and large rectangular corner stones. However, the roof of the building was completely missing and the heat had been so intense that a large part of the stone wall closest to the street had caved into the interior, the slabs cracked by the intensity of the blaze. Inside, the building had been completely destroyed. The ash and debris were piled up on the floor of the barn and numerous body parts and pieces of clothing were protruding through the wreckage. Eloise gasped as she surveyed the carnage in front of her. This had obviously been the site of a major loss of life.

The ash was still warm as they moved slowly into the barn. Gabrielle whispered softly to Agathe so that Eloise wouldn't hear, "There are dozens of bodies in here, and from the looks of it they are all men. I just get a horrible feeling about this place."

"Me, too," replied Agathe quietly. "If Pierre was in the village when the Germans started to round people up then he must have been killed. We have seen so many male bodies that very few men of the village can possibly have survived. And we didn't find Pierre at any of the other sites…" She then corrected herself so as not to appear too pessimistic. "But let's pray that he's not here either."

By now, Eloise had almost reached the far end of the barn, where there was a door into an adjoining building. Clinging to the handle of the door was the charred upper torso of Pierre LeClerc.

"Oh my God, no, no, no!" screamed Eloise, "please not Pierre, my darling, it can't be you."

But there was no doubt. The shape of his head, the wedding ring still visible on his left hand and the collar of his red jacket, which nestled around his blackened neck, all testified to the tragic end to the life of Pierre LeClerc. He had done better than most, at least reaching the door from which he could have made his escape. But the holes in the remains of the door left no doubt as to how he had died, riddled with bullets as he desperately grabbed the handle of the route to safety. A few seconds more and he might have made it.

Eloise was sobbing uncontrollably as the others rushed over to comfort her. She kept screeching, "It can't be true, it can't be true!" but the evidence of the reality of this horror was right in front of her. Up until this point, Agathe had been able to reassure Eloise that somehow Pierre had survived but now there were no words of comfort that could be given. She must just plunge into the depths of despair with the grieving wife. Death was now enveloping her like a blanket. First Dominique, then the Steinrich girls, now Pierre LeClerc. Death had its sting, the grave its victory, she thought, doubting the apostle Paul's words to the contrary. She thought of all the other relatives who would be grieving over fragments of the bodies of their loved ones, which would be pulled from this and the other pyres in the village in the coming hours. It was just too much to bear and Agathe wept from the very depths of her soul.

* * *

Otto was desperate to help the distraught Eloise. This was partly from compassion but, in truth, partly from a desire to distance himself and indeed other decent German citizens from this barbaric atrocity. But he was dumb. He couldn't speak French and, even if he could, had no words of comfort or explanation to offer. He could only contribute practical help. Finding a wooden box which, apart from some charring around it, had miraculously survived the inferno, he delicately started to place the remains of Pierre LeClerc inside. At least Eloise would be able to give Pierre a proper burial in the knowledge that he rested in peace in the earth of the town that he loved. Many others would not be so lucky. They might have no physical remembrance of their loved ones, so fierce had been the blaze in the building, reducing bones to powder indistinguishable from the ash of the barn's timbers. He worked reverently, making sure that he picked up all the fragments of body parts in the vicinity of Pierre's outstretched hand.

He could hear Eloise's sobbing as she nestled into Agathe's shoulder for comfort. But then he was shaken by a piercing scream and, turning, saw the flailing limbs of the bereaved women bearing down on him. The blows raining down on his head and back stunned him with their power and frequency. It was like being trapped in the spinning arms of a threshing machine. Eloise was hysterical and thundered at the top of a voice which seemed to have been raised an octave by her grief,

"Get off him you murdering Nazi bastard! How dare you touch my precious husband with your stinking German hands. Scum… scum… scum… I hate you… I hate all of you!" and she cradled the remains of Pierre close to her chest, his torso disintegrating further at her touch.

Otto moved away from the sobbing woman. She was right. He was a murdering bastard. He had never spoken out as Das Reich had marched through southern France killing anyone who got in its way. Yes he had been cynical in the way he had carried out his duties, even relishing in the sneering disdain of his more zealous colleagues, especially the Alsatians. But he had saved no lives and this atrocity was the consequence, the inevitable conclusion of his acquiescence, and that of thousands of other German soldiers who just didn't care enough to risk their own lives in order to try and save those of innocent civilians. He had been disgusted when he heard of the French civilians hanging from the lampposts in Tulle but he did nothing. He should have known that it wouldn't just stop there, that further bestiality would follow. But yet he kept quiet. He had even carried the box of explosives into the church at Oradour without questioning his orders. History's judgement on him and his kind would be just as severe as on those who had actually

lit the fuses and on those who had shot Pierre LeClerc. Eloise was right
to brand him a murderer and he had felt the shame and guilt of the
whole nation as she had lashed out at him.

Otto left the building, slipping silently past the other women, who
were moving forward to comfort Eloise. He waited out in the street,
each cry, emanating from inside the barn, resonating through his body
just as the physical blows had done. There was no escape from the
present as there wasn't from the past. This horror would be with him
for the rest of his life, which, at the moment, he hoped would be as
short a period as possible. He longed to share in the fate of the villagers
of Oradour. Perhaps the soldiers would come back and finish him off
too. He would put up no fight – better to die now than be tormented
for all the days that he had left on this earth.

He wanted to walk, but to where he didn't know. Anywhere was
good enough, away from this madness – into a void, the emptiness of
which would swallow his remorse and shame. Otto headed away from
the barn and back towards the Champ de Foire. He could still hear the
sobbing from the barn, magnified as the sound ricocheted from the
walls and escaped through the open roof. He covered his ears and
started to run. He knew that, if he didn't escape that sound, it was likely
to haunt him for eternity. His hands clasped his head tightly as he left
the fairground and headed along the open road into the countryside. He
didn't even notice the fork in the road and was thus spared having to
make a choice of direction which, in his disturbed frame of mind, he
would have been unable to accomplish. However what he then saw
struck a visceral blow to his fragile emotions.

Staring at him from the graveyard were the headstones, pock
marked with deposits of lime, and they seemed to shout out at him,
"Murderer, slaughterer of women and children. Here lie some of your
victims, you cowardly slime". Otto wept as he passed by the cemetery,
imagining that each grave contained the corpse of an innocent victim
like Pierre LeClerc.

Suddenly he stopped. Was it the wind making a moaning sound?
Were the very elements also crying out against his iniquities? But the
night was still. Perhaps the spirits of the dead were coming to torment

him in the same way as the living were railing against him. Looking more closely among the gravestones, he thought he could see something moving – a flash of yellow. Otto ducked down under a stone wall that ran round the perimeter of the burial ground. Surely it couldn't be a German soldier left behind by his departing colleagues? Maybe it was another deserter like himself? Otto peered over the wall and could now see more clearly. The shape was small, no bigger than a child, and it was writhing deliriously, groaning as it thrashed from side to side.

Otto looked around and, when he could be sure that he wasn't being observed, climbed over the wall. He headed out towards the middle of the cemetery, to a tall memorial stone, behind which the body was partially hidden. His tread on the dew laden grass was soft and deliberate so that he didn't startle the boy, whom he could now clearly see tossing and turning behind the stone. The young lad looked about thirteen or fourteen. He was wearing long brown shorts, full length beige socks, which had now slumped down to his ankles, and sturdy black shoes. However he could only see flashes of yellow on his flannel shirt vibrant against the dirt and blood with which it was now caked. The boy's face too was streaked with blood which had matted his hair and seeped into every orifice. Only his eye sockets had escaped a coating but, in his delirium, his eyes were rolling around highlighting the madness of his movements. Otto approached the boy slowly and carefully, kneeling when he was about a metre away.

For some moments, Otto just stared at the agitated body. He daren't speak, since the sound of a German voice might terrify the lad. Otto was certain that he was another victim of the appalling atrocity that had gradually been revealed to him in Oradour. He resolved to do everything in his power to ensure that the child did not become a permanent resident of this necropolis. After a while, Otto edged closer and gently touched the boy on the shoulder. Surprisingly to Otto, the lad quietened at the unexpected sensation. He was clearly trying to focus on the source of this physical contact. His head was still rolling from side to side but his eyes were calmer, as if he was using all his residual powers of concentration to assess the provenance of his companion. Otto was grateful for the farmer's outfit, in which he bore a passable resemblance to a typical French peasant. The boy too was reassured and with his good arm reached out towards Otto. The German held the outstretched hand and gave it a gentle squeeze.

Despite this moment of clarity, the boy's movements were still frenzied. He needed urgent medical help. Otto was sure that the child was incapable of walking. After all, he had made no effort to get up when he had stretched out his arm. Such was the seriousness of the obvious wound to his arm that Otto doubted whether he could make him comfortable in any carrying position. He needed something that would provide some support. Otto held up the palm of his hand indicating to the boy that he should wait there. He then realised how pointless this action was, given the boy's immobility, but at least he had done his best to reassure the child that he would return.

Otto skirted round the outside of the cemetery, earnestly scanning both the interior and exterior of the burial ground for any suitable vehicle for transportation. His attention was drawn to a small shed in the northern corner of the cemetery, which was almost hidden under the branches of an apple tree. The shed door had not been opened for some time, judging by the rotten wood and rusty hinges, but he was just about able to force it open despite the protests of its ancient fastenings. Inside, he found exactly the object for which he had been hoping – an old, dilapidated, but still reasonably sturdy wheelbarrow.

Urgently, Otto grabbed the handles of the barrow and pushed it out of the shed. His progress along the gravel path that led from the building was slow, as the barrow seemed to have a mind of its own and careered regularly into the grass at the side. However, by the time he got back to the boy Otto had worked out how to compensate for the deviation in its steering. It would be a harder proposition trying to balance the barrow with the weight of the boy inside, especially as he appeared incapable of supporting himself. It would be a long journey back to the village.

The next big task was to get the child into the cart. Without words, Otto would have to rely on gestures and the boy's eyes were rolling, making it difficult for him to focus on any object for very long. Otto decided to get the boy into a sitting position, propped up by the upturned wheel barrow. He pointed at the cart and wheeled it round behind the boy tipping it up so that the handles were pointing at the sky. He grabbed the boy, wrapping both his arms around his waist in an effort to steady him. Several times the child slipped from his grasp, and started thrashing around on the floor again. Eventually Otto worked out that he would have to manhandle the boy more roughly. If he could prop his back against the floor of the barrow he could hopefully tip up the cart almost in the same movement and the child would slide down inside. It would be agony for him with his injured arm, but at least Otto could then take him to safety. The child cried out as the German yanked him against the barrow and, simultaneously, pushed down on the handles and up against the lip of the box, but the job was done. Otto dragged the child by the shoulders into a more comfortable position so that he was almost sitting up, with only the bottom part of his calves protruding from the lip of the barrow.

Oddly, the jolt had calmed the boy somewhat. He was still tossing around but less violently than before. This was fortuitous as his presence had unbalanced the barrow and Otto was veering sharply from side to side. It would have been impossible to make any progress at all without some co-operation from his passenger. It seemed to take an age for Otto to negotiate the uneven and indistinct path out of the cemetery, but once on the road his journey became less challenging. For the first time he became consciously aware that he knew nothing about this boy and the circumstances by which he came to be lying so badly injured in the cemetery. He had also been so bound up in planning how he could safely transport the child that he had given no thought to what he should do when he got to the village. Should he just wheel him around until he found someone who knew who he was? And then what? If his parents were dead or missing who would look after him? And the most important question of all was how could the boy get medical attention in a remote French village where, no doubt, the only doctor was either dead or in hiding? He needed to find Sister Agathe if she was still in the village. He must head back towards the barn.

Otto quickened his pace as the barrow became easier to manouevre and the buildings on the outskirts of Oradour came into view. There was no-one about. It occurred to him that he and the women may have been the first people into Oradour that morning, quite possibly the first to venture into the village since the atrocity. If so, his chances of finding anyone else to help were remote and, even if he did, it would not take them long to find out that he was German and…Otto shuddered at the likely consequences. Still, if only he could find someone to care for the boy his mission would have been accomplished. He cared little for his own life after Eloise's onslaught but, if at least some good could come out of his actions, his presence in the village that day would not have been totally in vain.

Otto headed off towards the barn. The scene was exactly the same as when he had left the site but there was no sign of the women. How long had it been since he was there? Otto calculated that it must have been at least half an hour, possibly more. Perhaps they had gone back to the farm, but then again surely Eloise would still want to look for her son. It was eerily quiet in the village, the vacuum left by the departing troops had not yet been filled by local people seeking to identify the dead. He wondered anyway how many families had any surviving members left to search for their missing loved ones. Most of those who had gathered on the Champ de Foire had appeared to be in family groupings. They would, by now, all be dead.

The boy had now become largely quiet and still, lulled almost into a trance by the swaying motion of the barrow as it meandered past the barn. Otto was starting to feel the strain, hunched as he was over the cart trying to cushion the impact of each bump in the road and keep his passenger as horizontal as possible. He daren't stop in case the boy became agitated again and because he desperately needed to find someone to take the youngster to hospital. He coughed as the acrid air, laden with its sinister aroma of burnt wood and flesh, tickled his throat. It was a smell from which he knew he would never escape, trapped in his nostrils and released slowly whenever the memory of this dreadful place threatened to fade. Otto shook at the thought of it.

He continued shaking as he felt a sharp, cold sensation in the fleshy part of his neck to the side of his spinal cord. He had applied such pressure on his victims himself during this war and immediately recognised the cold, naked tip of the barrel of a revolver.

Otto was bundled to the surface of the road by what appeared to be two men, who flattened him agonisingly onto his stomach with his arms crossed and yanked behind him. One of the men then sat heavily on his back, thrusting the barrel of the gun deep into Otto's neck. Neither of his attackers said a word. Otto was simply aware of the sensations of fear and silence, the one reinforcing the other as he desperately tried to ascertain his likely fate.

"Kill the Kraut," one of the men snapped at the other, his comments all the more menacing because of their brevity. Obediently, the man who was restraining Otto pressed his gun deeper into the German's neck, to ensure his life would be ended with a single bullet.

A high pitched scream pierced the miasmic air. The two men turned with a start as they saw a shape topple out of the wheelbarrow and stagger shakily towards them. The crazed child held onto the upright man, almost dragging him to the ground as he slid down his body in a vain attempt to stand.

"Please don't kill him. He saved my life, he saved my life…" bellowed the boy as if using up all the energy that he had been conserving during his long wait in the cemetery.

His screams had been heard throughout Oradour, slicing through the silence which the tragedy had imposed on the village, like a sharpened scimitar. It was a dream like sound which filled the ears of Eloise LeClerc. At first she was sceptical of the reality of the familiar voice that she was hearing but at the same time she sensed that it might just be him. Eloise tore back up the road towards the fairground screaming Claude's name and trailing the other women in her wake.

By now Claude had collapsed on the ground, all energy spent by his dramatic intervention, but still able to point at Otto and mouth "non" until he could be sure that Otto's life would be spared. Eloise kissed her son repeatedly, protective of his wounds but desperate for physical contact with the offspring she had feared lost. Sister Agathe pleaded with the resistance men to spare Otto's life, certain now that, not only had he saved her life but that of Claude too. She blurted out the events of the last few days and, despite the warnings she had been given not to disclose any involvement with the resistance, told the maquisards how their comrades had helped her and the Jews escape to Oradour. As she continued with the tale she could sense the man's grip on the trigger weaken. It was not easy persuading those who had seen their comrades executed by the enemy to accept that there was such a thing as a 'good German'. But such was the intensity of her plea, the passion in her argument and the integrity that her nun's habit bestowed that the men moved away from the prostrate foreigner.

"Quick, help us carry the boy to our car. He needs treatment at the hospital, hurry, we can't waste any time."

The two men and the women carefully lifted Claude into the black Renault which was parked a few metres away. As they sped off down the road, Eloise threw a glance towards Otto and smiled.

CHAPTER TWENTY SEVEN

"Papa, chase me", shouted Grace Karamira, "I'm over here." The six year old waved her arms excitedly as she jumped out from behind one of the thousands of plastic shelters that extended as far as the eye could see. Never far from her big sister's side, little Marthe also came out from her hiding place but all she could do was dissolve into a fit of giggles, an enormous smile consuming most of her face in a flash of white teeth and pink tongue.

"There you are," sighed Samuel, "I've been looking everywhere for you. I'm completely worn out chasing half way round this camp trying to catch you."

He lollopped over to the girls, pretending to be a huge monster seeking to devour them and letting out an enormous roar. This made them scream even more, but they didn't run away. The tension was too great for their small bodies to absorb and they just waited for their father to protect from this fearful ogre. Somehow it didn't matter to them that he was one and the same person.

Samuel cradled both his daughters in his one good arm, kissing them repeatedly on the tops of their heads. Physically he was making a good recovery from his injuries. The lacerations to his head had healed and his hair had regrown so that at least from a distance there was no sign of his wounds. The skin that had been sewn over the stump of his left arm had knitted together well and he was now ready for his prosthetic limb to be fitted. But it was at times like this that he became more conscious of what he had lost. No longer could he sweep his girls up into his arms and hug them. No more could he hold each of them high into the air, whirling them around above his head as they kicked out their legs in sheer delight. His physical condition forced him to be more restrained. His natural exuberance with his children had to be tempered by his bodily frailty.

"Come on, girls, let's go home. Mother will be waiting for us with our dinner. You know what she's like when we're late back. Mind you, I haven't a clue where we are, you've led me half way round the camp."

Samuel smiled, not really cross with his daughters, as the chase had been a welcome diversion from the reality of his situation and the monotony of every day survival, which had become a routine at Benaco. Not many weeks before, his routine had been a day's teaching at his school in Nyarubuye followed by a leisurely walk home to his bungalow, where Chantalle and the children would be waiting for him and where he could eat his dinner while listening to their excited chatter about the day's events. Now he had a different routine. Chantalle and the children were still there, except Jonathan of course, and he still had a home of sorts and, if they queued long enough at the feeding and drinking stations, they could obtain enough provisions to eat a meal together. It was, he thought, ironic how quickly one routine replaced another, yet the circumstances were very different.

"It's this way, Daddy" shouted Grace, pulling her father and Martha between the rows of blue plastic huts and pushing between the crowds of people who had gathered outside each one. There were fires everywhere, flames lapping up around large black pots and smoke rising perpendicularly into the still Tanzanian air as if constrained by some invisible chimney.

"How do you know, Grace?" questioned Samuel.

"Because I'm a girl, that's how," giggled his daughter, mimicking her mother's stock answer to any question that seemed to challenge her common sense.

Samuel was happy enough for the moment to be dragged along by his daughter, as he could see they were heading for one of the big compounds that housed supplies for the camp. They were always sited close to a main thoroughfare so that the growling lorries could discharge their loads at any time of the day or night.

They approached the wooden fence that surrounded the compound and, despite the presence of a guard patrolling the perimeter, couldn't resist the temptation to look inside through the gaps in the wood posts. There were several large tents, all of which were shut tight, apart from one where the flaps were wide open as large sacks of grain and rice were being unloaded from a lorry. This did not seem to be progressing too quickly as the only human activity appeared to be a man leaning against the side of the delivery vehicle smoking a cigarette. Samuel shrugged his shoulders. Even as a native Rwandan, the slow pace of life in his country frustrated him. When there were so many starving people around, couldn't they unload this vehicle a little quicker?

Martha shrieked at the sight of such a big truck, grabbing Samuel's arm and pointing at the towering vehicle, while jumping up and down at the same time. The smoking man turned round to face the direction of the noise and puffed a cloud of white smoke towards its source. As the smoke thinned, it revealed a large, forbidding looking man, scowling at this unwarranted intrusion into his cigarette break. Samuel froze feeling his legs buckling beneath him and sweat seeming to extrude from every pore of his skin. The person looking directly at him was none other than Julius Ndagijimana.

"Igendere" he barked in Kinyarwanda, in the same dismissive tone of voice that he had used to murder innocent civilians in Nyarubuye church. Samuel's mind was flashing back to the sights and sounds at the church as the Bourgmestre's voice resonated through every bone in his body, shaking him to the core. He felt again the stinking dog licking his face as he lay with the dead and saw the coin in the fist of the man who had been shot. He turned and saw the piles of bodies spreadeagled in hideous contortions but worst of all he could see the red and blue colours of Jonathan's clothes staring up at him from the meagre earth of a lonely roadside. For all Samuel knew it might have been Ndagijimana who had pulled the trigger. This monster was heading in Samuel's direction with hatred burning in his eyes in the same way as he may approached his innocent and defenceless son.

But now was not the time for revenge. Composing himself, he grabbed the two girls and ran from the compound, and was out of sight before Ndagijimana reached the fence. As he walked purposefully back to their hut, Samuel was no longer shaking. How he had thought about the day when he would come face to face with the Bourgmestre again. He had run through the scenario hundreds of times in his mind playing out on his mental stage the means of his retribution. But now it was for real – now he knew where to find his nemesis. The final scene was about to be acted out.

* * *

As more and more refugees arrived at Benaco camp and the relief agencies were able to provide more staffing and supplies, life started to become more normal and predictable. Refugee teachers combined with UN educationalists to set up makeshift schools. They had no books and only the occasional blackboard and piece of chalk, and lessons had to be conducted in the open air, but, for children deprived of any positive stimulus for weeks since they had left Rwanda, any form of schooling was a welcome diversion.

Traders had set up stores selling anything from pots and pans to jewellery. Refugees could now get their hair cut, their teeth fixed, sing and dance with impromptu bands and even eat out in restaurants. Most of these facilities were pretty basic and available most easily to those with hard currency, but bartering was commonplace and goods and services could be often obtained by those who had something to exchange in return. A black market in food and clothing had existed from the early days of the camp, stoked by unscrupulous Rwandans who were assisting the aid workers while also siphoning off their own personal supplies. Everything had its price and its value was known by everyone.

Trauma centres were being established throughout Benaco, where trained counsellors could help the victims of the genocide come to terms with their appalling experiences and grieve for lost loved ones whose bodies they might never find and never be able to lay to rest.

Sister Agathe Deladier and Mary Edwardson had reunited hundreds of Rwandans with their loved ones but, as time went on, it was becoming harder to do so and success rates began to fall.

"Mary, do you realise that it is now three days since we last tracked down a relative? This is soul destroying. All this work," she pointed to the piles of index cards and papers strewn across the tent, "and no reward."

"I know, Sister, the problems are getting more intractable with every day that passes. And I know that you are feeling bad that you haven't found Etienne." The large Englishwoman got up and moved over to her tiny companion and put her arm around her shoulders. "I'm sure we'll find him soon, but the camp is so big and there only seem to be two of us doing this work."

Agathe touched the large hand that was almost crushing her slight shoulders.

"Thanks…but it's just that every time I see Naome she looks at me so hopefully and every time I have to disappoint her. There must be something else we can do."

"Sister, you're the nun – perhaps we should pray about it."

The two women sank to their knees and in turn poured out their worries to God, entreating Him to help them find Etienne, or, at least be certain of his fate. The earnestness and conviction of their prayer was so intense that neither was aware how long they had prayed before finally running out of words to say. It was only then that they were conscious of someone standing at the door.

"I didn't mean to invade your privacy…I…I…was just coming to see if you had any news of my nephew," said a large, open-faced, middle-aged man in a slightly guilty and hesitant manner. He made to leave, but Agathe called him back,

"Olivier, you are a minister of the church, don't be embarrassed at finding some of your flock at prayer from time to time." She pulled the pastor into the tent by the sleeves of his jacket. "You looked so surprised that anyone could be talking to the Almighty in such a hopeless situation." Agathe chuckled as she stared at the quizzical look on Olivier's face.

"No, please, you should be praying. Forgive me for my lack of faith in the power of intercession…even in this wretched camp." He waved his large, round arm in the direction of the door and in an arc around the tent. "But it's just so long since I heard my congregation speaking the name of the Lord. There's been no worship in the place...no singing...no Bible reading...it's as if God is still a refugee from the genocide and none of us have found where He is yet."

"Maybe we need to set up somewhere for Christians to meet together then....to find God again...to worship together and comfort each other. Perhaps that's the next stage for us." Mary looked enthusiastically towards Agathe, immediately energised by the thought of some positive action that they could take.

"If we can't unite many more families, at least we can provide those who are left with somewhere to go for fellowship and support. Give them some hope. Sister, surely the UN could give us an old tent for a church. You could ask them? They would listen to a nun. Maybe you could go too, Olivier. You know how the old blue helmets love to put a local person in charge of a new venture, and you are far more worthy than all those crooks who run the food dumps."

All three laughed, happy that the church could now be put back into the centre of the community, just as it had been in Rwanda.

Before sunset, the UN had provided a large white marquee, the official in charge of procurement being delighted to give the restless refugees something that would occupy their time and stop them moaning to him about the quality of the bedding and groundsheets or how indigestible the maize was. It never ceased to amaze him how quickly people whose very survival depended on the generosity of others turned against them and became grasping, demanding, ungrateful whingers. If they spent time on their knees they might realise how lucky they were in comparison to the dozens of corpses that were daily being delivered to the Benaco mortuary and the thousands that were still lying unburied in Rwanda. The official even found a quantity of wooden planks and nails that could be fashioned into benches and tables.

Soon the Church of Christ, Benaco was a working reality and Pastor Olivier was proudly officiating at Sunday services and even baptisms, weddings and funerals. The people of God were on the march once again.

*　*　*

An occasional worshipper at the church was Samuel Karamira, not because he believed any more – how could he when this God had been silent as his son and everything else that he held dear had been destroyed? – but because he sought salvation in human contact, in the warmth of proximity to others. He had become something of a loner, a man who didn't need companionship, who even sought respite from his own family if their demands for a piece of him became too overpowering. Maybe he could return to the fold of humanity in this place of worship and re-establish his human credentials.

But each time he attended he felt more alone, isolated by his experiences, unable or unwilling to share the deep recesses of his soul with others who wouldn't understand. Deep down too he was unable to release his hold on his desire for revenge. He would find deliverance, not through a relationship with the divine or the human, but through justice. Not that insipid, mechanistic judgement that the courts would one day enact but a full bloodied, immediate and personal retribution, planned and plotted in secret. It was nearly time and Samuel had now conceived an appropriate method by which the sentence could be carried out.

CHAPTER TWENTY EIGHT

"Hey, you, come over here," Julius Ndagijimana bellowed at an unfortunate minion who was attempting to unload grain from the latest truck to arrive at the compound.

"Imbecile!" he snapped as he hit the man broadside on the left cheek with the butt of his rifle. As a trusted associate of the UN, Ndagijimana had been given the weapon when he complained that it was impossible to keep order during the distribution of food without the threat of force. The UN official, not wishing to have to attend each distribution himself, was more than happy to accede to the former Bourgmestre's wishes, just for an easy life. He and his colleagues were less and less willing to venture out from the safety of their own compound into the increasingly violent atmosphere of the camp. Scores were starting to be settled as victims of the genocide identified those who had been involved in the atrocities which had affected them and their families. Only yesterday, a Tanzanian UN soldier had been killed as he intervened in a dispute between a group of Tutsis and a Hutu militiaman. So, to have a senior and seemingly respected local government leader offer to take a problem away from him was just the ticket for a lowly official too poorly paid to regard such action as an abrogation of duty.

"How many times have I told you, spineless wretch, to put every other sack into my tent? How do you expect me to satisfy my clients without plenty of stock available?" Ndagijimana looked at the man as if he had raped his mother.

"But, Bourgmestre, even my own family aren't getting enough grain, and we haven't sufficient cash to pay your prices. Do you want us all to starve?"

"Is it my fault that you've been such a miserable failure that you haven't scraped together a few coins to provide for your own flesh and blood? I look after you don't I? You can't expect me to support every urchin that you may have squired in a moment of passion. If you hadn't followed your urges everywhere, you wouldn't have had all these problems. Now get working."

Ndagijimana kicked his inept subordinate, still smarting from the heavy blow to his head, back towards the truck.

Now, back to business, he thought as he pulled a handwritten note out of his pocket. As ever, it was unsigned, but that was the way of commerce in Benaco camp. No questions asked, no answers given. No refugee wanted to appear to have a private source of funds, to buy little luxuries or extra supplies, so that no spongers or gangsters came to the door pushing for a piece of the action. Negotiation was done in secret and goods collected under cover of darkness.

Still this note intrigued him. The writer was obviously a major player. Unusually he had enclosed ten US dollars as a downpayment. It wasn't much, but he obviously had money to spare and he was promising more, much more. That's what the Bourgmestre needed – a wealthy, well connected middle man. Someone who could take away the tedium of dealing with dozens of penniless peasants begging to have a few more grains in exchange for their pitiful mites. To deal with a man of substance, who would be making bulk purchases at top prices, was an attractive proposition.

* * *

It was about 4p.m. as Julius Ndagijimana settled onto the wooden bench in the spartan marquee and took in the surroundings. Beyond a simple wooden cross on the table, which prosaically represented the altar, there was little sign that the modest white canvas shelter was a place of worship. Good job too, thought Julius. He had no time for any display of religion, any spiritual mumbo jumbo, that got in the way of money and power. These were his gods.

Yet somehow he felt strangely uneasy in the chapel. Those feeble brained losers at Nyarubuye church had put their trust in religion and look where it had got them – a place of honour on a pile of rotting flesh. Faith was no match for a sharp machete or a loaded revolver. The sword was mightier than the word, he chuckled. Yet somehow faith had survived. He rationalised this anti-evolutionary fact by surmising that the witless failures in the camp had nowhere else to turn. Better to hope in an illusion than have no hope at all.

"He should be here by now," muttered the Bourgmestre impatiently, "I've got more business to do."

"Sorry to have kept you waiting," mumbled a nervous voice from the entrance to the tent. Ndagijimana looked round to see a gaunt, serious man holding a wicker bag with his one good arm as he shuffled towards him.

"I'm a very busy man," snapped Julius unimpressed by the 'businessman' who was ambling uncertainly towards him.

"While I was interested in your note, I can only do business with people who have the appropriate collateral. Can we please get straight to the point. If you want grain, it's three US dollars per sack and I require payment in advance."

"Oh, Bourgmestre," replied Samuel, more confident now. "I fully intend paying you in advance. Here I have my payment right here in this bag."

Samuel reached into his bag and pulled out a gleaming machete sparkling even in the fading light of the late afternoon. At that moment two stocky young men emerged from the side of the tent and walked menacingly towards the Bourgemestre.

"What is this?" Ndagijimana was starting to appear flustered. "What have I done to deserve this? I've never met you before."

"Oh yes you have," Samuel replied, "you've seen me before all right but you wouldn't have noticed me hidden under the pile of dead bodies, men, women and children murdered by you and your mocking henchmen. Get on your knees."

"How dare you speak to me like that?" Ndagijimana was desperately trying to reassert his authority. "Do you know who I am?"

"Of course I do." Samuel lifted the machete above his head menacingly. "That's why I'm telling you to kneel on the floor. I don't suppose you would have seen me scrabbling around under the pews at Nyarubuye, trying to avoid the blows that you had ordered. Now just do as I say."

Samuel was now screaming at Julius, who was by now very anxious and sweating profusely.

"Listen," said the Bourgmestre, trying a more conciliatory approach as he sank to his knees. "Why don't I just give you some money. You've got the wrong man but.... we all make mistakes from time to time and I don't hold grudges. You're obviously very upset about something, but I'm sure we can work it out."

Julius reached into his pocket and held out a pile of coins in the palm of his hand.

"If you let me go, I will bring you some more. I can make you a very rich man in Benaco."

"You vile inyenzi. You made your victims pay to be killed by a bullet rather than a machete. Keep your filthy cash. You're going to die just as you made all those wretches at Nyarubuye die." This was the signal for the two youths to jump on the Bourgmestre and wrestle him to the ground.

Julius never felt the first slash as it sliced into his shoulder, just the warm sensation of the blood running down his back. The power of the blow pushed him forward and under the bench in front of him, his head sticking out from under the seat. The second blow virtually decapitated him, forcing his head upwards under the bench so that it appeared to be staring out from underneath it.

"Now you know how it feels, shitbag." Samuel spat at the body in front of him as it lay prostrate on the bare earth.

In his bag he had a canvas sack. Samuel had wanted to take his revenge entirely from his own resources but with only one arm this was an impossibility. But you could hire anything in Benaco camp if you had some cash. A few coins and you could find someone to do anything you wanted, no questions asked. He threw the sack at the two youths and motioned to them to bundle the Bourgmestre's body into it.

Even with two people, it was hard manhandling Julius's body into the sack, for he was a big, heavy man but there was one other duty Samuel had to perform.

Julius Ndagijimana had left the keys in the Ford pick up truck, which he had left outside the chapel. This was just one more privilege that he had been able to wangle from the UN. If he was responsible for the distribution of food then surely he needed a vehicle in order to make deliveries to outlying areas, to supply those who were too ill to get to the feeding station, his argument ran. In reality it was a convenient means of transport for getting round the camp to do as many illicit deals as possible in the shortest time possible.

Samuel and the youths loaded the Bourgmestre's body into the back of the truck, taking care to attract as little attention as possible. Not that they needed to worry. There were dozens of men loading sacks into UN vehicles right across the camp. No-one batted an eyelid. Samuel noted with satisfaction that the fuel gauge indicated that the tank was nearly full. Julius was nothing if not fully prepared. Always ready for a quick getaway.

It was dark by the time the truck approached the Rusomo bridge. The Akagera river was in full flow, crashing through the chasm and hurling everything in its path from side to side against the rocks.

Samuel parked the truck some distance from the border post on the bridge and killed the lights. With any luck the border guard would be asleep or drunk, or both. The three men dragged Ndagijimana's body towards the bridge, creeping past the somnolent guard, his feet planted on the desk and his head flopped backwards over the top of his chair. At the mid point of the bridge they levered the body over the railings and let it drop down into the raging river below, like thousands of others before him.

"Get back to Ethiopia yourself, you cowardly, stinking rat," pronounced Samuel, rather like a priest at a funeral committing the deceased's body into its final resting place. But this was no valediction – it was a curse. A curse on all those like Ndagijimana who had ripped the heart out of Samuel's beloved country and created an unspeakable evil. Those who had murdered the innocent and then played the victim themselves. Those who, even now, were squirming out of the justice that was the proper reward for their actions, pulling the strings to blame others or bribing those who might make any accusation against them. Samuel would track them down and bring them to this place. Samuel prayed that Ndagijimana's body would get caught under the branches of a tree in a distant lake miles downstream from Rusomo, and there it would rot, pieces of flesh torn from it by the bloated rats who gorged on this harvest of decaying flesh. Justice was his, he would repay.

* * *

Jennifer's tea was cold by the time Agathe re-emerged from the house in Gahini. By now the setting sun had vanished and the night had cast its blanket of chill and darkness across the missionary compound. The old nun sat beside the young medical student and laid her tiny hand on the girl's arm. Jennifer shivered, not from any feeling of unease but because she was suddenly conscious of the cold which had involuntarily crept up on her. For some time she had not been aware of any external stimuli, lost as she was as in deep thought about the genocide that Agathe had briefly introduced to her.

"Jennifer, perhaps it's time that I told someone about my life. You see, many terrible things have happened to me and I have never felt able to share them properly with anyone. I believed that it was a burden God wanted me to carry all by myself, but I am old now and may not have many opportunities to pass on my memories. It's important that the world never forgets the appalling atrocities that one man inflicts on another. It's not that I expect such events to cease, because they never will, but we mustn't forget the truths that they reveal. Here, you must share my blanket to keep out the cold."

The two women huddled together on the bench under the blanket as Agathe recounted the events of her life and poured out her soul to her young companion.

"My dear, I expect you're wondering why I stayed here after all of this?"

Her arm swept around in an arc of 180 degrees, not pointing at anything in particular but seeming to encompass 60 years of trauma, as if wherever she pointed there would be some sign of man's inhumanity to man. It could be on a small hill in Rwanda or in a sleepy village in France, in a rice field in Asia, a school in Russia, a skyscraper in America or a bus queue in Iraq.

"You see we're all tribal in a way. We each have our scapegoats, those we look down on, those who get the blame for anything that goes wrong. And sometimes that tribalism gets out of hand, starts to be manipulated by spiritual forces, magnified into cosmic proportions. That's when we have to decide which side we're on, who we're going to fight for. I can't just walk away from it. Everyday I see God in the victims here, those who have lost everything – family, health, property, innocence, trust. That's my battle, bringing them hope and assurance, so that Satan doesn't win. Can you understand?"

"I think so," Jennifer held the nun's sparrow like hand, "but what I can't fathom out is why you identify with these victims as you call them. At another time they might turn into killers, fighting for the other side in this spiritual war. Are all Hutus bad and all Tutsis good? Are all Germans evil and all French righteous?"

"Of course not, but while they are victims I must love and support them. It's not my role to sit in judgement, to decide who's right and who's wrong. It's enough to see that that they are people in need whom I should defend and encourage. I can appreciate that it's difficult for you to understand that but, you see, I know what it's like to be abused and despised, hated by my own people, spat at, treated as a traitor. I know that this treatment can turn people into killers, into those possessed by the Devil in order to do his will. I have always fought against that in myself and in others. God wants me to do that Jennifer. I know He does."

"Sister, you say that you know what it's like to be hated and abused. How?"

"Jennifer, do you remember that I told you about Captain Vomecourt and other soldiers from Alsace-Lorraine who fought for the SS. The Nazi troops looked down on them because Alsace wasn't properly German and the French despised them because they were regarded as traitors. You see the one thing I didn't tell you, Jennifer, is that I too am from Alsace."

POSTSCRIPT

The original village of Oradour-sur-Glane has never been rebuilt. To this day it remains a ruin, a memorial to the lives so tragically and pointlessly lost in June 1944. There were only six survivors. Only one German officer was jailed for his part in the massacre.

The church at Nyarubuye has also been preserved. The remains and possessions of some of those who died have been retained at the site. The main perpetrator of the atrocity was tried in 2003-4 and is serving a life sentence.

One can only imagine the effect of such brutal slaughter on the lives of those who survived. French and German relations are now strong. Rwanda is being rebuilt and reconciliation has been a more prominent motive in its renaissance than retribution. However, despite these encouraging signs, the problem of the human condition remains and we cannot say with any confidence "Never Again".